"I wanted to talk with you about something else, Annie."

"What could you possibly have to talk to me about? We've only just met."

"I have another reason for staying in Safe Harbor." Russ peered at her.

"Really?" She laughed nervously. There was something about those unusual eyes. "Well, according to the Chamber of Commerce there are a lot of reasons anyone would choose Safe Harbor."

"It had nothing to do with the Chamber of Commerce. I'd already decided to set up shop here, just not quite yet. But then my grandfather upped the ante. More particularly, his will did."

Something—a fizzle of awareness—shot through her. "Your grandfather's will said you had to live in Safe Harbor?" she whispered.

"No." He took a deep breath and looked her straight in the eye. "My grandfather's will said I have to marry you."

* * *

Safe Harbor—
The town where everyone finds shelter from the storm.

Books by Lois Richer

Love Inspired

12

†Faith, Hope & Charity
*Brides of the Seasons
‡If Wishes Were Weddings

LOIS RICHER

lives in a small Canadian prairie town with her husband, who, she says, is a "wanna-be farmer." She began writing in self-defense, as a way to escape. She says, "Come spring, tomato plants take over my flower beds, no matter how many I 'accidentally' pull up or 'prune.' By summer I'm fielding phone calls from neighbors who don't need tomatoes this fall. Come September, no one visits us and anyone who gallantly offers to take a box invariably ends up with six. I have more recipes with tomatoes than with chocolate. Thank goodness for writing! Imaginary people with imaginary gardens are much easier to deal with!"

Lois is pleased to present her latest book for the Steeple Hill Love Inspired line. Please feel free to contact Lois at: Box 639, Nipawin, Saskatchewan, Canada S0E 1E0.

INNER HARBOR

LOIS RICHER

Love Inspired

Published by Steeple Hill Books™

Special thanks and acknowledgment are
given to Lois Richer for her contribution
to the SAFE HARBOR series.

STEEPLE HILL BOOKS

Steeple
Hill™

ISBN 0-373-87214-3

INNER HARBOR

Copyright © 2003 by Steeple Hill Books, Fribourg, Switzerland

Visit us at www.steeplehill.com

Printed in U.S.A.

You are my refuge and my shield,
and Your promises are my only source of hope.

—*Psalms* 119:114

Prologue

The letter arrived by courier on Thanksgiving eve, a bulky missive with a legal firm listed as the sender.

A strange quiver of excitement rippled through Annie Simmons as she dropped the sandpaper block she'd been rubbing against a battered oak table and tore open the envelope with trembling fingers.

What now?

A legal-size white envelope with her name printed on it lay tucked inside, along with a letter. She sank down on the floor and scanned the typewritten words from the executor of Wharton Willoughby's estate, informing her the envelope's sealed contents had been discovered on his desk, addressed to her. She noticed that the stamp had never been canceled. Why hadn't he mailed it?

Annie slit the envelope, slid out three pages covered in a thick black scrawl. She began to read.

Dear Annie

It's been several weeks since I last visited you in Safe Harbor. I expect that you are well under way with your renovations now. Soon your bed-and-breakfast will be welcoming folks through its doors. Congratulations!

Annie, you've become the granddaughter I never had. We've shared so many things, allowed the other to pray over our worries. Perhaps that's why I trust you won't be offended by this letter from an old man who dares to make an outrageous request.

My grandson is very precious to me, and yet I'm afraid for him. R.J. has lost his way, lost touch with what really matters in this life. He's grown afraid of responsibility. He needs someone—someone to help him face his past, his future and all the potential it holds. For some time, I've believed you are that person.

I've got a bad case of pneumonia, so I can't talk to you in person, and the phone seems too impersonal for what I want to say, so I've chosen to write. Tomorrow I'll mail this. Perhaps you'll manage a visit to discuss it, and I can better articulate my hopes, but until then, here are my thoughts.

I can't allow R.J. to continue on the path he's traveling, Annie. So I've taken steps to direct him toward Safe Harbor. I've stipulated in my will that he cannot inherit the money I so desperately want him to use to expand his business—unless he marries you. It's presumptuous of me, and I'm sure you'd scold me severely for my interference if you were here. Perhaps that's why I've cowardly chosen to write this letter instead of facing you.

I know you very well, Annie. And I know my grandson. I know the burdens each of you carry. I've come to believe that you and R.J. belong together, that you could share those burdens and build something wonderful—together. That's why I hope you'll marry him.

Please, at least consider my request. Many times I've asked the Lord to watch over you both, many times I've pleaded for His direction. I believe this is His will. You're both hiding, hurt by the past, afraid to move on. You can help each other, love each other, serve Him together. And I will have my dearest wish—at last you will truly be my own sweet granddaughter.

You are my hope for R.J., Annie. I trust you will prayerfully consider this request from a lonely old man who thanks you for the many happy hours you gave him.

Sincerely,

Wharton Willoughby

Annie lifted the courier's envelope, hardly able to comprehend what she'd read. As she tilted it, a funeral announcement fell onto the floor. It was dated three weeks earlier, announcing the passing of a man who'd been the grandfather she'd never had. He'd died the day after he'd written her. He'd never had a chance to mail his precious letter.

Tears filled her eyes. Dear Mr. Willoughby. How she would miss him.

The letter, still clutched in her left hand, reminded her that while he might be gone, Wharton Willoughby, her friend and legal counsel, was still advising her.

Only this time she would not take his advice.

All those prayers she'd listened to had left Annie with a certain impression of Wharton's grandson, and he was definitely not what she considered husband material. R.J. would have to find someone else to marry, because Annie Simmons had no intention of repeating her parents' disastrous mistake. She would never marry.

Chapter One

"It's only the first of March, Annie. The remains of that storm last month are still melting. Don't start your worrying. Tourist season will arrive hot and heavy soon enough, and then you'll be wishing for some time to yourself. Trust me, this place is going to be full."

Her assistant's words did little to ease the nag of worry dogging Annie Simmons, though she nodded to be polite. Felicity was right, of course. Patience and time were all she needed to make her business a success. But banks didn't have patience. They expected her to repay that loan. That was fine. Annie wanted to pay them on time.

Failure had no part in her carefully crafted business plan for her brand-new Lighthouse Bed-and-Breakfast. But she'd had to borrow a little. Her mother's legacy hadn't quite covered all the renovations. Nor had Annie planned for the immediate expenses of a little boy who'd lost his parents at sea.

The search for a guardian had taken longer than anyone had imagined. At least now they knew the boy's mother, Rhonda, had a cousin. The details were vague. Annie knew only that this man was in some far-off location. Now it was just a matter of locating him, telling him about Drew. Then the little boy would be gone from her life, free to begin again with relatives who would love and care for him. Who wouldn't delight to have Drew in their home? Annie thrust away thoughts of him leaving. Family was important. She would let him go with a full heart, grateful she'd been able to help. She glanced at her watch.

No more wasting time, or she'd be late!

"I've got one stop on my way to the church. If I hurry, that is." She tugged on her jacket, then grabbed her sheet music. "If someone phones, I'm on my way."

"You'll be late." Felicity chuckled. "Somebody will stop you and want to chat—that's Safe Harbor. I've never seen such a friendly place. But just you remember, those kids have had a day off school and they'll be flying pretty high." Her eyes danced with fun. "You could always race them around the block first, I suppose. But I'm not worried. You'll whip everything into shape. You always do." Her eyes glowed with admiration.

"Thanks for your faith. I just hope it's justified. Without an organist, my little choral group isn't exactly melodic." Count on Felicity to cheer her on. She'd been a good friend since the day she arrived in Safe Harbor, looking for work. As Annie's part-time assistant, she was perfect.

"I don't envy you all those kids." Felicity pretended to groan. "I can barely handle one."

"You're a great mother." Annie knew how hard this young mom worked to be everything to her daughter.

"I try. You'd be a great one, too." Trust Felicity to be loyal. "Look how you've managed with Drew."

"I'm not sure I've done anything right with Drew. He's so quiet." Annie sighed. "It's hard to know what he's thinking when he stares back at you with those big brown eyes.''

''You need help with him.'' Felicity tapped one blue-tinted fingernail against her bottom lip. ''Maybe... something along the lines of a husband?''

Annie froze, thought about the letter, then dismissed her fears. Felicity couldn't possibly know about it. Besides, it had been months since that letter had arrived, and R.J. still hadn't shown. It was obvious he'd found a way to inherit without her. Good. That was the way she wanted it.

''Drew will be leaving as soon as his relative arrives. What would I do with a husband after that?''

''I can think of several things you could do,'' Felicity said, deadpan.

''Romance isn't in my picture.'' Annie ignored her friend's groan. A pang pricked her heart at the thought of never knowing the thrill of cuddling her own precious bundle of joy. Soon even Drew would be gone. And she'd be alone.

Again.

''I've got to get going.'' Annie checked that her ponytail was neatly in place, then pulled on her gloves. ''Drew's with Billy Martin. Billy's mom is bringing them to the church, so you don't have to worry about him. I'll see you in a couple of hours. Okay?''

''Yes, boss.'' Felicity saluted. ''And I'll mind my own business from now on, too.''

Annie smiled, then left. Felicity meant well, but she wouldn't understand. Sometimes even Annie didn't understand her reluctance to fall in love. Surely not all men were like her father?

As predicted, her stop at the Realtor's office took a few minutes more than she'd expected. Noting the time on the clock in Market Square, Annie strode quickly toward the church. Kids raced through the few remaining clumps of soggy spring snow, howling with laughter as they pelted each other with mushy snowballs. Annie deflected several missiles, then ducked inside the foyer to remove her coat.

They certainly were rambunctious. Directing them wasn't easy without an accompanist. Seven and a half weeks until Easter—was that enough time to pull off a miracle? She'd just have to trust that God would send the right person at the right time.

Annie laid the music on her stand, ordering it in the correct sequence for quick reference. Then she arranged the chairs precisely. After filling her lungs with a deep breath of faith, Annie stuck her head out the door.

"Come on, people. It's time to practi—" A cold, wet lump of snow cut off her words. Annie wiped away the few flakes that hadn't already dripped off her chin and grinned. "You're going to pay for that, you hooligans. Now, come on. Let's get started."

They trooped inside, silent, eyes downcast, suppressed giggles escaping whenever she turned her back. If they were just the tiniest bit worried she'd be mad, Annie was glad. Perhaps order would prevail for at least five minutes. Coats, boots and mittens dropped to the floor as they jostled each other with good-natured ribbing. It took forever until, one by one, the kids filed into the left side of the choir loft. Occasionally, a mischievous child peeked up, checking her face for some sign of disapproval. Annie kept her expression serene. Later she'd pelt them all with a barrage of snowballs, but right now she needed them to concentrate.

"Okay, guys." She began by smiling at each one, searching for a confidence she didn't feel. "You know the words. I think you know the melody, but just in case, I'm going to pound it out on the piano. Remember, you have to watch me to know when to come in.''

A little blond sprite in the front row turned to his neighbor. ''Not that again! Everything gets mixed up when she does that. Annie on the piano doesn't sound like Reverend Burns on the organ at all.'' A rumble of agreement rolled through the choir.

Annie chuckled. Nothing like the honesty of a child to dent the ego.

''It sure doesn't, Robbie. But right now, a piano is all we've got. Since Reverend Burns hurt himself, we're out of an organist. We'll just have to pray that God will send another one.'' Annie cleared her throat and played the intro. It took three false starts before they finally found their note and the correct entry point. Then, for some reason, their attention strayed to the back of the church. Annie ignored it. Probably another child, coaxing them to leave. Three tries later, she gave up on the accompaniment.

''Come on, guys.'' Should she call the whole thing off, before it was too late? No. This cantata was the focal point of their Easter service. She wouldn't quit. Annie left the piano and moved to stand in front of them.

''Think about what Easter means. Your best friend was killed. Now he's buried, and you don't think you're ever going to see him again. The world is dark, the sun's just under the horizon, and you're sad.'' She hummed the first few bars, motioning them to sing. ''Okay, now you're in the garden where he's buried and you see that the stone over his grave is moved.''

Three loud organ chords echoed through the church, resonant, triumphant and totally unexpected, grabbing the children's attention like nothing else could. Annie blinked. She must have left the music up there. Had Pastor Burns finally found her an organist?

Annie forced herself not to look around. She refused to waste this opportunity. Instead she tapped her pen on the top of her music stand. Every eye centered on her.

"Now sing!" she ordered.

And sing they did. Glorious swells of jubilant notes from the tired old pipe organ begged their full participation. Whoever was tickling those ivories knew exactly how to get the most out of each and every pipe. Annie could hardly wait to see exactly who her benefactor was, and when she did, she intended to beg, plead and implore him or her to play for them each and every practice until the final concert Easter morning.

For now, she continued to lead her kids through the cantata, page after page. Soloists chimed in exactly right, harmonies came together almost without pause, until the last glorious notes of Handel's "Hallelujah Chorus" died away.

"Hey, Annie. We did pretty good, didn't we?" Her godchild grinned from ear to ear.

"You did a fantastic job, Drew. All of you. Thank you." She included everyone in her smile, delighted by the effort they'd made.

Unable to control her curiosity, Annie turned toward the organ. A man sat there, a gorgeous man with glossy black hair that stood to attention in perfectly sculpted spikes. He had a to-die-for face—all angles and planes—and a smile that would kick any woman's heartbeat into overdrive. But it was his eyes that held Annie's attention. Silver gray swirls of glitter danced with sheer exuberance.

"What a group! Sorry for bursting into your practice like that, but that music was just too tempting." He stood, climbed down from his perch and stretched out a hand. "Russ Mitchard."

"Bless you, Russ Mitchard," Annie breathed, eyes riveted on that smile.

Annie let his big warm hand engulf hers. Then her eyes got snagged on marks covering the back of his hand. Those scars were the only flaw in his otherwise perfect image, so she could hardly be blamed for studying them a second time.

"I beg your pardon?" His eyes stretched wide, curious.

Annie flushed. What a time to lose her cool!

"Just—uh, thanks for playing for us. It's the best recital we've ever had. You were a real blessing."

"Well, I've been called a lot of things, but never a blessing. I think I like it." He grinned, his eyebrows twitching as he glanced at their joined hands. "A lot." He winked.

"Oh. Sorry," she murmured as she tugged her hand away. "Annie Simmons."

"It's nice to meet you, Annie Simmons. Very nice."

Something strangely serious underlay his words. It was almost as if he'd been expecting to meet her. What nonsense. Annie shrugged it off as the kids swarmed around him, grilling him about his playing.

Russ answered the best he could with so many voices demanding his attention. His smile remained easy, his attitude relaxed as he tapped out a few songs they knew on the baby grand piano. Minutes later their singing was interrupted when several moms popped their heads inside, stared at Russ and Annie for a few awkward moments, then called their children away.

"Annie, I'm going with Billy. Okay?" Drew hopped from one foot to the other, barely able to wait for her permission.

"Yes, all right. Billy's mom said she'll bring you back before dinner." She watched Drew race out the door. As far as Annie could tell, he wasn't suffering any ill effects from her mothering so maybe she was doing something right.

With one last look at Russ, the rest of the children filed out until Annie was left alone with *him*.

"Your son?" Silver-gray eyes perused her curiously.

"Godchild. His parents died in a boating accident last fall. No relatives have come forward to claim him yet, so he stays with me, for now. We both like it." Why was she telling him this?

"Oh."

"I want to thank you for your help," she blurted, wondering how to phrase her next request. "You made all the difference today."

"Regular organist conk out?" He shrugged into a black leather jacket that fit over his turtleneck like a second skin.

"Something like that. Pastor Burns hurt himself shortly after I agreed to handle the Easter concert. He's having surgery, so he'll be out for a while. Unfortunately, his interim replacements don't play the pipe organ. Nor does anyone else around here."

"Tough break." He closed the piano, his hand gentle against the polished wood. "This thing has a gorgeous tone, but as someone I knew once said, nothing can replace the full-blooded intonations of a pipe organ. I'd forgotten that."

Annie followed him down the aisle, almost jogging to keep up with his long stride. Her curiosity got the better of her.

"Are you visiting Safe Harbor, Mr. Mitchard?"

"It's Russ." He stopped, glanced at her. "Sort of." He tilted his head one way. "Maybe." A decided negative shake. "No, not really."

"Nothing like a straight answer." Annie peeked at him in confusion. "Could you explain that, please?"

"I guess I'd better. Let's see—where to begin?" He laughed, a burst of pure pleasure that echoed around the sanctuary. He never looked away from her the entire time he considered his answer. His expressive eyes fluctuated from pewter to steel, then glowed like polished silver.

"I used to come to Safe Harbor every summer with my parents when I was a kid. Mom and Dad had a cottage just outside of town."

"I see." She didn't, really, but she pressed on, anxious to know how long he'd be around. Suddenly the nippy spring afternoon seemed warmer. "So you're back to take a look, relive the memories of your youth?"

If she hadn't been staring at his gorgeous face, she would have missed the flare of pain that snatched the joy from his eyes. A minute later the look was gone, roguish grin firmly in place.

"No, I'm not interested in the past. I'm interested in the future. I'm going into business here. Perhaps you've noticed my shop—The Quest?"

Annie blinked. This hunk owned The Quest?

The gossips were going to be put out. They'd insisted some tacky tourist outfit was setting up shop in their quaint little town and had all but voted to boycott the place. Nobody in their right mind would boycott this charming man, whatever he was selling.

Nobody but her, that is. He might be good-looking, and he was certainly attractive, but she had no intention of getting involved. Not that way. She just needed an organist.

"Well, have you? Noticed my shop?" he prodded.

Annie snapped back to reality, caught the sparkle of pride glinting at her from those silver-gray eyes. She knew that feeling, felt the same way whenever she caught a glimpse of her bed-and-breakfast.

"I noticed." Who could help it with all the cargo being unloaded daily?

"I've been forwarding a lot of my stuff. I hope it's here."

She nodded. "Actually, right after the sign went up, the crates began arriving. I think you'll find everything is there."

His chest seemed to expand. "My sculptures," he told her.

Sculptures? Annie frowned. Stone carvings, she decided. That's why his hands were marked. As usual, her mind slipped into its creative mode and began fashioning a background story. The chisel must have slipped and—

"I'm a silversmith. My specialty is lamps. I had a lot of equipment sent here, too."

"Oh." There wasn't anything else she could say. The reality was so far beyond anything anyone in the entire town had imagined, her included. "Drew's parents used to rent that space for their bookstore. The Book Den."

"Ah." He seemed surprised. "I agreed to keep the books, to sell what I could. I wondered why the owner insisted they went with the place." He held her coat while she slipped her arms inside, then turned her and did up the buttons as he spoke.

"There's a lot of work in progress here, isn't there? Some places look spanking new, others look old and tired. I guess that's the charm of a tourist town. Past, present and future all bound together. I'm hoping Safe Harbor will live up to its potential this summer. In fact, I'm counting on it."

"Me, too." Annie just hoped the potential would arrive sooner rather than later.

"It looks a lot better than when I was a kid, though." He pulled on soft leather gloves, easing each finger in as he spoke, apparently unaware that she'd spoken. "All I remember are a few older buildings, streets so bumpy they could trip you, and the dock. That dock was like a second home."

"Sounds like you had a lot of fun here."

"Sometimes." The glow in his eyes seemed to dim a little. Then he smiled. "I'll admit, I never cared much about anything but the water." He held the door open for her.

Annie flicked off the lights, then stepped outside, grateful that the sun still shone, that the days had lengthened. Winter was almost gone, and she was glad. She loved the rebirth of life spring always brought. It meant hope, new beginnings, a chance to change.

"The water?" she murmured while wondering how to make a graceful exit.

"I was addicted to water. Am addicted." He grinned at her puzzled look. "Boating," he explained. "Give me a sailboat and a light breeze, and the rest of the world fades away."

The way he said it, eyes flashing silver glints like wave crests rolling across the midnight deep, snagged Annie's attention. Drew's parents, her best friends, had been like that, totally relaxed in the world of water. They'd hoped to impart that love to their small son, but since their deaths, Drew hadn't been on a boat, hadn't expressed the least interest in them. That was one area in which Annie felt she'd failed her dearest high school friend—not teaching Rhonda's son the joys of sailing. If the cousin took him soon, she'd lose her chance. Sadness at the emptiness of a life without Drew gripped her.

"That's one reason I chose this place to set up my shop." His stare grew more intent. "Though there were several other factors."

It sounded like he was hinting at something. But Annie had no idea what that could be about, and she needed to get back to work.

"I see. Well, goodbye. And thanks." Annie skipped down the church steps and traveled on the sidewalk toward home, a faded memory gurgling up from the depths of her mind.

Russ Mitchard reminded her of her father. Though he'd been dead for ten years, killed in a car accident in some far distant place, what she remembered of her dad bore a remarkable resemblance to the man at the church. No, it was far more than his tall, handsome looks. Her father's reputation as a charmer, smooth, glib, funny, with the glitz and charisma that drew people like bees to jam, worked exactly the way Russ Mitchard had drawn Annie's attention with his dancing eyes that promised so much.

Her protective radar beeped an alarm. Her father had cruised through life on his personality and wit. And he'd made her mother's life a misery. Of course, she and Russ wouldn't have much contact, but she'd be doubly careful. She had her business and Drew; that would take all her time. Besides, a handsome, rugged man like him would hardly be interested in Annie Simmons.

"Are you going somewhere?" Annie realized she was halfway home and he was still there, beside her, as they waited at the corner for traffic to pass.

"Of course I'm going somewhere." He matched her step for step across the road, his hand slipping beneath her elbow when she tripped on a crack in the pavement. He chuckled. "Some things never change, especially potholes." He volunteered nothing else.

"Well, this is my destination." Annie tugged her arm away from him and stepped back. "I own the Lighthouse Bed-and-Breakfast."

"That's nice. It looks a lot better than the last time I saw it. You've done a lot of work." He stared at her, head tilted in a lopsided way, asking a question without saying a word.

What he was asking wasn't immediately clear. But something about that stare and the familiarity of it kicked her heart rate up a notch. Annie shifted, avoided his glance. Her mouth was dry, her palms sweaty. She swallowed, searched for something to say that would break his focus on her.

"Have you lived in Safe Harbor all your life?"

She nodded.

"I don't remember you. You'd think I'd have run into you once or twice back then." He smiled that playboy grin that sent her heart rate soaring.

"I assure you, I was quite forgettable as a child," she told him dryly. "Shy, boring. Not at all the adventurous type. Besides, I didn't spend much time near the water. I had other interests." Like looking after her mother when her father's usual promise of a summer vacation fell through—as it always had.

"Still, I think I'd have remembered you. If we'd met." He smiled.

"Yes, well—" She turned, pulled open the door. "Good—"

"Oh, not goodbye, I hope. Not yet." He stepped in behind her. "We've barely become acquainted." Russ grinned again, that provocative smile flashing white against the rich, healthy tan of his face.

She didn't want to become better acquainted. Not with him. She'd never been good with men. And this particular man made her more nervous than usual. Her palms were sweaty even though the spring breeze off the water chilled the outside air. She shifted nervously.

"I have to go now." She walked toward the counter, turned and saw him standing there. "Can I direct you somewhere?"

"I'm already there—er, here. But thank you." He fiddled with the brass ship's bell that hung just inside the door. "You've kept some of the relics, I see. We used to dash in here and ring this whenever Mr. Potter was out in his garden." A winsome smile flickered, tilting the corners of his lips. "He chased us with his flyswatter."

"Us?" Annie wished she'd bitten her tongue when his startled glance leaped to hers, eyes darkening once more to that sad, forlorn pewter that drowned all the fun.

"Just some other kids." He avoided her stare. A noise behind Annie drew his attention, and the glint reappeared. "Ah, another beautiful lady to brighten my day. How goes it?"

Felicity Smith nodded at Annie, but her attention was all on him.

"I see you've met Russ." Felicity grinned, cheeks glowing pink at the wink he sent her way. "Russ will be staying with us for the next month or so."

"He will?" Her first customer, and he had to be a flirt!

"He's opening The Quest. He'll be selling silver lamps." Felicity fairly oozed with admiration, her brown eyes melting with adulation. "I think it will be wonderful to have the place open again, Russ."

"Thanks, Felicity."

Annie felt an overwhelming need to break up this mutual admiration society.

"Yes, it will be nice." She walked behind the counter and glanced at the ledger. Apparently Mr. Russ Mitchard, of no fixed address, was to be her only customer. One client was better than none, wasn't he?

"I hear an unspoken 'but' in your voice." Russ leaned against the counter, shadowed chin propped on one palm.

"I'm glad the bookstore is able to remain open." She shrugged. "It's full of character. I used to go there often when my mother was alive, but lately…"

"I heard about the accident. I understand." He nodded, his voice sympathetic. "I can imagine it hasn't been easy on your godson, either." He shrugged. "Perhaps seeing the place open again will ease his memories, help him see life goes on." His attention shifted to Felicity. "I'll bet Annie was one of those little girls who lost themselves in fairy tales and dreamed of her own Prince Charming."

He was so exactly on target that Annie drew into her shell.

"Actually I studied birds," she informed him. "I had a thing for birds."

"Still do. Birds and wildflowers. Which anyone who looks through this place could tell right off. Her watercolors are all over the place." Felicity grinned, then shrugged into her jacket. "I've got to get going. Saturday is our play day, and my daughter doesn't like waiting. See you, Annie. Bye, Russ." She disappeared like a whirlwind, her long legs carrying her out the door and down the street in mere seconds.

"When she goes, she really goes." Russ swiveled his head, watched Felicity's lithe figure disappear. "She seems nice. Straightforward." He was looking at Annie again.

"As straight as they come." Annie wished the phone would ring. Anything to get his focus off of her.

"Unlike you."

"What's that supposed to mean?" She glared at him. "I'm no crook."

His finger grazed her cheek, cupped her chin, forced her to look at him.

"I didn't mean that. But you've got secrets, Annie girl. Anyone can see that. Sad secrets buried in the glacial silt of those blue eyes. It's going to take some work to dig them out."

"Don't be silly. There's nothing glacial about my eyes. They're just plain old blue." She jerked her chin away, then stepped out from behind the counter. "Besides, in a place like Safe Harbor, it's impossible to have secrets."

"Do you think so?" He sounded strange, almost hopeful.

Annie took a deep breath and refocused. She was his hostess. Time to earn her money and act like it.

"Did Felicity show you to your room?"

"Changing the subject, Annie?"

"Yes. Did she?"

He nodded, his mouth tilted in a wicked grin. "She did. Thank you."

"Good. Fine. Excellent." She was babbling. "Well, make yourself at home then. Let me know if you need anything." She turned, walked through the dining room and into the kitchen. There she made a pot of coffee, chose a freshly baked cinnamon bun from the rack.

When she turned again, he stood leaning against the door frame, leather jacket gone but still the charmer in black cashmere and worsted slacks. If she'd snapped a photo of him, Annie would have titled it The Ultimate Flirt. Funny, she'd thought she'd heard him leave.

"Wanna share?"

"Oh. Well, it's up to you." What else could she say? He was her guest. She poured two cups of coffee, then motioned toward the cinnamon rolls. He put three on the plate she offered.

"I'm good at sharing." He laughed at her look. "I'm also starved."

"I see that."

They sat down at the small bistro table under a bank of windows that overlooked a tiny flagstone patio and Lake Michigan beyond. Suddenly Annie remembered.

"Since you're going to be living here, I wonder if you'd be interested in playing for our children's choir—the same music you played today. Easter morning." She rushed on, blurting out the facts in no particular order. "They're good kids, but I can't direct and play, and they need to practice to memorize their parts. We haven't yet begun to coordinate with the readers, and that will take a lot of work to get the timing right, and—"

"Okay."

"And then, of course, there are the robes to think of. Someone else is handling them, but I expect—" She stopped, stared at him. "What did you say?"

"I said I'll play for you. The organ?" His eyes sparkled with mirth. "That was what you asked, wasn't it?"

"Oh. Yes, it was." Annie gulped. That easy? "Thank you."

"You're welcome." He licked the white Danish icing off his fingertips, then took a sip of coffee before leaning back in his chair like a satisfied cat just finished a bowl of cream. "Actually, I wanted to talk to you about something else."

"Talk to *me?*" she demanded, suspicious of the odd smile twitching at his handsome mouth. "Why?"

"Calm down. It's nothing horrible," he assured her. "I can see the worst ideas flickering through your eyes."

"What could you possibly have to talk to me about? We've only just met."

"Remember I told you we used to come here in the summer?"

She nodded.

"My parents are both lawyers in Chicago. They're very busy. Back then they lived in Green Bay and they wanted a place nearby where our family could get away from work and relax together." His voice tightened a fraction.

"Oh, yes." She still didn't see what that had to do with her.

"My grandparents would come sometimes, too. My grandfather wasn't crazy about leaving work. He was a workaholic, and lazing around made him very uncomfortable. But my mom loved having her mother visit us at the cottage, and my gran adored the lake. They spent a lot of time talking. My grandfather didn't dare put a damper on that because Gran was the love of his life." Those unusual eyes darkened with emotion. "Their marriage was perfect, exactly what everyone thinks of when they say the word *love*. Unfortunately Gran died eight years ago."

"Oh." Where was this going? "They were your only grandparents?"

"The only ones I knew. Dad's parents died before I was born. They lived in New York."

Mitchard. The name pricked her memory. A newspaper article, what, a month ago? Something named in memory, wasn't it? Annie stared at him. "The land developer?"

He smiled. "Uh-huh."

"Oh." What else was there to say? Russ Mitchard's grandfather had been a household name and certainly a workaholic. No wonder he hadn't wanted to put grandiose building schemes aside to traipse around Door Country like the tourists. If she remembered correctly, the son, Russ's father, was an only child and had inherited everything when Mitchard Senior had a heart attack. Curiosity got the better of her.

"With that history, it seems strange you'd choose the

career you have. I'd have thought you'd follow your grandfather, build more office buildings.''

"There's nothing wrong with what I do."

The belligerent words startled her.

"I didn't say there was. I just thought—" She stopped when his face darkened. "Never mind." She sipped her coffee, thinking. "So you came back to Safe Harbor because of your memories."

"I came back because the marketing studies I commissioned showed great potential for my business here." The words stopped abruptly.

"Good for you. And welcome to our town." She tried to lighten the tone.

"I have another reason for staying, though, Annie." He peered at her.

"Really?" She laughed nervously. There was something about those unusual eyes. "Well, according to the Chamber of Commerce there are a lot of reasons anyone would choose Safe Harbor."

"It had nothing to do with the Chamber of Commerce. I'd already decided to set up shop here, just not quite yet. But then my grandfather upped the ante. More particularly, his will did."

Something—a fizzle of awareness—shot through her. "Your grandfather's will said you had to live in Safe Harbor?" she whispered.

"No." He took a deep breath and looked her straight in the eye. "My grandfather's will said I have to marry you to collect my inheritance."

Annie stared with shock into that cool gray gaze. So this was R.J. She wished she'd been prepared. But then, wasn't that why Wharton Willoughby had written her, to prepare her?

As she watched him, a mask slid into place, shielding

his expressive eyes from her. How much did he know, she wondered. Was he aware of the relationship she'd shared with his grandfather?

"What did you say your name was?"

He frowned. "Russell James Mitchard. Most people call me Russ. My gramps used to call me R.J. Why?"

All hope that this was a case of mistaken identity flew away. Annie swallowed.

R.J. This was the beloved grandson, the man her dearest friend had chosen as her husband. A husband she didn't want.

Ignorance was bliss. And it was worth a try if it deflated this crazy idea before it got airborne. She'd pretend his proposal came as a shock.

"Proposing marriage to someone you've only just met is preposterous. I'm afraid I'll have to turn down your proposal, Mr. Mitchard. I'm not interested in getting married."

"Now?" he asked, one eyebrow quirked.

"Ever."

The mask dissolved. His eyes narrowed, intensifying their scrutiny of her, probing for answers. He wouldn't give up easily. Annie felt her heart sink to her shoes. She'd liked Wharton Willoughby a lot, but marriage? No way.

She'd tread her life path alone, and keep her heart safe.

Chapter Two

"**Y**ou have to marry me!"

Several minutes elapsed while the world regained its balance. Russ watched Annie Simmons's face darken, blue eyes frost over. He winced at the smothered fury in her voice, wondering why the possibility she'd refuse had never occurred to him. Gramps had given the impression he'd spoken with her, but if not—

"I don't *have* to do anything." Annie Simmons shook her head, but her stare never left his face. "You said your grandfather was leaving you something, didn't you? I didn't mishear that part?"

"You heard correctly, Annie. He left me a substantial amount of money so I could move up my plans to expand my business. I'd been telling him about some new equipment and—never mind." He looked away from that stare, felt slightly abashed at his temerity in blurting it all out. He should have found an easier way. But what easier way was there to explain Gramps?

"But—" She stopped. Her lips worked, but no sound emerged.

"Trust me, I know how you feel. I felt the same way when I found out his conditions—stunned. But it's true. My mother is an excellent lawyer. She inherited his law firm and his house. She assures me it's all legal. My grandfather specifically worded his last wishes—in order to collect my inheritance I have to marry you within six months of his death."

He saw her swallow, hesitate, look away, then back at him.

"No offense, but is there a history of mental illness in your family?" Annie's fingers folded and refolded in her lap.

Nervous energy, he decided, though she didn't sound as surprised as he'd expected. Why was that? What was she hiding?

"Not that I know of." He grinned. "Though you might think so if you'd known my grandfather. Normal wasn't in his vocabulary."

"I'm beginning to realize that." Her blue gaze remained wide and fixed—on him.

Russ took another sip of coffee, sorting through his words carefully.

"Grandad was a character." He stared into the black brew, remembering the old man's penchant for running things. Then he chuckled. "But no one ever suggested Wharton Willoughby didn't have what it took in the courtroom."

"There's something you should know."

He watched Annie swallow, take a deep breath.

"Your grandfather was my mother's lawyer," she whispered.

Russ Mitchard met her frown with a shrug. He hadn't known that, but then there was a lot about his grandfather he was just beginning to uncover. "I didn't realize he actually knew you." His brain began processing. "Though if he did, that explains his insistence on you as the chosen one."

"But—" She frowned at him, her eyes intently scrutinizing his features. "So he was your grandfather. Hmm."

She was holding back. Russ watched her puzzle something out in her mind and wondered what was going on.

"My mother's papa," he confirmed with a nod. "Died a little before Thanksgiving. If you met him, you must understand about the will. Eccentric was his middle name."

"He wasn't eccentric when I knew him. He was kind and gentle, comforting. A father figure who also happened to be my mother's lawyer."

He saw genuine tenderness fill her eyes.

"He helped me settle her estate. He's the one who suggested I use the money she left me to buy this place. He helped me negotiate the sale, then came back to check on my renovations several times. But I hadn't seen him since winter arrived."

"He didn't like snow very much. He caught pneumonia before he died."

She glanced at him, chewed on her bottom lip for a moment, then blurted out the duty phrase he'd heard so often.

"I'm sorry. I would have gone to the funeral if I'd known. But with this place, and Drew to think of, I wasn't paying much attention to the news."

"I understand." Russ could see how tightly she controlled the words. She was definitely hiding something. His senses perked up.

"Why me, do you think?" Annie faltered over that question as if she weren't sure how he'd take it.

"I haven't figured that out yet," he confessed, watching

the swirl of conflicting emotions darken her eyes. Should he tell her? "My hunch is that, while he was ill, he dreamed the whole thing up."

"Was he ill a long time?" she whispered.

"Several weeks. He couldn't shake that cold." Russ closed his eyes, thought it out. "My guess is he concocted one of his ideas, then purposely brought us together. He certainly knew I was doing studies on the area as a potential business site. In fact, he's the one who originally pointed it out as a possible location, then told me not to bother. He knew very well how much I'd loved my time here as a child."

She blinked innocently, but Russ saw a shadow flicker through her eyes. Something about this whole thing bothered him. Annie Simmons didn't seem nearly as flabbergasted by his proposal as he'd expected.

"If I knew Gramps, and I did, he manipulated my whole situation for his personal convenience. He'd been after me to move closer to home for ages." More flickers. Russ frowned.

"Manipulated? He didn't seem conniving to me. Just very kind." She avoided his stare, studied her fingers.

"Gramps was kind. He was also very big on marriage. Maybe because his own was so great." He paused, then decided to tell the whole story. "He and my grandmother were married after her parents died. It was a marriage of convenience that provided a home for her baby sister and gave him the society wife he wanted. But they fell in love, and everything worked out for them. They had a great marriage, the envy of everyone who saw them together. I guess that's why he thought it would work if he forced the two of us together."

If Russ closed his eyes, he could see his grandparents, hands clasped, eyes shining with a rich, deep joy he'd never known. Maybe if he could feel that kind of emotion, be so confident that nothing he did would disappoint, he would be more interested in the institution of marriage.

But Russ was smart enough to know he was not his grandfather. Nor his father. When people depended on him, they were disillusioned. Invariably. He didn't do it deliberately. Responsibility just didn't work with him. Whether it stemmed from selfishness, or from years of being expected to follow in the family career path, he'd never managed to be the man they wanted, had never come close to stepping up to the plate and handling the responsibility they wanted to give him.

"Now that you mention it, I do remember he once said he missed her presence more than anything else he'd ever known, that she'd gone from being a stranger to becoming a part of his heart. The way he talked about her—it was so sweet."

She drifted away on some memory Russ couldn't share. Clearly Annie Simmons knew his grandfather well. But how—

"So your grandfather named you as his heir?"

Nodding, Russ steeled himself to face her. "One of them."

The next part would be touchy. There was no easy way to say it without sounding crass and greedy, but neither was he quite ready to divulge his true reasons behind this strange proposal.

"His plan goes like this. We marry, and I collect my inheritance. I get my business on a solid footing, charm the tourists with my creations and start work on some bigger projects I've been itching to try, once I buy some more equipment. It's actually quite simple."

Simple? It was a nightmare, one Russ would have avoided like the plague if he hadn't allowed himself to be persuaded by the cajoling words in that letter Gramps had left behind. He'd only come here, asked her to do this, out of respect for the old man and because he wanted to see what Annie Simmons had that had bowled over his crusty old grandfather so much that he'd taken it upon himself to arrange a marriage.

Gramps's opinions on marriage were no secret to him. It made a man stronger, grounded him, gave him purpose and a helpmate to lean on when things got tough. He remembered their last conversation vividly. The right woman would help Russ realize his dreams. Well, Russ was realizing his dreams just fine—gaining increasing fame with his work, landing contracts, building a base of studio buyers.

Gramps knew Russ had committed every dime he could spare to open that shop—and that wasn't counting the loans he'd taken to move everything to this tourist Mecca. His studies had shown the potential here, the support for craftsmen willing to work hard and build their business. Russ desperately wanted to prove himself, but he was at the sink-or-swim point. If Safe Harbor didn't work out, he'd have to dip into his savings, and that was a last resort. Gramps had known that, and apparently he'd come up with this solution.

Marriage.

Russ might have walked away without a second thought, dismissed the whole idea as the romantic machinations of a delusional old man if he hadn't had that last conversation with his grandfather, hadn't felt the conviction in the old man's voice that Annie Simmons was his soul mate. Hadn't listened to his fervent prayer for Russ's future happiness. Hadn't received the letter.

Even so, after the funeral, after the will had been read, he'd worked six ways through Sunday, unpacked his law books and plied every legal tactic he could remember to break that will, until finally he'd been forced to admit defeat. The will was unbreakable. Gramps would have it his way or Russ would lose his opportunity and break the trust his grandfather had placed in him. The latter would hurt far more than losing any money.

He looked at Annie. She didn't speak, didn't say a word. Her mind seemed to be somewhere else. Russ shifted uncomfortably, tented his hands, then unfolded them and shoved them in his pockets.

"So? What do you think?" he blurted, unable to keep silent a moment longer. He'd never been so uncomfortable in his life. He didn't want to marry her, knew he couldn't be what his grandfather had been to Gran. Annie didn't need her life messed up by him. But Gramps—

"I'm thinking that I need to get away from you."

"What? Why?" He ordered his mind to pay attention.

"This is a quiet little town, Mr. Mitchard. People don't walk into my bed-and-breakfast and suggest I marry them so that they can inherit an estate! It just doesn't happen here." The speech burst out of her as if it had been prepared some time ago.

"It probably doesn't happen anywhere else, either," he admitted dryly. "My grandfather never did anything the ordinary way. He liked to be—original." Okay, that was a vast understatement of the facts. He tried again.

"The marriage wouldn't have to be the ordinary kind of marriage, Annie." He tried to comfort her. "It could be whatever we wanted—a business arrangement between us, if you like. I fully expect to split the inheritance with you, anyway. Gramps would have wanted that."

"Pay me, you mean? For marrying you?" She was outraged. "No."

Russ raked one hand through his hair and desperately

wished his grandfather were here right now to explain what will-o'-the-wisp dream had engendered this situation in his fertile mind. Gramps knew exactly how little Russ wanted the responsibility for someone else's happiness—anyone else's. Apparently Annie felt the same way. He didn't blame her.

"No, not pay you." He retracted the words, trying to find new ones as he stared into her angry face. "I just meant that I wouldn't expect you to disrupt your life for nothing. I know this will inconvenience you."

"Inconvenience me? Getting married? Oh, perhaps just the teeniest bit, Mr. Mitchard." She laughed, a sharp, grating sound that told him the state of her nerves. "This whole thing is impossible! He should have known that."

"Maybe." Russ reached out a hand to stop her from leaving. "But it's also reality." And it got worse. Russ dredged up one last ounce of courage and laid it on the line. "I have to be married to you within the next three months."

If he had to wait that long, he'd give up. As it was, he'd had to summon every ounce of courage to ask someone he didn't know to marry him. Only the memory of his grandfather's whispered words pushed him forward. But Russ kept that knowledge to himself, silently chiding his grandfather for his manipulations. Bad enough Gramps had used him. But Annie? She seemed a sweet, innocent person. Why involve her in this?

"Three months? Three years. The answer is the same. No." She shook her head, her eyes huge as she leaned away from him, jerking her hand out from under his.

"Annie, I've done everything I could think of to find some way around this, but the will stands."

"I don't know about the will. I only know I'm not marrying you. I loved and respected your grandfather. I'd like

to do as he asked. But that doesn't mean I'm willing to
marry you.''

Russ wasn't crazy about marriage himself, but the way
she said that made him feel like a slug. He wasn't that
bad, was he?

''But—''

''Forget it.'' She jumped to her feet, grabbed her coffee
cup and carried it to the sink. ''No. No! No way.''

''I see.'' He frowned, tilted back on his chair and studied her, stuffing down his doubts. ''What's the problem?
Is it me or just the general idea of marriage that you object
to?''

''Both!''

''Ah.'' So he didn't appeal to her. Well, that was hum-
bling, but probably good. Romance complicated things,
and Russ had enough complications in his life. She was
pretty and graceful and efficient, but he'd never intended
to tie himself down. Responsibility was the one thing he
always failed at. This wouldn't be an emotional commitment, it would be business. ''It wouldn't have to be anything personal.''

She choked. Russ moved to stand beside her.

''That didn't come out right,'' he muttered. ''I meant
that it's just—''

''Business? Yes, I guessed you'd say that. Let me explain this to you.''

He noted the way she smothered her emotions, her fingers clenching at her sides.

''I'm not trying to be difficult,'' she explained in a quiet
voice. ''I'd like to help you out, if I could. I'm sure it's
perfectly normal for you to want your inheritance.''

He frowned. She did understand—at least as much as
he'd told her. But it wasn't the money—

She read his face and rushed to finish. ''I can't help

you. Not that way. I am not marrying you. Wharton shouldn't have asked me.''

"Asked you? But—'' He stared at her, understanding dawning. She had known. "He wrote you?'' Russ murmured.

She nodded.

"Yes. I didn't get the letter until after he'd died. At first I didn't connect you with his R.J.'' She looked sad for a moment. "But this is not even up for discussion. I'm Drew's temporary mother. Think about him. How would I explain such a thing to him? No. Drew needs security from me, not a whole new set of changes.'' She shook her head vehemently, obviously appalled at the thought of being tied to Russ.

"You said they'd found a relative.'' Russ caught her frown of dismay. "You'll only have yourself to think about when he leaves.''

"I'll deal with that when it happens.''

Something on her face told him she didn't want to contemplate Drew leaving. Why was that?

The telephone broke the silence. Annie grabbed the receiver off the wall.

"Hello?''

"Annie.''

Russ was standing near enough to hear a man's voice.

"Which date did you prefer? Day after tomorrow?''

"I—uh, that is, I haven't had a chance to look at your notes yet. I just got back from choir practice.'' Annie turned her back to Russ. "I'm glad you found a buyer, but I don't really think they need me to decide whether or not they want my mother's house.'' She held the phone away from her ear, wincing at the jovial tone.

"They claim they do. I want to get this settled, strike while they've got their loan approval. We've waited a long time for a hot prospect, Annie. Let's not lose them. I'll tell them we'll meet at the house this Tuesday after lunch. Okay?''

Russ thought Annie looked like a hunted fox. She glanced here and there around the room as if a sudden way of escape would open up.

''Unless you want it sooner?''

''No! Tuesday's fine, I suppose. I just don't see why they want me there.'' She snuggled the phone close, but Russ didn't even pretend not to listen. The conversation was fascinating, at least Annie's side of it was.

''Oh, they saw that, did they? Well, I guess if they like it—''

The person on the phone kept talking.

''Everyone?'' She seemed to shrink a little. Her voice rose. ''I don't want to be the object of people's gossip. I want my personal life to be private.'' She sighed at his guffaw. ''Yes, I know. Privacy is impossible in Safe Harbor. All right. Goodbye.''

She hung up the phone, but stood staring at it for several moments. Eventually she moved to the table, but only to stack the rest of their dishes. Russ watched her stuff the white crockery with its delicate blue flowers into the dishwasher.

''Is everything all right?''

She looked at him, gave a half laugh that was not at all amused. ''No. Absolutely nothing is all right. But I'll manage. I always do.''

He got the impression she wanted to do much more than manage. What had happened to cause that sheen of happiness he thought so much a part of her fade away after one phone call? Where did she go when her eyes glazed over and her face stiffened into that mask of rigid self-control?

A sound broke the silence between them. Russ started out the door, twisted his head, noticed she wasn't following.

"Annie?" She blinked, focused on him. She looked sad, about to burst into tears. He walked back, brushed a hand against her cheek. "I think someone needs you."

"Oh. Okay." Annie nodded, turned, walked through the doorway.

Russ followed her.

"Yowl!"

He quickened his step. Uh-oh. He'd meant to explain first.

A man with gray-streaked hair, granite jaw and midnight blue eyes that begged for their help waited in her foyer.

"She won't leave me alone," he muttered. He seemed glued to the spot.

"Who won't?" Annie frowned, her eyes sliding down his frame until they arrived at the monstrously huge body of a marmalade-colored cat curled around his feet, purring a loud contented rumble. A smile twitched the corner of her mouth. "Oh, I see."

"I'm not very good with cats," he murmured, his face pinched in distressed lines. "Usually they don't like me at all."

"Well, this one does."

"Apparently." The man tried to move, but the cat counteracted his motions with her own.

Russ stood silent, watched as Annie tried to figure out a way to free her guest from its clutches.

"Were you wanting this place in particular, or did she chase you in here?"

"She was here when I arrived. But the sign says no pets." His words sounded hesitant, confused. His eyes revealed little of his thoughts. "I'm Nathan Taylor. I'll be coming to Safe Harbor for the next several months, but only on the weekends. I'd like to rent a room.''

''Wait a minute.'' Annie studied him more closely. ''I remember you. The man who saved Aidan. You were at my grand opening.''

His face darkened with embarrassment. ''Yes.''

''I'm glad to see you again.''

She did look happy, Russ decided. The glare he'd been favored with had disappeared, replaced by a friendly smile.

''Well, we can certainly accommodate you here. As soon as we free you, that is.'' Annie glanced at Russ.

He did his best to hide his guilt, but he knew from the furrow of her eyebrows that she'd seen some flicker of it in his face.

''I—er, I may be able to help.'' He walked over and scooped up the monster cat. Instantly at peace, Marmalade curled herself over his shoulders and settled down to sleep. ''I'm afraid she's mine,'' he admitted quietly.

''What?'' Annie frowned at him. ''But surely Felicity told you our policy of no pets.''

''Yes, she did.'' Oh, why hadn't he explained the cat's presence earlier? Now it looked like he'd been trying to slip one past her. Which he had.

''You knew? Then why—''

''I thought that if I explained, you'd understand. She's completely house-trained. She doesn't scratch things or tear up shoes. Mostly she sleeps.'' He shrugged, trying to appeal to her decency and love of animals, though to be frank, he wasn't certain she did like animals. She certainly kept well out of reach of his cat.

''Marmalade is another legacy from my grandfather. I brought her in from the truck a few minutes ago.''

Annie ignored her newest client to direct visual darts of suspicion toward Russ Mitchard.

"As I'm positive Felicity explained to you, we don't allow cats here. I can't afford the damage claws could do to the quilts or the curtains, not to mention that woodwork." She blanched a little at the mention of it, her eyes on the oak paneling. "It's one of the rules I just can't break."

She wouldn't budge. Russ knew that as surely as he knew his name. Annie Simmons was very protective of her business, very proud of what she'd accomplished. He'd noticed it earlier in the way she slid her hand over the gleaming stainless steel range in the kitchen, her quick mop up, which returned the shining glass table they'd eaten on to its pristine condition. She delighted in what she'd made here and she didn't want it ruined. He didn't blame her.

Of course, Marmalade wouldn't hurt anything, but Annie didn't know that.

"There are no animals allowed in this establishment. If that means you're unable to stay with us, I'm very sorry, Mr. Mitchard. But I cannot and will not break my rule." Her lips were pressed together in a firm line that brooked no argument.

"No problem." He lifted the cat and walked to a corner by the desk. From behind a potted palm he pulled a black pet carrier. Within seconds, he'd stored the cat inside.

Russ wasn't going to argue. He'd landed enough on her today. If he wanted to make any progress on the marriage issue, he needed to correct this mistake in judgment. He lifted the carrier and walked to the door, then stopped and faced her.

"I'll find a place for Marmalade and then I'll be back. She's been declawed, so she wouldn't hurt anything. But I don't want to break your rules. I'll see you later."

He walked out her front door, headed for his truck. Today was not going the way he'd intended. But then, what did he expect? To walk in on Annie Simmons, announce that she needed to marry him so he could finally fulfill a dream and expect her to meekly agree? Put like that, it wouldn't matter how many letters she'd read.

"Thanks a lot, Gramps," he muttered, only half under his breath. "After today, she'll probably never talk to me again. Let alone marry me. Then what will you do?" In the recesses of his mind Russ could almost hear the old coot chuckle with delight.

Annie bit her lip as she watched Russ Mitchard walk away with his cat, wishing she'd rephrased that. She'd sounded like a stuffy old spinster who couldn't allow a cat to muss her home. But getting the bed-and-breakfast finished had taken such a long time, been so much work, eaten up every dime her mother had left her. Besides, the quilts had come from the Women's League. She couldn't imagine asking them to make her another because a cat had ruined one!

Then she remembered the reason Russ was here and felt even worse. How embarrassing to be proposed to for money, even by that sweet old man's grandson. He'd put a nice face on it, pretended that wasn't the only reason, but Annie knew he couldn't want to marry her any more than she wanted to marry him.

She'd had to refuse his proposal, surely he understood that? *If* he came back, it would be better to keep things on a business plane and pretend his offer of marriage had never happened. Perhaps if she acted nonchalant, she could spare both their feelings.

A cough broke through her musings. Annie pasted a smile on her face, then turned to the man standing in front of her desk.

"I'm sorry, Mr. Taylor," she apologized quietly. "Now let's get you settled in." She dealt with the registration, took an imprint of his credit card, all the while trying desperately to force Russ Mitchard out of her mind.

"I hope I didn't interrupt anything." He looked confused.

Annie knew the feeling. Nothing was going the way it should have today. Two new customers, and she was mad?

"You didn't interrupt a thing. If you'll follow me?" She made herself calm down as she showed him to his room.

"I take it he's another guest?"

"That remains to be seen." Annie met his curious stare but did not elaborate. "Breakfast is served from six-thirty to nine. I hope that will suit you, Mr. Taylor?"

"Sure. Whatever. I'm here to relax." He set his duffel bag on the bed.

"I'll leave you to get settled in, then. Please make yourself at home." She moved toward the doorway.

"If I correctly remember our introduction at your opening, you're a native to the area, aren't you." It wasn't a question.

Curious, Annie turned back, one hand on the doorknob. "Why, yes, I am."

"Then you know Constance Laughlin."

"Everyone knows Constance." Annie smiled. "She's like our den mother. Anything to do with Safe Harbor has to do with Constance."

He nodded. Annie studied him, watched his cheeks flush a rich red. He turned away from her scrutiny to peer out the window. Why Constance, she wondered idly.

"You don't happen to know where I'd find her this afternoon, do you?"

The words tumbled out in a rush, as if he were embarrassed to ask. There was something strange about him, almost furtive. As if he were hiding something. And yet, when she looked into his eyes, they seemed honest, clear. It was just that Russ Mitchard and this crazy day had confused everything.

"Constance?" She pretended to think. "Probably at the church. She'll be checking the spring bulb collections in the flower beds. Constance has a thing about those bulbs. You might try there. First Peninsula Church." She gave him directions.

The screech of brakes and a child's yell cut off her explanation.

Drew!

Annie tore down the stairs, raced out the front door. What had the child done now?

"You could have gotten yourself killed! Me, too, if my reactions hadn't been fast enough. You never run into the street after something. Didn't your mother teach you anything?"

Him again!

Annie saw Drew's little face crumple at the mention of his mother. He hunched over in the street and bawled.

Annie marched out the door, right up to Russ Mitchard and glared at him.

"Did your mother tell you to think before you speak?" she hissed, glaring at him with the frostiest look she could muster as all her protective instincts swam to the fore. At his blank look, she boiled.

"He hasn't got a mother," she told him in a half whisper of pure fury. "I told you that." She ignored his groan of dismay to crouch beside Drew. "Come on, honey. Let's get you inside. Everything's going to be fine."

"Somehow, Annie, I doubt that with you around things will ever be merely *fine* again." Russ's silvery eyes flashed with an inner fire.

Now what did that mean?

Russ brushed her out of the way, bent and scooped the boy into his arms. He carried him into the bed-and-breakfast.

"At least he's not hurt. Are you?" He set Drew on a chair. Then his hands moved carefully over the small limbs, checking for fractures.

"I'm okay." Drew dashed one hand across his eyes. "I'm sorry, Annie. I just wanted to see the cat. It was huge." Drew's tear-smudged face begged her to understand. "I've never seen a cat that big. She almost let me pet her!"

That cat. Again. Annie risked a look at Russ, watched him shrug, as if this, too, wasn't his fault.

"I thought she was in her carrier?" she demanded softly.

"She was. But I had to let her out. She cries if I keep her in there. That's why I let her out in here. I was afraid she'd start howling before I could explain." He flushed. "I just didn't get around to explaining before—"

"She cries. Uh-huh." Annie rolled her eyes. What a line.

"Hey, mister? Is that big orange cat yours?" Drew blinked at Russ, hero worship glowing in his pale face.

"Yes. Her name is Marmalade. And your name is Drew. I didn't recognize you at first, especially when you took off across the street like that." Russ raked a hand through his black hair, ruining its perfection.

Did his fingers tremble just a little?

"You scared the daylights out of me, Drew."

"I'm sorry." The apology was perfunctory. "What are daylights?" He studied Russ for a minute before a new thought took precedence. "Hey! You're staying here, right? Felicity told Billy's mom a handsome man had moved in.''

Excitement lent Drew's eyes a glossy chocolate sheen.

''So that means your cat will be staying here, too. All right!'' He jumped up, twisted to face Annie. ''I can play with her, can't I? I never had a cat before. My mom—'' He stopped, gulped hard but stoically continued, a sheen of fresh tears glossing his eyes. ''Remember, Annie? Mom was allergic, so I couldn't have any animals at our place.''

Russ cleared his throat. Annie ignored him. She was going to have to eat crow. She didn't need him to rub it in.

Drew had lost everything. His little world had shifted, changed irrevocably when he'd lost his parents. She had a business to run, but was that a good enough reason to deny Drew the comfort of an overfed orange feline? No. She was all for anything that would make Drew's life a little happier. Wasn't that what parenting was all about?

''You can't deny the kid a cat,'' Russ whispered in her ear, satisfaction resonating through his rumbling voice. ''Marmalade is here to stay.''

But you aren't, she thought, twisting to look into his silvery eyes. *You won't be staying here long.*

She'd known him only a short while, talked to him for less than an hour, but she knew a lot about Russ Mitchard. And somehow she just knew that settling down wasn't in Russ's long-term plans. She had a hunch from something Mr. Willoughby had once said that as soon as Russ had his business running smoothly, he'd be off searching for greener pastures. Wasn't that what had worried his grandfather so much—the fear that R.J. was running away from life?

Still, as long as he was a guest at her bed-and-breakfast, she'd have to face him every day, be civil. Probably even explain repeatedly that there was no hope of him marrying her. The thought of that daily contact left her both wary and excited.

Why was that?

Annie was afraid she was going to find out.

Chapter Three

"She's a big old girl, isn't she?" Drew tenderly swiped his hand down the cat's sleek back. "She purrs louder than a bullfrog."

He laid his head on the floor beside the cat and closed his eyes, listening for the rumble of contentment.

"You're my bestest friend, Marmalade."

Russ had to look away or bawl. Drew reminded him so much of Adam, the Adam he remembered—before the accident, the one that had claimed his brother's life. If only he'd taken his responsibility to Adam as seriously as Drew took his toward that cat.

"I made hot chocolate. That should tide you over till dinner. I'm afraid I got a little behind today." Annie stood in front of him, her blue eyes bright with the frustration of his presence here.

Russ grinned. At least she wasn't indifferent to him. A marriage of convenience would be difficult enough. A marriage of indifference would be intolerable. Strangely, he understood Annie's discomfiture around him, even felt the same way. She kept him on his toes, slightly off center.

He never knew exactly how she'd react. She certainly wasn't like any other female he'd ever met. For one thing, she always spoke the truth, no matter what. It didn't do a thing for his ego, but he found her bluntness refreshing, just the same.

"Are you going to take this mug or not?" she muttered just low enough so Drew wouldn't hear.

Clearly she wasn't thrilled that he'd become more than simply a guest.

"I'm going to take it. Thank you." He peered at the peppermint in it, then glanced at her. "What about Drew?"

"I already drank some juice. I gave Marm some milk." Drew turned to the cat. "She likes milk."

"Thank you for taking care of her." The boy's attentiveness surprised Russ. At that age, he'd had a lot of pets. Had he ever been so careful of them? Maybe that's when this problem with responsibility had begun.

Annie seated herself away from Russ, in the big brown armchair by the fire. It was a deliberate move, distancing him. Russ knew he was supposed to take note of that. Which he did, with a smile at her prim face. Then he promptly shifted seats so he lounged across from her. Keeping up with Annie was like playing chess. He adored chess. Gramps had taught him the game years ago. *Check, Annie Simmons.*

He lifted the red and white striped peppermint stick. A drop of chocolate dangled on the end. Russ licked it off. The chocolate flavor blossomed on his tongue, made richer by the hint of mint. He caught her stare.

"I had some peppermint sticks left over after Christmas. No point in throwing them out." Her eyes glittered defensively.

"None whatsoever," he agreed, leaning back to savor

the atmosphere she'd created. "It's excellent. So is this room."

The soft glow of firelight on the oak paneling and the comfy furniture set around the fireplace gave the room a well-lived feel. Annie, having started dinner, had changed from her jeans into a long velvet jumper the exact color of her eyes. Her hair glowed silver in the firelight. She was very much lady of the manor.

Taken as a whole, this was a picture-perfect example of home. The air was redolent with the succulent aroma of beef stew, fresh rolls and something with cinnamon that Russ prayed was apple pie. The flames, the quiet peace, all of it combined to relax the visitor. She'd achieved her aim and then some.

At the moment Annie ignored him, the same way she'd tried to ignore him most of the afternoon while he'd settled into his room, gone back and forth to his shop and taken Marmalade out for a walk with Drew. Russ stifled a chuckle at the way she tilted her nose in the air and focused her attention on the ceiling to avoid looking at him.

"Something smells very good. I hope my staying for dinner isn't an intrusion." He paused deliberately, found himself waiting for her comeback with anticipation. Their verbal sparring intrigued him.

"This is a bed-and-breakfast." She deliberately emphasized the last word. "We don't serve dinner to our guests."

He could almost hear her thoughts. *Check that, R.J.* Annie Simmons was looking at him, maybe not the way he wanted, but at least she wasn't ignoring him. He studied her in return. Marrying her wouldn't be any hardship. She was gorgeous. But Russ knew his grandfather had seen more than that in her. Gramps was a stickler for inner beauty, the character inside a person no one could see, which spilled out in the tough times.

"I realize you don't usually serve dinner. But Drew invited me." He hid his smile when she glared at the unsuspecting boy. "I could hardly refuse when he said you always made way too much and if I stayed, maybe he wouldn't have to eat leftovers."

"Remind me to speak to you later, Drew," she muttered, lips pinched in pretended annoyance. But the gentle glow on her face gave her away.

"Okay, Annie." The boy returned to ignoring them both, his voice barely audible as he hovered over Marmalade. "You're so pretty, Marm."

"Did you think about—" Russ glanced at Drew, then straight at Annie "—um, what we spoke about earlier. Have you decided?"

"Drew, honey, I think maybe you should take Marmalade for another walk before dinner." Annie's eyes warned Russ to hush. "Just outside by the bushes, okay? Don't go too far. Dinner will be ready soon."

"Okay, Annie. Come on, Marm." Drew jumped up, snapped the cat into her leash and headed toward the door. A second later they heard it thud closed.

"I decided right after you asked me, Russ. I gave you my answer then. It's still no. That isn't going to change. I'm not the marrying type." She leaned forward, her voice low, eyes flashing a warning. "According to what your grandfather told me about you, neither are you."

"No, actually I wouldn't be interested in marriage at all—under normal circumstances." Boy, was that the truth. He caught her glint of irritation and rephrased what he'd been about to say. "Though I think I could be quite good at marriage." That didn't sound right. Russ tried again. "Not that I was suggesting anything permanent between us." *Clear that up right now, Mitchard. No responsibility.*

"You take one step forward, then two back." She ticked

his misdeeds off on her fingers. "You want marriage, but not a permanent one. You think you'd be good at it, but you're not willing to give it a full commitment." She shook her head. "Maybe you need to think this idea through to completion."

"I'm merely asking you to help me achieve a goal," he clarified, then wished he hadn't said it.

It *was* unreasonable to expect a stranger to marry him without some justification, but Russ had no desire to explain about that letter. She wouldn't understand the feelings it aroused, nor could she comprehend the obligation he felt. Sometimes he didn't understand it himself. He just knew he'd loved his grandfather dearly, that he wanted to finally live up to the old man's expectations, do what Gramps had asked of him, fulfill that one last request.

"Your goal being marriage for money?" Annie's arched brows rose. "You don't seem the type."

"It's not exactly like that," he protested. "I'm not a gold digger. I earn a living with my work." Well, almost a living.

"Really?" Annie stared him down. "So why do you need your grandfather to find you a wife? Why do you need his money?" she challenged.

He didn't. It would be nice, but he could manage without it. Still, maybe if Annie felt sorry for him, maybe if he pretended he desperately needed his grandfather's legacy... The idea mushroomed in his mind. This way he wouldn't have to reveal Gramps's words.

Annie had a soft heart. Look how she'd taken in Drew, made him the center of her world, even though he was only there for a short while. If Russ could just elicit a little of those tender feelings, maybe later he could explain.

"I have two reasons for proposing." It was hard to know exactly how to say this. "I can manage without it, but I'd hate to see the old man's life savings go to a cat charity.''

"A what?" Annie blinked at him, her bewilderment showing.

"A cat charity. Marmalade was his cat. One of seventeen.''

"Seven—'' She gulped. "You're not bringing more, are you?''

Russ burst out laughing at the look of horror that spread across her expressive features.

"Don't worry. I gave the rest away. Gramps had several lady friends who love cats as much as he. They've all got good homes.''

"Oh.'' Relief didn't begin to cover the emotion washing through her blue eyes.

"But you do see why I couldn't give Marm away, don't you? She was his favorite. He specifically asked me to look after her. I couldn't let him down.''

"I suppose I can understand that.'' Suspicion lurked in the depths of her voice. "Actually, he often talked about Marmalade. I just didn't know Marmalade was a cat.''

"It's a bit inconvenient. Marm had the run of Gramps's house, and now I'll have to keep her in a cage. But what else can I do?''

"Ah.'' She ignored his wistful hint. "So you need your grandfather's money to get a home for the cat?'' Annie squinted at him dubiously. "Uh-huh.''

Russ read her thoughts. "He wasn't crazy. Just a little eccentric.''

"Forcing your grandson to choose between marrying someone he doesn't know or losing his inheritance to a cat charity is eccentric?'' She tilted one eyebrow into an inverted V. "In Safe Harbor we call that crazy.''

"Gramps obviously felt he had a good reason to insist

on our marriage. He was a smart man, he knew me, knew what I wanted to do with my work. I may not understand all of his reasons, but I expect that in his own warped way, he was trying to help me by arranging this.''

Russ clamped his lips closed. He wasn't going to explain the empty barren years after he'd left the law firm, years he'd filled by taking on any challenge that came along, years that had sunk him in plenty of hot water. Gramps had understood his decision to quit law, but he'd never understood Russ's restlessness or what lay underneath it. If he knew his grandfather, the old man had conceived this idea believing it would tie Russ down.

''Help you?'' Annie stared. ''You're sure there's no history of insanity?''

''Quite sure.'' He smiled, pleased that she'd dropped her attitude.

''I'll take your word on that. For now.'' She tapped one slim finger against the fabric of her skirt. ''You mentioned two reasons. The cat charity and what else? What other reason do you have for marrying to get your grandfather's money?''

How far did he take this pretended greed? The answer wouldn't be silenced—far enough to do what his grandfather had asked. He owed him that. Russ thought fast.

''I have plans for the future. I want to expand my shop, develop more lines, maybe take on an apprentice while I travel, hold exhibitions. Silver's expensive. It takes time to build up a repertoire, recoup your expenses.'' He shrugged. ''There are things I want to do with my life, and it takes money. Why shouldn't I have what my grandfather kept for me?''

''Maybe. But still—marrying for money?'' Her lips turned down in distaste. ''It sounds so sad.''

''There are a lot of reasons to get married. Money isn't

the worst one. Besides, we wouldn't be marrying for money." It felt good to say that, emphasize it, even. "We'd be marrying because my grandfather arranged it. What's so bad about that?" He stabbed his toe into the carpet, wishing he knew how to word that differently.

"Hmm." She tapped her bottom lip with one forefinger. "Where to begin?"

"I've watched my friends get married, Annie." Why not let her see some of the truth that had always driven him away from marriage? "They had no expectation of failure, but they still found themselves separating after a couple of years because their goals changed and the euphoria that carried them into marriage couldn't sustain them through reality. Life is difficult. There are only so many hours in a day, so many years allotted to each of us. I don't want to waste any more of them doing things I don't enjoy. Why should I give up my inheritance to a cat home when it could give us both a measure of freedom?"

"Said that way, it sounds reasonable. I suppose."

She didn't look convinced. Despite her agreement, Russ knew Annie wasn't comfortable with the idea of marriage, no matter how he worded it. He could see aversion written all over her expressive face. The question was, why?

"It is reasonable. I'm not the type to hang around anywhere for long. Too many things to do and see. That's why I told you the truth up front." Well, most of it. "I'm not out to cheat anyone. No secrets."

She nodded sagely, her plucky grin back in place. "Well, for your sake, I hope your inheritance is big enough to allow you that kind of freedom."

"Nine hundred eighty-five thousand dollars," he told her bluntly, watching for her reaction, hoping to see the character Gramps had spoken of.

"Nine—oh!" She blanched, and her blue eyes seemed

to swell with worry. "You mean you'll lose all that money if we don't get married?"

Guilt. Russ recognized it immediately. And wished he could abolish it. The last thing he wanted was for her to marry him out of guilt. He knew too much about that emotion already.

"Well, yes," he admitted. "I wasted a lot of time trying to contest his will, but it's rock solid. Anyway, Gramps would be mad if I did that. He must have had a thing about you."

"A thing? About me?" Distaste flooded her face. "He was like my grandfather, Russ. He was sweet and honest, a shoulder when I needed one. That's all there was between us. Friendship."

Russ nodded. She was so transparent, so easy to read. A man would know exactly where he stood with Annie Simmons. She accepted others at face value. He had a hunch she wouldn't try to change him. She hadn't with Drew. She'd mentioned earlier that the boy still didn't talk about his parents much, but she didn't push him. When he was ready, she'd said. That spoke well for their future, didn't it?

"Maybe friendship was part of it. But I still think there was something that made him come up with this idea, and it wasn't me. Until he phoned me that last time, we hadn't talked in quite a while." And that was his fault, Russ admitted. He'd been ashamed, and embarrassed.

"What kind of 'thing' could your grandfather possibly have about me?" She seemed genuinely puzzled.

Which was odd. Gramps had said he would explain all of it to her. Russ considered relating what the old man had said to him but quickly changed his mind. Wouldn't it make an already tense situation worse to admit that he'd spoken with his grandfather about her? That they'd discussed her behind her back?

"Did you hear me?"

Russ blinked, then nodded.

"Sorry, yes. I was just thinking of something he said." What was the question? Why her? "Gramps claimed he got an impression of people the first time he met them. Knew right away whether they were guilty or innocent. That's why he was so successful in his practice. People seldom managed to bamboozle my grandfather."

She caught her bottom lip between her teeth as if she were rehashing something from her past. Russ decided to probe further.

"Gramps met you several times, didn't he?" Russ was flying by the seat of his pants. He knew only what she'd said about their relationship and what Gramps had hinted. But he'd sure like to find out more. "When you settled your mother's estate—that's how you met?"

"I went to his office for a number of reasons. I'd never done any of it before, you see. When my father died, your grandfather was also the attorney, but my mother handled everything. I barely knew him then." She shook her head, sighed. "When Mother died, I had no idea how to proceed. Fortunately, her death wasn't unexpected, and your grandfather had already been to town once or twice to have her sign some papers, so her estate was settled quickly, without problems. He was very kind to me."

"I'm glad." If he knew Gramps, and Russ had known the old guy very well, every *t* was crossed, every *i* dotted. In fact, if you read between the lines of Gramps's last letter, Annie Simmons was like the granddaughter he'd never had.

"He visited me, you know. Every so often." She nodded at his look of surprise. "Really."

"For what, I wonder." Russ frowned. "He never cared much for this town when I was a kid. Claimed a person could get snagged in the relaxed lifestyle and never make anything of themselves. One day last summer he was talking about the potential I'd find here. By fall he said he'd made a mistake in ever recommending the place and warned me away, said it didn't have what I needed." Which was one reason Russ had chosen Safe Harbor. He'd been fairly certain his grandfather would not interfere in his plans.

Suddenly he wondered how deliberate that move had been. Another of Gramps's chess plays?

"I don't know about that." Annie blinked her surprise. "He only told me he had business in town. I never knew what it was. He'd stop by the house, have a cup of tea, and we'd talk."

"About what?" Russ couldn't wrap his mind around this image of his cranky old grandfather sipping tea with a bereaved young woman.

"Everything. His youth. How much he loved his wife, places they'd been. Things he wished he'd done."

She was leaving something out, he knew it. Russ held his peace, waited.

"We even talked about you. He was very concerned about you, you know." She stared into the fire. "Your grandfather was always concerned about the people he dealt with. It was he who encouraged me to buy this place. He'd offered me a job in his office, but I wanted to stay here."

"He offered you a job? In his office?" Russ stared. Gramps must have been smitten. As far as Russ knew, Gramps had never allowed anyone but Millie Fitzgibbons in his office.

Annie avoided his stare, looked at her hands, knotting and unknotting them over and over. Finally she continued.

"I guess maybe I was one of those people he thought wasn't reaching her potential." A sad little smile crowded the joy from her face. "I didn't go to college, you see. I could have. I won a full scholarship for interior design. At least, my sketches did."

Ah, sketches. Now perhaps Annie would explain that curious phone call. But she didn't, only named a prestigious school Russ knew by reputation. Those scholarships weren't doled out to just anyone. She must have had great talent to win. He was puzzled about that.

"My mother was ill. Not just physically, but mentally, as well. I didn't want to leave her alone." Her voice dropped to a whisper. "She still missed my father terribly, you see. After all those years, after all the awful things he'd done, she still cared for him when he died."

Did she realize how much she gave away with those few words? Russ watched and waited, his focus entirely on her bowed head. The room was silent save for the flicker of the fire.

In the periphery of his vision, Russ saw Drew creep into the room, settle in the corner, Marmalade on his lap. Soon the cat's gentle snoring resonated, but Drew never said a word. He seemed to sense that Annie needed this moment to pause, regroup.

After a moment, she straightened, thrust back her shoulders and began to speak in a harsh tone.

"My father wasn't the kind of man to be tied down. He'd promise things, lots of things. But he never followed through. He'd phone her filled with glorious plans for the future." Annie's blue eyes darkened almost to violet. "She'd do as he asked, get things ready, cancel all her plans so she'd be ready for him. But he didn't show up.

He never showed up. She was so disappointed, but she always made excuses for him.''

"But you didn't?" He wondered if she'd answer him.

Annie's head jerked up. Her shoulders grew even more erect. Her eyes froze into blue chips of ice that fairly crackled across the room. The harsh, painful words burst out as if she couldn't contain them any longer.

"No, I didn't excuse him. Not when he kept hurting her over and over. He had no respect, no love, or he wouldn't have kept building up her hopes and then dashing them. He never kept his word, wasn't there when she needed him. My father thought only of himself, of *his* needs, *his* wants, the rainbow just beyond his reach. He couldn't understand that his irresponsibility was killing her spirit.''

She laughed, a sharp discordant sound that shattered the fragile bond of something akin to friendship they'd shared just moments ago.

"Isn't it strange that the only time he tried to keep his promise he truly wasn't able to?" Annie shook her gilded head as if to dislodge the memories. "He's been dead ten years, and I still remember the day they told my mother he'd died in a train wreck. She refused to believe it. Jim would be home, she said. He'd promised to be there for their twentieth anniversary, and she knew he wouldn't disappoint her." Annie snorted her indignance. "Like he hadn't disappointed her a thousand times before.''

"I'm sorry." Russ didn't know what else to say.

"So am I. She wasted her life on him, and he wasn't worth it." Annie jumped to her feet, her voice changing. "Anyway, you can never go back. You can only go ahead. That's something your grandfather told me during one of our many discussions.''

"I see." Russ had a lot to think about. Gramps had

come here, not just once or twice, but regularly. Intentionally. Why?

"Dinner's bound to be ready by now. Why don't we stop all this maudlin talk and go to the dining room?" She rose, disappeared through the door, skirt flying behind her as if pursued.

Russ lapsed into thought, startled when someone began to speak.

"Annie gets sad when she talks about her daddy." Drew leaned against Russ's knee, brown eyes sad as he cuddled the cat closer. "She doesn't have happy memories."

"I'm sorry."

"Me, too." The little boy tilted his head to one side like an inquisitive sparrow and studied Russ. "Do you have happy memories 'bout your daddy?"

Out of the mouths of babes. Russ took a deep breath.

"I mean, things like goin' fishing and stuff. Annie told me you used to visit Safe Harbor." Drew waited for an answer, his face expectant.

Suddenly Russ remembered a sailing trip he and Adam had taken with their father. He'd been what—four? And yet he could still feel the lash of the storm-driven waves against his skin, feel the fear snake up his spine as the boat rocked and water flew in. He could still hear his father reminding them that he would take care of things.

"Yes, Drew." He was surprised to hear himself admit it. "I have some very good memories of my father from when I was a boy."

"When you were little, right? Like me?"

Russ nodded, wondering where this was going.

"Don'tcha got no good ones from when you were big?"

"You can't keep running from life, Russell. You've got to face responsibility, own up to your duties. Following through on our commitments is what this firm is about."

"Not too many," he admitted, reluctant to go back into those hurtful times or to let Drew see how much they continued to bother him.

"Is your daddy still alive?" Drew leaned against his knee, brown eyes hopeful.

"Yes, he is. He and my mother both."

"That's good."

"It is?" Russ smiled at the funny little boy. Such deep thoughts for such a young child. "Why is it good?"

"'Cause you can still make some good memories. It's not too late."

"I see." Meaning that it was too late for Drew to make good memories with his father? Russ winced. Pretty harsh reality for such a little kid.

"Life is harsh sometimes, Russell. But if you've done what you know is right, you can weather its storms."

"Are you two ever coming? I'm starved." Annie stood in front of them, staring. "What's wrong?" she demanded when neither said anything.

"Nothing's wrong, Annie." Drew put the cat down, then walked over and threaded his pudgy fingers through hers. "We were just talkin'."

"About what?" Her gaze moved from Drew to Russ, suspicion lurking in the glacial depths.

"Man stuff. You wouldn't understand." Drew pulled her toward the dining room. "Do I have to eat salad?"

Annie frowned at Russ for one long moment before she allowed herself to be led into the glass-walled room.

"Of course you have to try it—at least one taste," she told him, her voice echoing to Russ. "Right after you wash your hands. Why? Did you think I'd changed the rules?"

"Did you think we would change the rules, just because you're our son? Rules apply to everyone, Russell. That includes you."

"I kinda hoped." Drew's high-pitched squeak broke through the daydream. "Come on, Russ. You can have lots of Annie's yucky old salad. I'm only tasting it."

Russ stood, brushed away the reminders of the mess he'd made of his life. Safe Harbor was his chance to start again. He wouldn't mess that up. He'd find a way to marry Annie without anyone getting hurt. He'd fulfill his grandfather's wishes, then he'd concentrate on his future. Once he'd done what he promised, Annie would be free, and so would he.

And the burden of knowing he'd disappointed the old man would finally dissolve.

Wouldn't it?

Chapter Four

"Are you ever going to be ready?"

Tuesday morning, Russ shifted from one foot to the other, forcing himself to remain calm in spite of his urge to be outdoors. Annie had called off this date twice in the past week. He didn't intend to let it happen again.

"You've been fiddling with that ledger for twenty minutes."

"It's called balancing." Her eyes glinted blue sparks. "That's the way we make sure our expenses don't exceed our income." She didn't bother to hide her meaning.

"Look, I've explained ten times that the check for room and board bounced because I changed banks." He took a second look into her gorgeous eyes, caught the hint of fun glittering there and chuckled ruefully. "You're teasing. Are you ever going to let that go?"

"The short answer? Probably not." She grinned her delight at his groan of disgust.

She did it deliberately, reminded him of his goof just to hassle him. Russ knew it, Annie knew it. But they kept up the game anyway, neither one averse to the verbal sparring.

The kind of mental fencing his grandfather would have adored. Only Russ figured her sword was a little sharper. Annie didn't mince the truth. For some reason that reassured him.

"If you don't hurry up, I'm not taking you out for lunch. My offer stands for five minutes longer. Then you lose." He glanced at his watch.

"I've been ready for half an hour. I was just putting in time." Annie moved from behind the counter, a giggle bursting from her. "You've been here for over a week and you still can't figure out when I'm kidding. Wise up, Russ!"

She glanced outside the front door, then at him.

"Where's Drew?"

"Staying for lunch with Billy at school. By the way, Billy's mother said she wants Drew tomorrow afternoon."

"Wants him?" Annie stopped buttoning her jacket to peer at him, confusion washing over her face. "What does that mean?"

"She's trying to paper the living room and Billy wants to help." Russ chuckled. "I think her theory works something like this. With Drew there, she can send them both outside. Billy will be kept busy, and she can finish the papering herself."

"Ah. Well, Billy's pretty determined. I hope it works." Annie called to tell Felicity she was leaving, then led the way outside. She breathed deeply, wrapped her arms around her waist. "It's gorgeous today. I can smell spring."

"Spring has been moving in since I got here—the day I wrote the infamous check." Russ made a face at her, then held open her door.

"Ah, yes. That day." Annie grinned, shrugged at his

lack of a comeback, then climbed in. "We're driving? Where to?"

"You'll see."

"You promised me lunch at the best place to eat in Safe Harbor. That's got to be the Bistro." She did up her seat belt, then leaned back, a smugly satisfied grin on her face.

Russ suppressed his laughter. Annie was in for a surprise, and he could hardly wait to spring it on her. He'd never mentioned the Bistro, so the mistake wasn't his. He relished the drive down the street, straight past the fancy restaurant.

"Hey!" Annie shifted to glance over her shoulder. Then she glared at him. "What gives?"

"Patience is a virtue." He continued down Lake Drive until they were heading out of town on Route 7. "Enjoy the scenery," he advised. He pretended to ogle her. "I know I will."

"Get over yourself, Russ," she muttered, but her cheeks were fiery red. "You can stop acting like some kind of lovesick beau. I'm not the type to be swayed by compliments and I'm not going over that ground again."

Ha! Little did she know. He intended to go over and over that ground until she agreed to marry him. The check *had* bounced because he'd changed banks, but if he had to, he'd pretend his finances were the main reason for his proposal. Opening up his shop hadn't come cheaply. But the main reason he wanted her to agree to his proposal was that he had very little time left to fulfill his grandfather's request, and this one thing he could not fail at.

Russ was glad to get out and breathe some fresh air. He hadn't been to the spot in years. But there, exactly where he remembered it, a gravel road veered off the highway toward the lakeshore. They bounced and jounced over the rutted path, climbing steadily higher until finally reaching the top of a hill with the most spectacular view he'd ever seen.

"Here we are. The best place to eat in Safe Harbor." He climbed out, then hurried around to open her door. "Come on, Annie. It's lunchtime. Aren't you hungry?" he teased.

"Technically, we're no longer in Safe Harbor." She allowed him to help her out of the vehicle, to lead her to the edge of the cliff where they could look out over the lake. When his arm crept around her shoulders, she shrugged it off. "Let go of me."

"Just making sure you don't fall." He lifted his hands up, waiting for her glare to dissipate.

Russ didn't take offense. She wasn't used to him, that was all. But he enjoyed touching her, enjoyed the soft rose scent of her hair, the alabaster smoothness of her skin, the way she blushed when he got too close. Annie was fun to be with, delightful to look at and a challenge to understand. For the first time, Russ considered his grandfather might have done him a favor. Russ had never met anyone like Annie.

"You're going to have to get used to having me around," he said quietly.

"Why?" She faced him head-on, golden eyebrows furrowed.

"When we get married—"

"Oh, not that again!" She slapped her hands on her hips, her eyes blazing. "I've told you a thousand times that I'm not going to marry you no matter how many times you beg, so you might as well stop asking me."

"I did not beg."

A flicker of annoyance twitched at him. He'd begun his campaign in earnest last Sunday morning, escorting her to church, joining in the potluck lunch while he stuck like glue to her side and endured a host of curious looks from what she'd called the Women's League. Walking home with her, he'd felt Drew's hand clinging to his and begun to wonder if marriage would be so bad. Drew liked him.

Since then he'd been back to church, endured the stares again, but Annie hadn't relented a bit.

What was she so afraid of? He wasn't an ogre, for Pete's sake.

"Find something else to harangue me with because that marriage song's gone flat." She turned her back and stared at the sparkling lake.

"I maintain I did not beg."

"Fine. You didn't beg." She sighed once, then ignored him.

"You like me, Annie. I like you. I like Drew. We get along together. Why shouldn't we marry as Gramps intended?" Frustration crept into his voice. "There's nothing wrong with arranged marriages. They happen all over the world. People looking out for their loved ones often choose a partner."

"Yes, they do. And there are lots of unhappy couples because of it. Why add to the negative statistics?"

Russ had an answer, but it slipped his mind when her bright hair whipped free of the topknot she'd created and swept across his face. It was like being brushed with silk. Her quiet voice, almost carried away by the wind, gently reprimanded him.

"Russ, what you're looking for isn't just an arranged marriage, it's a temporary one."

Progress? Russ considered her words.

"We could talk about making it permanent?" he offered tentatively, secretly appalled by the responsibility such an arrangement would entail.

She twisted around, her face alive with a grin of pure mischief.

"You want to be married to me forever, Russ? Me, Annie Simmons? The woman who agrees with you on nothing in this hemisphere? You really want to marry me—when my coffee is too strong, my vacuuming too loud and my friends too nosy?" She shook her head, her smile mocking him. "I don't think that supreme sacrifice will be necessary, thank you. Besides, yesterday your friend seemed to think you had a case to set aside the stipulations in your grandfather's will."

Weeks ago Russ had told a law school buddy he would not contest his grandfather's will. But Jerry specialized in loopholes and he'd been certain there was a way, in spite of Russ's insistence that he wanted to fulfill his grandfather's wishes. Jerry heard only what he wanted to and he'd pressed on. Russ wished he'd never invited Jerry to visit on Sunday afternoon, or to look at his briefcase full of advice. His mocking comments about marriage and divorce irritated Annie so much, she'd gone out of her way to avoid them both for the rest of the day.

He'd gotten rid of Jerry, searched for her to apologize. But Annie had disappeared. Forced to question the townsfolk, Russ had finally run Annie to ground at the park where she'd sat on a bench, watching Drew, her face smudged with dusty tears. He'd never learned where she'd disappeared to earlier or why she'd been crying. Even Drew wouldn't tell, though Russ had bribed him mercilessly by coaxing Annie to let him take them out for pizza.

"Is there any lunch involved in this expedition?" Annie's voice forced him back to reality. She tossed a pebble over her head and watched it sink into the water. "I'm hungry."

"You're always hungry." Since the debate was tem-

porarily closed, Russ strode to his truck, removed the picnic basket and thermal pouches he'd stowed there earlier.
He led her to a grassy spot under a towering spruce dap-
pled with sun. "Take the corner of this, will you?"

She helped him spread the blanket, then sat down on
the edge farthest from him. That annoyed Russ greatly.

"I don't have the plague, Annie," he muttered, exag-
gerating his stretch across the blanket to hand her the
chicken pie he'd ordered for their picnic. Though the sun
was warm, the day pleasant, a fragrant steam wafted up
from the delicacy still enclosed in its aluminum jacket.
"I'm not infectious."

"Glad to hear it." She tasted a corner of the flaky pas-
try, closed her eyes and sighed. "Heaven."

"Not my idea of it," he retorted. Annie picked out the
peas and daintily set them aside. "Hey! You make Drew
eat his vegetables."

She winked at him. "I promise I'll stop when he hits
eighteen." Suddenly aware of what she'd said, her face
fell. "If he's still with me, that is."

She was a confusing blend of gorgeous woman and
whimsical child, and she frustrated the daylights out of him
with her refusal to consider his proposal. But Russ
wouldn't have changed places with anyone just then. He
sat content as the sun's rays sank through his jacket and
warmed his body.

"Annie, if you don't marry me, I can't buy that used
equipment I showed you in the catalogue. It'll be gone,
and I'll pay twice the price later to get new stuff. I need
it."

"Like Drew needs a baseball glove?" She wasn't buying his sob story. Instead, she reached out and plucked the
bowl of salad from the blanket where he'd set it. "Thanks.
I love salad."

"What don't you love?" he demanded, watching her nibble the tender greens. "Besides peas."

"Men who won't take no for an answer." She raised her eyebrows at him meaningfully, then bent her head and continued with her meal.

"But I had plans!" When no response was forthcoming, Russ began eating. But he didn't taste a thing because in his mind, his hopes of atonement for the past were disintegrating like wax over a flame.

"Change your plans, Russ. Find a different way. Nobody said there's only one way to skin a cat." Her fork halted midway. Her head jerked up, and her huge eyes blinked at him. "Oops! Sorry. No offense to Marmalade."

"Ha! Don't bother pretending." Russ pretended to glare. "I know what you've threatened her with, Annie."

"Drew," she guessed, with a giggle. "That kid and I are going to have a talk about secrets."

"Won't work." For the first time in this conversation, Russ felt he had the upper hand. And that delighted him. Annie was a changeling. You never knew what she'd chuck at you next. Better to be one step in front.

"Why won't my talk work?" There was no softness in her voice. Just demand. "It always has before. Drew's an open book with me."

"Me, too." He smiled.

"Since when?" She looked worried.

Russ suddenly felt much better.

"Since I bribed him." He licked his fork with relish. "He'll tell me anything I want to know, Annie. Anything."

Russ chanced to glance up just then and caught the worry in her eyes. It was more than worry, it was pure fear. For the umpteenth time he wondered what she was afraid of. Maybe she'd tell him if he pressed.

"Anything," he repeated in a growl. "Your most personal secrets, where you hide your jewelry, what you love most. Whatever I want, Drew will tell. I've got him like that." He held up his thumb and forefinger pinched together.

Her face closed up. "Russ, I don't want you—"

And that about said it all, Russ figured. She didn't want him. He threatened her safe little world. A light clicked on.

Suddenly he understood.

"You don't want me—to what? Dig around in your past? Question your decision? Make you think about the possibilities?"

She frowned. "What possibilities?"

"Possibilities. What could be? What might have been?" He watched her blue eyes cloud. "Think about the fun we could have with all that money, Annie," he murmured, changing tactics. In his experience, most women could be swayed by money.

Annie glared.

"It would be like stealing—getting someone else's money without playing by the rules." She shook her head, golden hair swinging in a wide arc. "It's detestable."

"Those *are* the rules."

She glared. Okay, scratch the lure of money. Either she didn't need it, which he doubted, or she was one of those rare individuals who really didn't care how much money she had.

"I didn't make them up, you know. My grandfather did. He said that to inherit, I had to be married to you." Russ blinked at her. "I'm not breaking any rules, I'm just trying to fulfill his last wishes."

Her face froze. So did her hands. Annie didn't move for a minute. When she did, her motions were the deliberate ones of a person forcing herself to remain calm. What had he said?

"Is that really what's behind your proposal?" she finally asked. "You're just trying to do what he wanted?"

The intelligent blue gaze widened. "Did he leave you a letter?"

How had she known? Russ nodded, though he didn't want to talk about that right now. Gramps's words were personal. Allowing someone else to read them would give too much away about Russ's mistakes.

"I thought so, since he sent me one, too." She set her dish on the blanket, her face a mess of confusion. "By marrying you, I would be breaking other rules, Russ. My own. I'd be going against my personal beliefs about the sanctity of marriage. I can't, I won't do that."

"I'm not disputing that. I agree. Marriage is sacred. This marriage wouldn't violate that. It would be a partnership. A mutually beneficial partnership, if we wanted it that way."

When she shook her head, frustration nipped at him. Why was she being so stubborn? For some reason Gramps had been adamant about this, and Russ intended to do what he could to fulfill the old man's stipulations. He owed him that, at the very least. He decided to try another tack.

"Well, it's your call." He leaned back on his elbows, allowing the sun to touch his face.

Annie picked a nonexistent bit of fluff off her jeans.

"Yes, it is. I liked your grandfather, Russ. But the answer is still no." She jumped to her feet. "Thank you for lunch. But I've got to get back. I've got a meeting."

"Now?" He checked his watch. "But we haven't even had dessert, or coffee." He frowned. "What's so important about this meeting?"

"Did I say it was important?" She sat down, but fidgeted.

"I know you believe this whole thing is my greedy way of getting his money. But it's not true. Believe me, I didn't know a thing about it. Besides, Gramps specifically named you as my wife candidate. He must have had a very high opinion of you to include you in this." Which was something he didn't yet understand completely. Why had Gramps named Annie?

"I can't speak for your grandfather, Russ." It was clear she was not going to discuss it further. "You said something about dessert?"

Russ stashed the leftovers into an empty bag, then pulled out his pièce de résistance.

"Ta da! Black forest cake." He waited for her admiration, frowned when it wasn't forthcoming. "You don't like black forest cake?" he demanded, unable to hide his disbelief.

"I like it. It's from the bakery, isn't it?" She nodded. "They're the best."

Something was wrong. Russ cut two slices, handed her one, then poured them each a steaming mug of coffee. She set down the cake, ignored it, but accepted the cup, staring over its brim to the lake beyond, her face drawn tight with tension. He had to know what was going on in her mind.

"Annie?"

Her head jerked up, and she stared at him. "Yes?"

"Will you tell me what's bothering you?"

She said nothing, but her blue gaze stayed fixed on him.

"I can see there's something. If it's about Gramps, I'd like to help, if I can. Why don't you share?"

"It's not about him." She laughed, a harsh, bitter sound that held no joy. "Some things just can't be shared, Russ."

Lord, did he know that! Russ pushed his past away and concentrated on her. "Talking sometimes helps."

Her eyes left him, returned to their scrutiny of the bay. "Not this time. But thanks for the offer." She took a deep drink, her fingers white and clenched around the mug.

"Who is your meeting with?" Russ pretended to concentrate on his cake, but his favorite dessert had lost its appeal.

She sighed, as if to tell him to leave it alone. But something about her body language told him she needed to talk. "Anyone I know?"

Her lips tightened. "A Realtor." One quick side glance. "And some people who want to buy my parents' house."

Not *her* house, but her *parents'* house.

"And you don't want to sell?" he guessed.

"I can hardly wait." The words burst out, her eyes flashing. "I want to be rid of the place, rid of everything it reminds me of—my mother's bane, my father's folly." She stuffed her fist against her mouth to stop the words and blinked hard.

Russ frowned. Annie too upset to speak? What was this about?

Her ragged voice told him the rest. "If I could, I'd abandon it and never put a foot inside it for the rest of my life."

"But you can't." He nodded, knowing exactly what she meant. "I'm sorry, Annie. I didn't mean to—"

"Sure you did." She turned on him, eyes shooting blue arrows of anger. "You wanted to know all about me, even to marry me, remember? Well, marriage isn't going to happen, not in this lifetime."

"But Gramps specifically—"

"I'm sorry about his wishes. He had good memories and he thought everyone else would enjoy the same love that he did with his wife. But I've seen what marriage can do to someone, seen the humiliation, the pain, the abandonment that never quite goes away, no matter how hard you try. There is no way I will allow myself to live like that, to drown in loving someone else so much that I lose my own identity. I will never marry, Russ. Not you. Not anyone.''

She dashed away the tears, set down her cup and picked up her dessert. After tossing Russ a defiant glare, she began eating it, one tiny bite at a time.

He didn't know what to say. "I'm sorry." How weak, ineffective it sounded.

"So am I." She took another sip of coffee, drew a deep breath and exhaled. Her dessert, half-eaten, was discarded. The faintest trace of a smile tugged at her mouth. "Is there any more of your dishwater coffee?"

He silently refilled her cup, watched her snuggle the warmth of the cup against her cheek. When she spoke, her voice was sad.

"That house was not a happy place for me, Russ."

"I gathered." He wasn't sure exactly how he should proceed.

"I want to sell it, but the prospective buyers want me to go through it with them, point out the defects, suggest renovations I would make if I intended on living there myself. They want to make Safe Harbor their vacation home. Eventually, they'll bring their family here."

"Won't knowing the problems drive the price down?"

She shook her head. "They've already agreed to buy, provided I do what they ask."

"But why you? Surely an architect, or a designer—"

"You'd think so, wouldn't you?" Annie laughed, but the joyless sound pained him. "Apparently they were at Harry's Kitchen, and Harry blabbed about some suggestions I made to a few other homeowners. This couple saw those houses, liked them so much, they wanted me to draw up some ideas for their new home.'' Her lips twisted as if she couldn't imagine her old home comforting anyone, no matter how it was altered.

She'd mentioned a scholarship to a design school. He'd seen sketchbooks around the house. Obviously her dreams hadn't completely died. Something clicked in his brain.

''You did the plans for the bed-and-breakfast, didn't you?''

She nodded. ''I had to have someone go over them, of course, to make sure everything was up to code. But I did use my own plans.''

Russ dredged up a memory of the building as he'd known it seven years ago, when they'd come to the cottage for a family weekend.

''Congratulations, Annie Simmons.'' He held out a hand. ''Well done. I remember what the old place looked like and know what you've accomplished.''

''Yes, well, it was a labor of love.'' She blushed a rich ruby, avoided his stare and his handshake.

''So why not do a few sketches for these people? They'll buy, you'll be free of the place. What's to lose?''

''Me,'' she whispered, her eyes huge as they met his. ''I'm afraid I'll go into that house and lose me. I'll become that stupid girl who kept hoping her father would show up and make her mother happy.''

Russ shifted until he could wrap his arm around her shoulder, shield her from both the freshening wind that had kicked up, and the sad memories engulfing her. As he sat in silent comfort, just for a moment his mind strayed to the sailboat he dreamed of owning. A wind like this was perfect for sailing.

At Annie's sniff, his attention returned to the woman at his side.

"Listen, honey," he murmured, squeezing her shoulder. "You're you, you're strong and competent. How many women do you know who could teach Sunday school, look after a kid who's lost his parents and build her own business?"

"Lots of women—"

"Lots of women work nine to five, go home and call their life their own. I saw you making those special blueberry pancakes for Nathan last Sunday morning. You had a hundred things to do, but because he mentioned he loved them, you decided we needed pancakes."

"That wasn't anything." She brushed off his compliment but didn't move away.

"Wasn't it? How about that phone call at twelve-thirty last night?"

She blinked at him. "You heard that?"

"I thought something might be wrong so I came down to help. Does your class often phone you at that hour to talk about their problems?"

"No. Celia's a special case. Her parents are divorcing, but she's so mature about it. She just needs a shoulder to cry on once in a while." Her eyes came to life again, glowed rich and blue. "She wanted to talk."

He nodded. "So you listened to her for an hour and a half, even though you were dead tired." He hugged her close. "Woman, you've got your life firmly under control. What in the world do you have to fear from a few memories tucked up in a silly house?"

She thought about it for a minute. He could see the hope rise, almost bloom, only to disappear with doubts.

"I can't go back there," she whispered.

"Yes, you can. You have to. You have to free yourself

from the memories, regain control. Then you can finally get rid of the past.''

She twisted to look at him.

''You sound like you know,'' she whispered.

He held her stare. ''Someone once told me the same thing.''

''And did it work?''

Her quiet question touched a little too close to home, reminded him of the debt he owed his grandfather. Russ lurched to his feet, gathered up their things and packed everything away. Then he held out a hand.

''C'mon, Annie. I'll go with you. We'll face the monster together.''

After a long moment of silence, she reached up, took his hand, allowed him to pull her to her feet, then leaned down to pluck up the blanket and fold it. Together they walked to his truck.

''Thank you.''

To Russ, the warmth of the afternoon had somehow dissipated. Oh, the sun still shone, the grass still sprouted, spring was still in the air. But the world had shifted just a fraction. He'd realized that not only wasn't Annie Simmons who he'd thought she was, he'd just volunteered to help her. He was getting involved.

Russ helped Annie into the truck after storing everything, then took his seat and eased the truck away from their picnic area. With every mile they covered, Russ felt guilt cloak him as quickly as Annie's tension returned. What business did he have advising her about anything when he'd messed up his life so badly?

''You'll have to direct me there.''

She did, and five minutes later they'd arrived at a crumbling old Victorian house. A man and woman stood on the walk, hands clasped as they peered at the once gorgeous structure, now beaten down by age. The Realtor, a tall, lean man in a faded sports jacket, hurried over to the truck.

"Annie, I was beginning to wonder if you'd changed your mind. The Wilkinsons are waiting."

She climbed out of the truck, introduced Russ as her friend, shifted her bag onto her shoulder, then slipped her hand into Russ's, her eyes questioning his intention to stick by her. What else could he do?

"Let's go face the past," he murmured, squeezing her fingers, wryly amused by his own words. He'd moved here to finish with the past, to figure out a future. Who was he to help her? And yet, he couldn't abandon her.

Annie held her breath for several long moments, then nodded. "I'm ready." The look on her face spoke volumes—she might just as well get it over with.

After they'd greeted the Wilkinsons, Russ pushed the front door open. At first glance, the dirty white tumbledown house was as bad inside as it was out. When Annie didn't move, he gently tugged on her hand.

He noted her furtive glance around, the way her eyes dwelt on the fireplace in the living room. The couple behind them said nothing, their eyes casting to and fro about the room. Somebody had to break the ice that held Annie frozen in its grip. Russ figured it was up to him.

"At least that fireplace looks solid."

"It's sound enough," Annie murmured, blue eyes cloudy. "Just never drew very well. Maybe it needs cleaning. There's marble underneath, you know."

"Really?" He squinted at the ugly painted wood. "Why cover marble?" He turned to glance at the couple. "I'd have that removed first."

They nodded, and the man scribbled something on a pad he held. Annie stood frozen, so Russ moved on, half-pulling her behind him into the kitchen.

"Drew would love this room," he murmured, trying to help her get past whatever memories made her face pale. "I can see cherry red cabinets in here, stuffed with all kinds of good things." He sniffed. "I smell cinnamon coming from a huge range over there. Maybe gingerbread cookies? Just like home."

She turned to him, eyes huge with doubts.

"Do you think it would be better for Drew to be in a home than sharing the bed-and-breakfast with me?" She chewed her bottom lip. "I didn't think about that. I've tried to make my place into his home, but I'm never certain that he feels comfortable there. This mother stuff is just so new to me."

What was this about? Did she doubt her ability to care for the boy?

Russ dropped his poetry about the kitchen. Truth to tell it was a mess that no amount of make-believe could disguise. He turned his back on it, smiled at her and squeezed her arm.

"Trust me, Annie, that little boy feels very comfortable with you."

"Do you really think so? It's just that I have so little experience at mothering anybody." She made a face at the mess. "This place needs gutting."

Russ agreed. It was obvious she'd moved out of the house some time ago, sold much of the furniture. He kept going.

Annie didn't seem to notice that they'd moved beyond the kitchen or that the couple had followed them.

"This room is a beauty. Look at those cherry floors. Perfect condition." He trailed one hand through the dirt covering the gorgeous dining-room table. "This is in good condition, too."

"We never really used this room much. Except—" She stopped.

Russ knew she'd been about to say they'd never used it unless her father came home. He glanced at the table again. That's why she'd left it here. Memories.

"Not much work needed here," he told the couple in an undertone. "A good cleaning should do."

He checked Annie's white face and guessed she was having trouble with the nostalgia, so he changed the subject to Drew while leading her out of the room. She started up the stairs, and Russ followed closely. She began speaking, halfway up, her voice soft, brimming with concern.

"It's hard to know exactly what to do, whether I'm doing enough for him. He doesn't have any close relatives nearby so I have no sounding board. He never asks for anything, never tells me I'm doing something wrong or forgetting something." She twisted to face Russ. "Do you know what I mean?"

He studied her face, noting that, for the first time, she genuinely wanted his opinion. Her eyes brimmed with a thousand worries. How could she not know she was a terrific mother to Drew?

"Honey, you're doing a great job. He loves living with you." Russ wrapped an arm around her shoulders, hugged her. "He shows all the signs of a well-adjusted kid, Annie. I think you're worrying needlessly."

"Maybe." For once she didn't move away from him. "I've tried to make him comfortable, to feel he can tell me anything, but how do I know if that's enough? Maybe he needs more time with men, time to do male things. Maybe I'm smothering him or something."

"I could spend a lot more time with him, if you'd marry me. He could come to me any time with his problems," Russ whispered in her ear, unwilling to let the others hear.

She did shift from under his arm then. "You're staying at the bed-and-breakfast, Russ. He can come to you any time now."

"True. But it would be better if we were a family, don't you think?" What had made him say that? Russ studied her downcast head, sensed she wasn't as confident that Drew didn't need a surrogate father as she'd sounded.

"Maybe. But they've found a relative, you know. Not a close one, but a man and his wife who might be able to raise him. I'd like him to be around his family, if he could." As if suddenly aware of where she was, she scanned the room, paled, then turned as if to flee.

Russ gripped her hand for encouragement. He turned to the others. "It's a bit painful for her to come back," he murmured. "I hope you don't mind if we just go through and reminisce."

"Oh, no." The woman's eyes filled with sympathy. "It must be terribly hard to sell your family home. Believe me, we don't mind at all. We'll just listen in now and then." The other two nodded.

They had the wrong idea, but Russ wasn't going to be the one to correct them. He silently followed Annie into the master suite.

"This is way too small," he muttered, glaring at the dark, glowering room.

"It isn't small. It's the right dimensions for a Victorian bedroom." Annie took a second look around, as if she hadn't noticed all the details before.

"Well, let me tell you it is way too small for a king-size bed. If I slept in there, my feet would stick out the end of that ratty old thing." There was a white iron bedstead someone had left behind. Russ could understand why. The thing looked like it would collapse under the least pressure.

"You could always knock out the wall here." Annie pointed east. "There's a wonderful view of the garden that would give morning light to the whole space. Of course, you'd have to update the bathroom. It's quaint, but not very functional. My mother never used this room after my father died." She pulled her sketch pad from her bag and began drawing, unaware or choosing to ignore the others who watched her.

In a few deft strokes, the room took shape and began to charm with whimsical curtains that billowed in an unseen breeze, a white wicker chair and a huge vanity with odd little bottles and brushes on top, all illuminated by sun-kissed windows that flooded the area with light.

"It looks like a girl's room." Russ blurted the words without thinking, then stared dumbfounded as she added a few more details here and there, and the room was transformed into an elegant master suite. "Yeah. That's perfect! How'd you know to do that?"

"It's just something I do. I guess I read too many decorating magazines when I was younger." Annie blushed, shrugged. "You learn to detail quickly when you draw birds."

"I know people who would pay big money to have someone like you tell them how to change their rooms to suit their personality." He took the drawing pad and peered at it. "This looks exactly like a room you'd fit into."

"Thanks. I think." She took it, frowned. "It's not exactly what I was going for."

"May I see?" The woman stepped forward and nodded. "It's exactly what we want. May I keep this?"

Annie shrugged, tore off the sheet and handed it to her. "If you like." She glanced at her watch. "I'd better get going. Felicity's left by now, and Drew gets back from school in half an hour. I've been away from the bed-and-breakfast too long as it is. You can't compete with the bigger places if you're not there for the customers.'' She touched her head.

"Is something wrong, Annie?'' Russ frowned at her pale face.

"I don't feel well today. I didn't sleep much last night. Now I've got an awful headache, and my stomach is doing this odd little dance—'' Annie twisted around, half smiled at the Wilkinsons. "I hope I helped. Maybe we can get together again, but I have to go now. Goodbye.''

Before they could answer, she hurried down the stairs and out to his truck. Russ knew Annie well enough to recognize that she'd reached her limit. For now. He'd bring her back, after the Wilkinsons had made some changes. Let her see this place in a new light, and maybe she'd let go of some of her dark memories.

"I suppose the summer tourists will be flocking pretty soon,'' he agreed, joining her in his truck moments later. He shifted into gear and headed for the bed-and-breakfast. "We've got that in common, Annie girl. We're both dependent on someone else for our livelihood. I'll have to hunker down at work, too. Can't sell silver if the door's locked.''

She didn't respond, and he didn't coax her, simply watched as she leaned her head back and closed her eyes, her white face drawn. Let her rest. Little by little, bit by bit, sooner or later she'd come to realize she had nothing to fear from him.

As his truck rolled down the hill toward her business, he caught a glimpse of a man standing outside her door.

"Looks like you were right about missing business, Annie. Must be a new customer.'' He parked by the curb and climbed out. Annie lifted one hand to her head, but climbed out on her own, beating Russ to the front door.

"I'm sorry, sir. I had to go out." She unlocked it, her words slightly slurred as she led the way inside. She wavered a bit, then regained her balance, one hand curved around the marble counter. "My, I feel strange." She summoned a smile. "Now how can I help?"

Russ watched the burly man scan the room, take in the desk, the business setup, the comfortable sofas and chairs. He didn't look dangerous, Russ decided. Merely out of place.

"Are you Annie Simmons?"

She coughed, drawing his attention. Russ frowned. Something was definitely wrong. Annie's white cheeks blazed with an unnatural color.

"Yes, I am. I own the Lighthouse Bed-and-Breakfast." She licked her lips, her eyes glassy.

"Thought so." He nodded, thrust out a hand. "Blake Kincaid," he announced.

"It's very nice to meet you." Annie shook his hand, her eyes huge. She glanced at Russ, blinked in confusion, silently asking for his support.

Something was wrong. He knew it by the way her shoulders tensed, her feet moved primly together, her lips pursed. Russ stepped up beside her, slid his arm around her waist.

"Kincaid," she whispered.

"What brings you to Safe Harbor, Mr. Kincaid?" Russ asked.

"Rhonda's boy, of course. Got a phone call that the boy needed help. I said I'd do what I could, of course." The sunburned face lost its animation. "It's just that I'm never home for long anymore. Still, I suppose he can home-school wherever we are. That's what some of my friends do.''

"Your friends?" Russ had trouble concentrating. He was worried about Annie. Her skin burned where it touched his.

"Other researchers." Blake Kincaid frowned. "I don't know exactly how it would work, but the boy will enjoy some adventures with me, I can tell you."

"Adventures?" Annie straightened, licked her lips, her eyes drained of everything but fear. "Wh-what exactly do you mean?"

"I'm the boy's kin, Rhonda's second cousin. Drew, isn't it?" He checked the piece of paper in his shirt pocket, then nodded. "Yes, that's what they said. Well, since there's no one else to take him, I'm here to see if young Drew will come with me to Wyoming. And in a couple of months I'll be heading to South America. I've got another expedition planned. I'll need to make sure Drew has his shots up to date. He should fit in down there."

He didn't exactly sound enthusiastic, Russ decided. More like resigned.

"Fit in?" Annie sounded distant, as if her mind were somewhere else.

"Yes. I realize its not a done deal, of course. But I said I'd come, see what the whole story is. A fellow's got to be prepared before he makes a commitment like that."

"You're going to take Drew away?"

What was wrong with her? She sounded befuddled, confused. Not at all like his usual efficient Annie.

"I'll do my duty. He's family, and the boy needs someone."

Russ's grip tightened on Annie's slender waist. He held her close against his side, certain that only he heard her whispered prayer, felt her shiver.

"Kincaid. I remember. A cousin." She closed her eyes, sighed, then finally dragged them open again. "So that's it. Drew will leave, and I'll be all alone." She sagged as if dealt a mighty blow. "I don't want him to go." She stared at them both. "I love him."

"It's okay, Annie. Just calm down." Worried by her pallor, Russ strove to infuse some of his strength into the delicate hand that rested in his. He hugged her close. "I think you need to rest."

"I feel so strange." She stared at him, blue eyes enormous in her wan face. "Tired." Her head drooped against his shoulder.

"If you'll excuse—"

"I wish I could keep him," she whispered. "He's the only child I'll ever have, and I love him so much it hurts. Help me, Russ."

Then, with a sigh of distress that ripped away a slice of his heart, tough, self-reliant Annie Simmons fainted.

Chapter Five

Annie was never sick. Everyone knew that. So when she awoke days later and found herself lying on top of her own bed, shivering and feverish, she knew it couldn't last long.

She pushed off the quilt the Safe Harbor Women's League had finished last Christmas and struggled to sit up, head whirling with the effort. Which way was up?

"I suggest you stay put, Annie."

"Why?" she tried to ask, but her voice emerged as a dull squawk. She lifted a hand to touch her throat where it burned like fire.

"I suspect staying put will be a lot more comfortable than the alternative." Nathan's kindly blue eyes twinkled at her.

"Which is?" She frowned, trying to assimilate the fact that her weekend visitor was sitting in her room, holding one of her hands.

"Falling face first on the floor?" He patted her hand, put it on the bed, then pulled the quilt to her neck. "You don't have to worry about a thing. Everything's running smoothly.''

''Everything?'' She croaked the word, worry nipping at her foggy brain. ''What everything?''

''You have three new customers that I know of. But then I only arrived last night. Russ took their money, settled them in and promised them a breakfast they wouldn't forget.''

That worried her. She could just imagine Russ making breakfast. After drinking his horrible coffee, her guests would check out faster than snow in a hot sun.

''I had no idea he'd worked as a cook on a boat. He's fairly inventive.''

Annie could do no more than squawk a response she hoped he understood as patent disbelief.

''If you'd like a sip of water, I put a glass right here. Dr. Maguire's been over, checked you out. Says it will take a couple more days to work through this bug, but you should be fine—if you stay put. Most of that nosy Women's League have tut-tutted their way in and out, too. Constance gave me a whole slew of directions, which I didn't need.'' He snorted his indignance.

''Yes, I remember Constance's voice. And Drew?'' It hurt so badly to say the word. Annie swallowed carefully, pressing her head into the pillow to ease the ache.

Then she remembered. A man was taking Drew away. A relative who would give him a normal home with a yard to play in. What kid didn't want that?

''Did you hear me, Annie?''

She blinked, then focused on the man at her bedside. ''Pardon?''

''Russ said you weren't to worry about anything. He'll look after the boy until you're feeling better.''

''Look after Drew?''

"Yes. Uh—there was some problem about his relative."

"Problem?" She frowned. Where was Drew, anyway?

"Yes. Some social worker came to speak to him." He stopped abruptly.

"Where's Russ?"

Nathan smiled.

"I figured you'd be asking that pretty soon. Russ is at the church right now. Apparently you scheduled a choir practice today. Constance sent me to check on you. Again." Nathan's eyes darkened to a brooding blue that reminded her of a storm at sea. "As if I hadn't done it ten times."

Annie almost smiled at his grumpy words. Why did she feel safe with him, as if she could trust him? She hardly knew this man, but there was something about him that reassured. Why?

"So if you'll be all right by yourself for a bit, I'll just go clean up the—er—" His face darkened to a raw red embarrassed color. "That is, I mean I'll leave you alone for a while."

"Wait." Oh, it hurt to holler. Annie took a deep breath and tried again, whispering. "What day is it?"

"Saturday. Saturday morning. From what I understand you've had a rough few days. Felicity's been with you most of the time, but I told her I'd take over today so she could get a break."

"Thanks."

He waited no more than ten seconds before scurrying out the door like a scared rabbit.

He was hiding something. Annie knew it as clearly as she knew she was lying here, useless, when there were a thousand and one things to be done. Primarily, make sure Drew would be safe and happy with his new family. But it sounded like something had gone wrong.

Suddenly it didn't matter that she'd been afraid too many times to count. It didn't matter that she'd made more mistakes than seemed natural, that she often didn't anticipate Drew's needs early enough and had to scrounge for last-minute solutions when he needed something at school. It didn't even matter that she didn't have a big yard where he could run free, or a bunch of siblings to play with.

What mattered was that she loved Drew Daniels as if he were her own child. And no matter how right it seemed, it hurt like the dickens to let him go, send him off with some distant relative and hope he was happy. Drew had been born and raised in Safe Harbor. He knew the locals, and they knew him. The lake was part of his heritage. His parents' bookstore was here.

Drew belonged in Safe Harbor. With her. Annie needed that little boy in her life.

But more than any of that, Drew needed a home.

Annie edged up in bed, forced her arm to leave the warm cocoon and reach for the glass Nathan had left. She took a sip, letting the water trickle down her throat in a deliciously cool drizzle.

She had to make sure she was doing the right thing by sending him away. Rhonda had trusted her. But how to do that?

"Annie. Nathan said you were awake." Constance Laughlin bustled through the door, straightened the quilt, then opened the window a crack. She sank down into the chair Nathan had occupied. "It's so stuffy in here. I told him fresh air would do you good, but he got all offended. Such a prickly man. I never did care for moody men. Joseph never—" She stopped, coughed, then held out her palm. Two tablets lay there. "Swallow this, please. The doctor left it. How are you, dear?"

"I'm all right." Annie smiled, accepted the glass and

swallowed the pills, then took another sip. "Constance, do you know when they're taking Drew?"

"Well, I don't know that anyone's taking Drew, dear. At least, not right away. Foster homes are difficult to find, you know."

"Foster homes?" Annie tried to understand. "But Rhonda's cousin? What about him? I thought—"

"Oh, we all did, dear. But it seems the authorities didn't know Blake and his wife are divorcing. He seems a dear man, but I think he was a bit relieved when Mrs. Yancey told him she can't let Drew go off to South America without someone to care for him while Blake's working." Constance combed her fingers through her short, dark hair. "Truthfully, Blake's life does seem very unsettled. He got a call while he was here and away he went, rushing off to Peru. Sad for the boy, but there it is."

Annie saw the way she glanced around the room, the way her hands fluttered nervously when she spoke of the far-off country. Constance had lost her husband, Joseph, while he was on a missions trip to Central America. Rebel forces had attacked his camp, leaving none of the men from their group alive. Annie knew from things Constance had said that their marriage had been a strong one and that she still missed her husband.

"Peru?" Annie shook her head, trying to clear it. "You mean he's not adopting Drew?"

"I don't think he can, dear. Though he did say he'd come and see the boy when he was next in this country." She pleated her skirt, her eyes brimming with sympathy. "I'm sorry, Annie, but without relatives, there's no other option but to put Drew in a foster home. After all, he can't wait here endlessly, can he? He needs to put down roots, find a family to love him."

Was that why Drew had never really opened up—because he was waiting until he'd found a permanent home?

"But I love him," Annie whispered, sadness eating at her.

"We all do, dear. But sometimes things just don't work out the way we plan." Constance sighed as if she knew too much about that. "Don't try to talk, dear. I know your throat hurts. Just rest and let the men pitch in. They're doing a fine job. A little messy, perhaps, but then they're not used to cooking and cleaning. Goodbye, dear. Feel better soon."

"Bye." Annie tried to call, but her voice wouldn't cooperate. So she huddled into her covers and considered what she'd learned.

A foster home. Everything within her screamed no. Drew deserved to be loved and cared for by someone who was genuinely concerned for his welfare, not as some kind of stopgap measure, shuffled on to the next place when he'd just settled in, insecure, alone.

It wouldn't happen, Annie decided. Not if she could stop it. Drew was the most precious gift she'd ever been given. Rhonda had wanted her to keep him safe, happy, that's why Annie was his godmother. She couldn't stand back and let him be taken to a foster home when he might need her. She couldn't betray her friend's trust.

In a flash of insight, Annie knew what to do. She'd adopt Drew herself.

"You're not supposed to be down here." Russ refused to budge from his stance in the doorway, no matter how she hinted.

Thus blocked, Annie had to peek around him and into the kitchen. What she saw did not inspire her.

"How many new guests did we have?" she squeaked,

her voice raw and unaccustomed to use after days of bed rest.

"Eight. Go upstairs. I'll bring you some tea with lemon and honey."

"I'll be fine." She balanced on tiptoe to peek past his shoulder. Gaped. "It looks like a herd of elephants has been through there."

"I made the mess, I'll clean it up. Felicity's doing the rooms. You go to bed."

She shook her head.

"No way. I'm perfectly fine and I've got things to do." Since he wouldn't let her into the kitchen, she headed for her office. "I'll take you up on that tea, though."

He brought it as she was calling the woman who had conducted the search for Drew's relatives.

"Hi, Mrs. Yancey. This is Annie Simmons. Simmons." She held one hand over the mouthpiece and coughed into a tissue. "Sorry. I've been down with the flu." She waited a minute, then nodded. "Yes, I met Blake. He arrived the day I got sick. Apparently he's gone now."

Mrs. Yancey repeated what Constance had told her, added a few details.

"I'm sorry about that, Mrs. Yancey. It must be a disappointment to you, too, after going to so much trouble. What's the next step?"

As expected, Mrs. Yancey began discussing foster care.

"I'm sure you've done the best you could, Mrs. Yancey. And we truly appreciate it. The thing is—" she glanced over her shoulder at Russ, who stood in the doorway. "Do you mind?" she whispered fiercely.

"No." He leaned against the jamb.

Disgusted, Annie turned her back and continued to speak.

"Drew has been with me for several months now. He's

settled in very well, even seems quite happy. He's developed a routine, has lots of friends and feels comfortable here. If he was taken into foster care, Drew would have no one who was familiar.''

Mrs. Yancey explained her legal obligations.

''Yes, I'm aware that you have to do your job. And I know how hard it is. I guess I was just hoping that perhaps I could adopt Drew. That way he'd remain in a familiar place, among his friends, surrounded by people who knew and loved his parents. Surely that would be preferable to a foster home? I was hoping you would help me get the paperwork started.''

A long pause was her response. Mrs. Yancey never did anything without thinking about it first.

''I know it's a big decision and I have been seriously considering all the ramifications, looking at it from all the angles. I believe we'd both gain by this. After these past few months, Drew's at home with me. We share some strong connections. Rhonda was a dear friend. I think we've done very well together.''

Mrs. Yancey's words choked her enthusiasm.

''I do?'' She closed her eyes, winced at the tenderness of her scalp. There had to be a way to get around the requirements. ''Are you sure? But what about references? I've got lots of those.''

References were not going to cut it this time.

''I see. You're quite certain, then?''

Mrs. Yancey was very certain.

''Yes, I will have to rethink my plans. Thank you for your help.'' She hung up the phone, defeat draining what little energy she'd begun with.

''It didn't go well, did it?'' Russ held out her tea.

''No.'' Annie took the cup gratefully, sipped carefully,

relishing the soothing warmth of honey on her raw throat. "Not well at all."

"How 'not well' did it go?"

She smacked the cup into the saucer and glared at him. "It's not really any of your business, is it?"

"No, I guess it isn't." He turned to walk away, then wheeled around. "But I'm allowed to be concerned. I like Drew. I want him to be happy."

"And you don't think he will be in some foster home?" Bitterness echoed in her words. Then Annie had an idea. Perhaps if they could show Drew's reluctance…

"I think Drew is the kind of kid who will make his own happiness. He'll take whatever he gets and make the best of it." Russ stood there, tea towel over one shoulder, peering at her.

"But?"

A long silence. A sigh.

"If you're asking me if I think it's the best thing for him, then no, I don't. He doesn't want to leave you, Annie."

"He told you this?"

"Among other things. We've had a lot of time to talk with you up there sleeping." He grinned at her, but the flash of humor soon faded. "Drew's built a new life for himself with you. He's grown accustomed to your way of doing things. To uproot him is to ask him to begin all over again with someone he doesn't know. He's concerned that he'll be lonely."

"Yes, that's what I thought." She was delighted Russ shared her opinion, at least on this subject.

"I doubted the authorities would allow Mr. Kincaid to take him to the Amazon, though you never know. One relative is better than no one. But with the divorce—" He shrugged. "I think that pretty much cinched it with Mrs.

Yancey. She cares about Drew, too.'' He frowned. "Foster care is going to be tough on a little kid who's just lost his parents and barely begun to reorder his world.''

"Exactly. Now what do we do about it?'' The bell at the front desk rang, but as she half rose, Russ shook his head.

"Stay put. I'll deal with it.'' He'd no sooner walked out the door than his overgrown orange cat strolled in and leaped onto Annie's desk.

"Get off my desk,'' she ordered huskily. The cat sprawled across the oak top and began washing her paws.

"This is not your home. I don't even like cats much,'' Annie told her with brutal frankness. "Your master is out there. Why don't you snuggle up to him?'' Not for anything would Annie have admitted that the sight of Russ's broad shoulders filling the doorway was tempting to a certain female human.

"You'd better not diss my cat,'' he murmured, a smile twitching his lips. "Drew loves that animal. He takes her out for a walk morning and night, like clockwork. He told me Marmalade is his job.''

Annie knew it was the truth. Marm was all Drew talked about since Russ had shown up. The silly cat was his pride and joy.

"Was everything okay out there?'' she asked as a wave of tiredness swamped her.

"Fine. Just another reservation for tonight. They've gone sight-seeing for now.'' He frowned at her, laid one big palm across her forehead. "You're not well yet, you know. You have to take it easy.''

"I have to figure out a way to get Drew.'' She glanced at her watch, frowned. "If there are tourists around, why aren't you in your shop?''

"It's not open yet. My kind of customers don't come

as early in the season as yours." He grinned. "Did Nathan tell you about my crêpes?"

"Crêpes?" She tried to remember something from the fog of the past mixed-up hours. "I don't think so."

"A hit. A total success. If you don't get repeat business because of my crêpes, you've entertained some pretty messed-up people."

"Uh-huh." She'd wait on that opinion, hear what her customers thought. Suddenly Annie realized she was being very ungrateful. Russ had stepped in and single-handedly kept things going—with a little help from Nathan and Drew. And probably the Women's League, if she knew those ladies. She should be thanking him, not questioning him.

"Thanks," she told him sincerely. "I don't know how I'd have managed without you."

"Me, neither." He chuckled. "You were so out of it." He thrust out his chest. "I told you we'd make a great team."

He left whistling, but Annie only heard the first few notes as something flickered on the edge of her mind. What was it he'd said? A team.

Annie felt her spirits flutter, then soar as the idea took shape. She picked up the phone and punched redial, then asked the question that could mean the answer to everything.

"I could adopt under those circumstances?" She grinned at the response. "I'm not sure, Mrs. Yancey. I'm really just finding facts at this point, so please don't say anything to anyone. I've got a few details to hammer out."

She slammed the phone down, narrowly missing Marmalade's tail. After gulping the rest of her tea, Annie raced the cat out the door at something less than lightning speed and burst into the dining room.

"Russ? Where are you? I need to ask you something."

He emerged from the kitchen, soap suds up to his wrists, a big puff of white bubbles dripping down one angular jaw onto his denim shirt. His silver-gray eyes darkened with concern as he studied her face.

"I'm here. Your cheeks are red again, Annie. Are you worse?" He squinted, took a second look. "What do you want?"

"A husband. I want a husband. Would you marry me— say, next week?"

To say he choked would have been to badly understate Russ Mitchard's shocked reaction to her proposal.

"Annie, I think you should go back to bed. It's quite obvious to me that you are delirious and still not in your right mind." He swung her into his arms and carried her up the stairs. "If you ever were," he muttered.

Annie let him prattle, her mind busy with the future.

"Let's see. We'll need to get organized. We could go to Green Bay, get a license. No one will have to know until we're actually married."

"Why shouldn't anyone know? Who would care, anyway? Not that I'm agreeing to anything a deranged woman proposes." He set her gingerly on the side of her bed. "I think you'll come to your senses once you get over this bug."

"I am over it. Well, almost. And I'm in possession of all my senses. Sit down." She waited until he perched gingerly in the white brocade chair. "I agree to your terms, Russ. I will marry you. Not because of your grandfather's will, but because I want to keep Drew here, with me, in Safe Harbor."

"You need to marry me to keep Drew?" He looked shell-shocked.

"I need to marry you so we can both adopt Drew," she

corrected. She crossed her legs under her and told him what she'd learned. "So the courts will consider my petition, and more important, Mrs. Yancey will back my petition, if I'm married. They won't let single people adopt, hence Blake Kincaid's departure. But couples are perfectly fine. Since Drew's been staying here for so long and we have a routine already established, she thinks I'm a shoo-in. Particularly since Drew's uncle is now out of the picture."

"I see. How many pills did Constance give you?"

"It's not the pills. I'm agreeing to your proposal. Isn't that what you wanted?"

"It's why you're agreeing that has me worried."

Annie felt a faint flicker of satisfaction. At least he knew how it felt to be proposed to for something other than love. Then shame chased in, ordering her brain to grow up.

"But why keep it quiet?" He scratched his stubbled chin, eyes thoughtful. "I would think the good citizens of Safe Harbor would go all out to help celebrate something like this. I know they love Drew." He frowned at her. "You've lived in this town all your life. You grew up in First Peninsula Church. Why not tell everyone and gain their support?"

She shook her head, her limp hair flopping against her skin. Russ looked rakish, handsome. Next to him, Annie felt unattractively rumpled. She knew she needed a shower, but first things first.

"No, Russ. If Reverend Burns were here, this discussion would be over. He's always been my pastor, and I'd love him to marry me. But I don't want to be married in that church by anyone else. It wouldn't mean the same." She chewed her bottom lip, thought of Constance and the Women's League and knew she couldn't carry off a wedding in front of them. "Besides, think of all the questions I'd get if they knew."

"They're going to ask questions anyway." He frowned at her. "Lots of them. Some of your friends might not understand," he warned.

"I'll tell them the truth eventually, of course. There's no way around that. But until then, I want to keep everything a secret." She refused to be swayed.

"But, Annie, you need to tell Drew. If he objects—" His voice died away.

"I'll ask Drew if he'd rather stay here with us or go to a new home."

"Some choice." Russ's silver eyes chided her.

Annie ignored him.

"If he wants to stay, and I know he will, I'll tell him that I'm going to try and work things out. But I don't want to tell him anything about us getting married until it's over. He doesn't need any more upsets." She crossed her arms over her chest and stared at him. "Well? Are you going to marry me?"

"Annie, this is so sudden." Russ frowned, his eyes studying her. "Don't you think you need time to consider all the angles?"

"No." The more she thought about it, the more Annie knew this was what she wanted. "You'll be getting what you need from the arrangement, Russ. You can collect your inheritance without any problem. Isn't that what you wanted?"

"Uh, yeah. I guess." His voice had dropped to a whisper.

He should be jumping for joy, but he seemed more worried about her. Annie frowned.

"Wait a minute. The money wasn't the issue, was it?" She suddenly knew exactly why Russ had been so insistent on his proposal. "The inheritance was just a smoke screen. What you really wanted was to do as your grandfather had asked, to fulfill his last wishes, kind of make amends."

He hesitated a long time before he spoke, and when he did, his voice was low, quiet, his head averted.

"Yes," he whispered. "I never did anything else he wanted, you see. I could never seem to live up to his vision for me. I thought maybe obeying this one last request would be my way to make up for all that." He looked at her. "I wasn't lying. The money would be helpful. But no, it isn't my main concern."

"But why didn't you say that in the first place?"

"Would it have made any difference?"

She considered their previous relationship, her poor opinion of him and the way his proposal had made her feel. Finally she nodded. "Maybe."

"How?" He looked genuinely confused.

Annie took pity on him and explained her feelings about his original proposal and the way she'd felt forced into the situation.

"I guess I wouldn't have felt so much like a cheat if I'd known you were trying to get me to marry you to honor your grandfather and not because you were lusting after his money," she finished, hoping he would understand.

"Doing what he wanted—that makes marriage to me okay?"

"That and the fact that I want to honor Drew. I want to give him a secure, safe environment where he can feel at home." She leaned forward. "Think about it, Russ. We get married. You do your grandfather's bidding and you get the cash you need to expand, or whatever. I get to be Drew's mom, to make sure he has a happy, stable life in which he won't be shuffled around. What's wrong with a marriage like that?"

"Annie?"

Russ jerked to his feet. Annie froze.

Constance Laughlin stood in the doorway, her tousled coal-black hair giving her orderly appearance a windblown look. Her deep blue eyes moved from Annie to Russ.

"Am I interrupting something?" she asked after a long moment's silence. "I thought I heard the word marriage."

Annie forced herself to laugh, though her voice was growing hoarse.

"Marriage? Really, Constance!" She smoothed a hand over her covers, conscious of the other woman's frown. "I was feeling a bit rough again, so Russ helped me up here. We were just debating something. Russ doesn't want me to see what he's done to the kitchen. Poor man, he's up to his elbows in dishwater."

When Constance shifted to get a better look at Russ, Annie made a frantic motion for him to go downstairs.

"Russ has been so kind. He and Nathan have kept this place floating while I was sick. I don't know how to repay either of them."

Constance flushed, her attention diverted from Russ's glare. "Oh, yes. Nathan. Is he here? I'd forgotten I needed to speak to him."

"I don't know where Nathan is." Annie shrugged, glanced at Russ. "Do you?"

"What?" It was obvious Russ was thinking about something else.

"Do you know where Nathan's gone?" Annie stared at him. What in the world was wrong with the man? First he couldn't wait to tie the knot, now she agreed and he went all spaced out? "Do you?"

He nodded. "Yes. Nathan took Drew for a walk along the beach. They were going to look for shells for a school project, I think."

"Oh." Constance looked crestfallen.

"Did you need him right away?"

Annie studied the older woman curiously. As far as she knew, Constance and Nathan had met socially only once, at her grand opening. Sure, Nathan asked about the woman's whereabouts every weekend, spent a lot of time watching her with the town's police chief, Charles Creasy. But she hadn't thought Constance was the least bit familiar with her weekend guest. Apparently Annie had been wrong. Again.

"I just wanted to—er, talk to him. We'd been discussing something and—" Constance drew herself up, shook her head. "Never mind. It doesn't matter in the least. I'm sure I'll see him later. Or tomorrow at church. Either one is soon enough. No problem. Bye." She turned, walked out of the room.

Annie stared at Russ as they listened to her clump down the stairs.

"What was that about?" he mused, his exotic eyes wide with confusion.

"I don't know, but you'd better pray Constance is too busy thinking about Nathan to bother with whatever she overheard from us. If she figures out what we're planning, things will get very complicated."

"What we're planning?" He chuckled. "You're the one with this sudden brain wave, Annie."

"Are you reneging? Suddenly you don't want to marry me?"

"I didn't say that." He shuffled from one foot to the other. "It's just—I'm not great at responsibility, Annie. And taking on you and Drew is a lot of responsibility. For anyone."

"You are not responsible for me." She glared at him. "Drew loves you, you care for him. I know you well enough to know you'd never let anything happen to that little boy. I also believe a sudden increase in your finances right now wouldn't be a problem. Is that why your shop isn't open?'' She saw the truth reflected on his face and nodded. "I thought so."

"That's only partly true. I haven't got everything arranged the way I want, yet." He fidgeted. "Annie, I do want to fulfill the terms of my grandfather's will. But—" He paused, searched her eyes, his frowning face brimming with foreboding.

"You don't want to get tangled up in something you can't get free of?''

"Something like that, I suppose."

She smiled sadly.

"I understand, Russ. In some ways you're exactly like my father. You want to live without getting caught in the problems interacting with other people always brings. Maybe someday you'll realize it just isn't possible." She sighed, knowing how hard it could be to learn that lesson. "But in the meantime, how about if I promise that I won't expect any more from you than that you promise to be there for Drew if he should ever need you?''

He nodded slowly. "I think I can manage that." He saw her shoulders straighten. "But what about you, Annie?''

"I only want to get married so I can adopt Drew and give him a stable home," she told him. "If we accomplish that, I'll be more than happy."

"So we're getting married?" Russ looked as if he still didn't believe it.

Annie nodded. "As soon as possible."

He stared at her, his glance moving from the top of her head to the tips of her bare toes.

"Then I'd better go finish the dishes," he muttered, and turned and quietly left the room.

As plans went, Annie figured it was the least romantic proposal anyone had ever accepted. Which shouldn't have bothered her a wit. After all, she wasn't interested in romance with Russ Mitchard.

Was she?

Chapter Six

It was his wedding day, and Russ felt like an outlaw.

They'd conned Felicity into minding Annie's bed-and-breakfast all day, found someone for Drew to stay with after school. Russ had once more posted his Opening Soon sign at The Quest. And all the while he felt the curious stares of townsfolk, who already thought he was strange, scrutinizing his best black three-piece suit, white silk shirt and red tie.

He pulled at his neck. He hadn't worn a tie since he'd quit going to court!

Of course, they stared at Annie even harder. Gone was the usual fluttery flowered skirt and sweater set. Today she wore a cream jacket that hugged her slim shape beautifully and offered just a glimpse of delicate rose lace at the neckline. Oh, she still wore a skirt, but it was like no skirt Russ had seen her wear before. Fitted, above the knee, with a tiny pleat at the back, that skirt, combined with a pair of elegant heels, showed off spectacular legs.

In fact, Annie's entire outfit was so out of character in

Safe Harbor that Elizabeth Neal stopped dead in front of the Harbor Hills Apartments and just plain gawked.

"We're causing a bit of a sensation," Annie whispered, trying to squish down in his truck seat. "Can't you go a little faster? We're supposed to avoid notice, remember?"

Russ snorted.

Like anyone wouldn't notice Annie Simmons in that outfit. As brides went, she fit the category perfectly. And so did that bit of fluff and nothing she intended to put on her head later.

"Would you rather I got a speeding ticket?" he muttered, knowing Annie was as nervous as he. She hadn't swallowed even one of her usual four cups of stomach-eating coffee.

"Do you think they suspect anything?" She kept her eyes on the streets, then twisted to face him if she saw anyone she knew.

What Russ thought was that the entire town would be buzzing in about five minutes. He'd learned the first week that nothing in Safe Harbor stayed secret for long, and he'd repeatedly warned her about keeping secrets from her friends. Still, for some reason she'd never fully explained, Annie insisted they keep the ceremony private.

"This is between us," she'd insisted. "An agreement between you and me. No one else comes into it."

In a way, he was glad. Right now he was too nervous to pretend in front of a bunch of curious Georges, which was his term for what Annie called the Women's League.

"They'll know eventually," she'd said. "But it will be when we tell them ourselves."

Russ figured he'd be prepared anyway. If Constance Laughlin didn't figure what was going on after what she'd overheard, she wasn't as quick as he figured she was.

Once they reached the highway to Green Bay, he sped

up. In a matter of an hour, they'd be married. It seemed funny to think of Annie as his wife. Funnier still to think of himself as a husband.

But then he wouldn't be. This was a facade, a way of placating the authorities to help Annie adopt Drew. A way for Russ to respect his grandfather's last wishes. A mutually beneficial arrangement. Nothing more.

There was something rather sad about that, he decided, glancing once more at Annie's gorgeous outfit. Suddenly he realized he hadn't given her any flowers. Getting married in that outfit certainly demanded flowers. He decided to stop before they got to the courthouse.

The miles slipped past with each of them enveloped in their own thoughts. Finally Russ had to break the silence.

"You're sure, Annie? This is what you want?"

"Let's not go over it again, Russ. I proposed, you accepted. Let's get on with this."

Nothing romantic about that, Russ decided. But then, why would there be? Surely he, of all people, wasn't looking for romance?

He almost laughed at that. Of course he didn't want romance. All he wanted was to fulfill his obligations to Gramps and get on with his life. But he was worried about Annie. It wasn't like her to be so—categorical. She was the kind of woman he was certain dreamed of orange blossoms, filmy bridal gowns and six-tier wedding cakes. The kind of woman who got married and the whole town showed up. She deserved that. Maybe by agreeing to this cold, impersonal ceremony, he was cheating her of that.

"Do you have the license?"

"Safely tucked into my pocket. Two trips to Green Bay. The gossips will be speculating."

She frowned. Russ switched subjects.

"Are you going to apply to adopt Drew right away?" He risked a sideways look and caught her glare.

"We. Are *we* going to apply," she corrected.

"Sorry. That's what I meant."

"Well, you'll have to be more careful. It's going to take the two of us, or it isn't going to happen. And that, might I remind you, is the whole reason behind this marriage."

Did her words have a faintly hollow ring? Then he remembered.

"Not the only reason," he muttered, more uncomfortable by the moment.

"No. There's the will, of course."

"But that's not the reason for all this haste. I had another month and a half." What brought that on? Did he want her to forget their deal, pretend to be a real bride? It was totally unreasonable. Russ chewed his lip. "Maybe we should have—"

He caught the sound of her indrawn breath, turned his head, saw Annie glaring at him.

"Could we please," she asked through clenched teeth, "not rehash the could have, should have, maybes until after the ceremony?"

"Sure." He saw her hand move to her cheek, caught the faint tremor she couldn't hide. She was nervous? He'd seen her feisty, determined, sick, angry and excited. But nervous?

Russ had to do something, alleviate some of the tension before they both said and did something that would ruin this day.

"It's actually quite a good day to get married," he announced, pressing the gas pedal a bit harder. "Sunny, warmer than yesterday. Yep. I can definitely feel summer on the way."

She gave him that look—the one that said she wondered about his mental state.

"It's the kind of day you start to think about getting back on the water." Hey, that was a good idea. "Maybe I'll buy a boat," he murmured, the image rising in his mind to full-scale proportions.

"A boat?" She looked dubious. "Like you'll have time to sail in tourist season?"

"I'll make time. Gramps always said you can make time for anything if you want to badly enough." At the time, of course, the old coot had been talking about the fine art of studying at college, but Russ had no intention of relaying that. "Do you think Drew is ready to go back out? I take it he hasn't been on the water since his parents' accident?"

She shook her head.

"No, and I don't intend to push it. He's never said much about it. The counselors I spoke to said to give him time. That's what I've tried to do." Annie rubbed her finger against her bottom lip, then peered at him. "Do you think that was wrong—to wait, I mean? Should I have made him go back out right away?"

"I don't think there is any wrong or right in a situation like this. You do what you can, meet the challenges as they come. I think you're doing a great job of being his mother, Annie."

"Thanks." She beamed at him, looking for all the world like a kid who'd just been given a lollipop.

"You're welcome. Hey, I never did hear. What happened when you talked to the distant cousin? Kincaid?" He saw the flicker of concern she tried to cover. "What did he say? He didn't threaten something, did he?"

"No, nothing of the kind." She shook her head. "He was quite nice about my petition, actually. Said he understood that the boy needed two parents, that he liked you and thought you'd make a good father.''

Russ almost choked. Him? A good father? His stomach knotted a little tighter.

"Blake said he was glad Drew could remain in a familiar place and he wished us the best. I gather he'll be back from time to time to check up on us. When I told him I loved Drew, he seemed to understand.''

"I'm glad.'' Russ heaved a sigh of relief that they were nearing the city. He wanted to get on with things. "I meant to ask about him before, but I got off track after you proposed.'' He grinned at the sudden tightening of her mouth. "I've never been proposed to before. It's a strange feeling.''

"You'll get over it. Though if you tell anyone I proposed, I'll deny it.''

He decided to stop teasing.

"I never realized the effort it takes to run a bed-and-breakfast until you got sick. It's not easy, especially when they expect you to cook something other than crêpes for breakfast.'' He tried for humor. "I thought toast and jam and dry cereal wasn't a bad breakfast.''

He still felt slightly offended that one of her guests had criticized the sugary loops he'd set on the tables that first morning.

"I've been eating that cereal for ages and I've never had a problem.''

"Oh, I don't know, Russ,'' she teased, eyes flashing. "All that sugar could account for your inability to sit still for more than ten minutes.'' She giggled, her laughter light and carefree as it rang around the interior of the vehicle.

"I sit,'' he argued. "But I think it's very rude to call your host flighty.''

"It is,'' she agreed, and reached out to pat his hand.

"Don't worry. Nathan told me you soothed her ruffled feathers by telling her how great she looked." Annie laughed again, eyes sparkling with mirth at his pained look.

"I didn't lie," he assured her. "I only spoke the truth."

"I think it was more the way you spoke it." She chuckled, enjoying his discomfiture. "Apparently Nathan felt your description of her—uh, Titian locks was a bit—fanciful. *He* likened her hair to dried-up orange peels."

"I—er—" Russ needed a different subject. Now. He caught a glimpse of a florist and exited his lane. Who said you couldn't find a way out when you needed one? "Just stay put a minute. I'll be right back."

For once, Annie didn't argue. She was too busy laughing at him.

It took him three minutes to pick out six pale pink cymbidium orchids mixed with delicate feathery fern. It took five minutes more for the woman to make him a boutonniere. He triumphantly carried them to his truck.

"What were you doing?" Annie demanded the moment he opened the door.

"Getting you a bouquet." He climbed inside, handed her the cellophane wrapped orchids. "This is for you."

"Th-thank you," she stammered, staring at their beauty. Her eyes moved to the box he held. "What's that?"

"My flower." He took it out, stuck the barely opened baby orchid in his buttonhole, then twisted to show her. "See?"

"Somehow I never thought of you as the type for flowers."

Her voice sounded muffled. Russ squinted across at her, saw the flicker of amusement in her eyes and huffed out his chest.

"There's a lot you don't know about me, Annie Simmons. But you'll learn. This is our wedding,'' he said, pushing the box under the seat. ''I think we should make sure everything is as nice as it can be.''

He'd only done it for her sake, because she'd had so many reservations about their marriage before Drew's predicament. Buying flowers was probably a stupid thing to do. Maybe it made getting married seem more important to him. But it *was* important. Even he knew that. Sorting this out made his head spin. Better to keep going down the path he'd set out on.

Russ sighed, flicked the key and steered onto the road.

''Russ?''

He turned to look at her, surprised by the softness of her voice. ''Yes?''

''Thank you. They're lovely.''

He saw the truth in her eyes. She was glad he'd done it. He nodded, his tension easing.

''You're welcome. Now, I think we turn here. Ah, there it is.'' He pulled up in front of the brick building, turned off the ignition and waited. She didn't move.

''Well? Shall we go? We've only got a few minutes before our appointment with the judge.''

She handed him her flowers while she put on her hat, then nodded.

''Okay,'' she said after taking a deep breath. ''I'm ready.''

''Stay there,'' he ordered and got out to come around to her side of the truck. ''I'll help you down. Here, you'd better take these.'' He handed her the flowers, spanned her waist with his hands and lifted her to the ground, taking care not to bump her hat on the roof. ''Okay?''

''More than okay, I'd say. You two look pretty snazzy. What's up?''

At the sound of the familiar voice, Russ turned guiltily, knowing his red face echoed his thoughts.

"Hello, Charles. What are you doing in Green Bay?" He felt Annie's cold, clammy hand slip into his and squeezed it.

"Just some shopping." Charles Creasy, Safe Harbor's police chief, scratched his bald head, his eyes moving from Annie to Russ and back again. "Something you two want to share?"

"No." Russ almost kicked himself for that. "Not really, Charles."

He could tell from Charles's quick grin that he suspected something was indeed up. To stop any further discussion, Russ scrounged for his best-chum look and grinned.

"Nothing we can talk about. Annie and I have a meeting. An important meeting. I'm sorry, Charles, but we've got to go or we'll be late. See you."

"Uh-huh." Charles nodded but never moved. "See you."

Russ felt that scrutiny boring into his back, but he took Annie's arm and walked with her across the street to the courthouse as if they did this every day of their lives.

"Do you think he knows?" she whispered.

"No," he said. "Yes." He hurried her to the elevator and rushed her inside. "I don't know."

"Another clear answer." She giggled at his pained look. "I hope you don't say that during our wedding vows."

"Cute," he muttered. "Really, really cute. C'mon. It's over here."

An older woman named Marge showed them into Judge Peter Nelson's chambers, a dark, oak-paneled room occupied by a small rotund man of perhaps sixty years of age. He stood when they entered, studied them for several minutes, then nodded.

Staring at Russ, he said, "You remind me of someone. Can't quite place it." Finally he shrugged, turned to his assistant. "Everything in order? License?"

Russ pulled the paper out of his jacket. "Right here."

"Hmm. Safe Harbor, eh? Lot of nice people there. Why aren't you getting married there?" he asked curiously.

"We wanted it to be very private." Russ wondered where the words came from. He was as nervous as Annie. Even his palms were damp.

"Good idea." The judge nodded. "Marriage should be personal, private. Not anybody else's business. I've seen lots of folks get buried in all the hoopla weddings bring and forget all about the vows they're making to love each other till death."

Annie's already white face paled. She sank into a nearby chair, clutching her flowers like a lifeline. It was up to him. Russ accepted the challenge, tugged on her arm until Annie was again standing beside him.

"Sir, we're on a bit of a tight schedule. Could we please begin?"

"Certainly. Got the rings?"

Russ nodded, fished the ring box out of his pants pocket. He showed the judge the contents, handed the box to Marge.

"Fine. Now we can start. All right then, miss, I'd like you to stand here." He directed Annie to her position. "And you stand here, son. That's lovely. Take a picture of them, Marge. Something they can remember." He grinned when she whipped out a camera and snapped several shots.

"No, that's no good. You two look like a couple of scared rabbits. Put your arm around her, son. Give her a little kiss. That'll loosen things up."

Russ glanced at Annie and winked. He slipped his arm

around her waist and drew her close enough to brush his lips over hers, just long enough to satisfy the judge.

"That's better. Look at the stars in their eyes, Marge." He beamed as she snapped several more photos. "All right. Save some for later. Where's Stan?" He looked around for the other witness, nodded, then picked up a book, cleared his throat, and began. "Dearly beloved…"

Russ kept his arm where it was, snug around Annie's narrow waist. She trembled once, then seemed to collect herself. But she didn't step away. She seemed glad of his support. That was encouraging.

"Are you listening to me, young man?"

Russ snapped to attention, his eyes focusing on the judge. "Yes, sir."

"Be sure that you do. Marriage is a serious commitment between two people, before God. Are you prepared to give up some of your own needs for your partner? Because marriage is all about giving, and you can't wimp out when you don't get your own way or when things don't happen just the way you want."

What was wrong with the old coot, Russ wondered. They'd wanted a plain, simple ceremony that would legalize their union, not a speech that made him feel guilty for his actions. Beside him Annie shifted. Her eyes flew to his, dark with concern. Was she having second thoughts?

"You're sure this is what you want?" Beady brown eyes scrutinized them, dared them to accept his challenge.

"Yes." Russ wouldn't back down. He couldn't. He refused to disappoint Annie. She loved Drew, really wanted him to stay with her. He couldn't deny her that. "It's what I want," he told the judge firmly.

"Young lady?"

Russ saw the hesitation in her eyes, the guilt that lay in

the dark shadows. He saw the way Annie studied him intently, searching for something he couldn't quite name.

"It's okay, Annie," he whispered, leaning down so the judge wouldn't hear. "We're doing this for Drew. There's nothing wrong with that." Every nerve in his body tensed as he watched her fight her doubts.

"For Drew's sake, Annie."

At last she nodded, and Russ let out his pent-up breath.

"I'm ready, Your Honor," she finally whispered.

"Very well." He began to repeat the timeless words Russ had always avoided. "Marriage is an institution, initiated by God... Do you, Russell, take Annie to be your lawfully wedded wife. To have and to hold, for better or worse, richer or poorer..."

"I do." His response was so soft the judge made him repeat it.

"Do you, Annie, take Russell..."

It's just a ceremony, he told himself. *It's only temporary.*

"I do," she whispered, long seconds after the solemn words had died away. Her eyes stayed riveted on Russ, peering into his.

The judge watched them both for several long moments, then nodded. "The rings?"

Russ reached out, accepted from Marge the diamond encrusted circle he'd carried in his pocket and slid it on Annie's finger, hoping it could infuse her with a confidence he didn't feel.

"With this ring, I thee wed." It sounded so final.

Annie fumbled as she slid his grandfather's plain gold band on Russ's finger. She looked scared. Very scared.

"With this ring, I thee wed," she whispered, her wide blue eyes staring into his with a trust that shook him to his core.

"I now pronounce you man and wife. What God has joined together, let no man tear asunder."

No man. No man tear asunder. The words echoed inside his head. Had he made a mistake?

"You may kiss your bride, son."

Russ blinked, saw the twinkle in the old man's eye and realized it was over. They were married. His grandfather had succeeded in forcing him to do the one thing he'd long ago decided to avoid. But as he stared into Annie's solemn face, marriage suddenly didn't seem quite so terrible.

"You gonna kiss her or not?"

Russ bent his head and pressed his lips against Annie's sweet, rosy mouth. Though she didn't protest, she didn't exactly swoon, either. He figured she was still in shock. A flashbulb went off.

"Not much of a kiss, if you ask me, Marge."

Russ shook the older man's hand. "We'll practice later," he told him with a forced grin.

The judge nodded. "I suspect you will, son." His eyes brimmed with admiration. "She's quite a looker. That kind of beauty doesn't age." He snapped into his official role. "Now let's get these papers signed, and you can be on your way. I've got court in twenty minutes."

The old gent could move quickly when he wanted to, Russ noticed. Apparently he wanted to now.

"Russell James Mitchard." The judge's eyes widened, then he nodded. "Ah. Now I know why you seem familiar. You're Willoughby's grandson, aren't you?"

"Yes, sir." Russ could have groaned, but he might have guessed it would happen. Gramps had known everyone in the court system in Green Bay.

"Ah, then I'm doubly delighted that you two came to me. Wharton and I were old, dear friends. We had many talks about you, boy. Why didn't you—"

"I'm sorry, Judge, but we've got to get going." Russ interrupted him, not wanting Annie to hear how he'd deliberately avoided Gramps when he should have been there for him.

"Of course you do. A young pair of newlyweds don't want to hang around this stuffy place when it's spring outside. Even I know that, right, Marge? Everything in order, Stan?" He waited for the nod, then winked at his assistant and grinned. "Old Willoughby's grandson. Boy, I wish he was here."

He grabbed Russ's hand and pumped.

"Congratulations, boy. You, too, sweetie. May your marriage be blessed. I expect you to make the best of it and succeed. Hear? Wharton wouldn't accept anything less for you both. I'm glad to have had the privilege of marrying his grandson." He beamed as if he'd been given a gift beyond price.

"Thank you, Judge. Thanks very much."

Marge shooed them out the door. "We'll mail you the pictures. No charge. Goodbye." She closed the door firmly behind them.

Two minutes later they were standing in the elevator, staring at each other.

Russ couldn't help it. He burst out laughing.

Annie still looked nervous, but also frustrated. Little sparks of annoyance flickered in her blue eyes. "What, exactly, is so funny?"

"Everything. He practically bullwhipped us into line, gave us his best advice, completed the ceremony, and then she pushed us out the door almost without either of them taking a breath."

A smile flickered at the corners of her mouth.

"Well, we did say we were in a hurry." She shared his

amusement for a moment, then a cloud darkened her eyes to a rich sapphire. "Russ? About this ring—"

"You don't like it?" He lifted her hand, peered at the blazing stones, wondering if he'd messed up again. After all, a wedding band was kind of important to a woman. Maybe she should have chosen her own. "Should I have stuck with plain gold?"

Her fingers shifted so she could see the band he wore.

"I notice there aren't any diamonds in yours," she whispered. A single tear flickered on the end of her eyelash. "I forgot all about rings," she whispered. "I'm sorry."

"Hey, it doesn't matter. My hands are ugly, and in my work, I can't wear one anyway, so I figured Gramps's ring would do. He said I should use it when I married you."

Annie frowned at him.

"In that letter he sent me, there were lots of very specific details. I'm sorry if you don't like your ring, but I thought it seemed appropriate. I know you said we'd keep the marriage a secret, but eventually people will know when you tell them we adopted Drew. I thought this would be nice to show." Russ fiddled with the ring, admiring the setting. "If you hate it, I guess we could get something else."

"I don't hate it!" She tugged her hand from his. "It's beautiful. The most beautiful jewelry I've ever had. But I feel—I don't know." She blinked at him. "Guilty, I suppose."

He cupped his hands around her face and held her gaze with his. One thumb brushed the tear away.

"You've got to get over this, Annie. We're not guilty of anything. Except not telling all of Safe Harbor that we got married this morning. Okay?"

It took her a while, but eventually she nodded.

"Good." He stared into her face, noting the delicate structure, the faint blue beneath her eyes, the almost imperceptible tremble of her lip. "That old coot criticized me, you know. Made fun of me."

"Who did? When?" She stared at him, half bemused.

"When I kissed you."

"Oh." Silence.

Russ smiled. "This time no one's watching." He bent his head and kissed her very thoroughly. "That'll teach you not to stick up for your husband," he whispered, and laughed at her blush, before leaning in for a repeat performance.

Unaware that the elevator doors had opened, Russ jerked away when a burst of clapping drew their attention. Lawyers, clients and assorted justice personnel stood watching them embrace.

"Come on, wife. Let's get out of here." Russ bowed to the crowd, folded Annie's arm in his and drew her along. "I'm starved. I thought we could have a nice lunch before we went back."

"Oh." She blinked at him, then smiled so her whole face was transformed. "I could use a good cup of coffee."

"Coming right up."

It took five minutes to drive to the ritzy hotel. Two more to find the dining room, almost empty of its lunch crowd. They lingered over a lazy lunch, and Russ took every opportunity to tease her. Flushed and giggling, she finally shed the nervousness that had plagued her all day and returned to her usual snappy self, commenting on his choice of tie, his Italian shoes and his fondness for lobster, which she likened to jellyfish.

Then they toured around Green Bay, speculating on the owners of the poshest houses and who did what. Russ deliberately avoided the area where his grandfather had lived and the cemetery where he lay. One day he'd come back, on his own, and tell Gramps he'd done his bidding. But today belonged to Annie.

They had tea on the sunporch of a little Victorian cottage covered with ivy and surrounded by gardens that would soon be glorious. Russ fed Annie crumpets slathered in red currant jelly while their hosts, two eighty-year-old grannies, stood nearby, chatting the entire time.

When they finally reached the outskirts of Safe Harbor, Russ felt a solid connection to Annie Simmons Mitchard.

"My place is dark," she murmured, leaning forward to peer through the windshield. "That's odd."

"I noticed a lot of cars over by the church. Maybe something's going on."

"Maybe." She barely waited for him to help her down from the high seat before she scurried inside the bed-and-breakfast, snapping on lights as she went. "Is anyone here? Felicity?"

Russ stood in the doorway, watching. It *was* odd, he admitted, but only to himself. He didn't want Annie to worry.

The phone began to ring. Annie hurried as fast as her high heels would let her and snatched the receiver.

"Bed-and-Breakfast. Hello? Oh, hi, Constance. Wrong? No, nothing." She raised one eyebrow, glanced at Russ and shrugged. "Drew?" Her whole body went on high alert. "Yes, I'll be there immediately. Russ is here. He can drive me. Three minutes." She slammed the phone down, then raced around the counter.

"Annie, what's wrong?" He followed her out the door, watched as she locked it. "Annie?"

"I don't know. Drew, she said. Drew needs me." Her big blue eyes sparkled with tears. "The only day I'm gone, and this happens. Why?"

"You don't know anything's wrong. Calm down." He lifted her into the truck and raced around to his side, spinning his wheels a little as they pulled away from the curb. "Hang on, Annie. It's going to be all right." He squeezed her hand for courage.

At the church every light seemed to be on, blazing through the stained-glass windows in myriad colors. The parking lot was packed. Then, suddenly, the entire church went black.

"Oh, dear."

"It's okay. Wait and see." He held on to her hand, walking beside her into the building. "It must be a power failure. Maybe I should—"

"Surprise! Congratulations!"

Constance stepped out from the group, face beaming.

"Sorry for the subterfuge, but we had to get you two sly ones over here somehow. Drew's just fine." Her eyes snapped with excitement. "Why didn't you tell us you were getting engaged, Annie?"

Annie's grip on Russ's fingers tightened until her nails bit into his skin, though Russ knew she had no idea she was doing it. It would be up to him to get her through this. He was her husband. It was his responsibility to her to protect her from gossip that could hurt her, and he would.

Russ wrapped an arm around her waist, tipped her head and kissed her quite thoroughly in front of the entire Safe Harbor congregation.

"The joke's on us, sweetheart. They all know about our little wedding."

She stared at him, silently ordering him to be quiet. Russ ignored that. People believed what they wanted to believe, and right now, most of Safe Harbor wanted to believe he and Annie were in love. He bent his head and whispered in her ear.

"Play along. It's the only way out." He smoothed a tendril of her hair, mimicking a gesture he'd once seen his grandfather use, then threaded her arm through his. "Ladies and gentlemen, I'd like to introduce you to my wife, Annie Mitchard."

He leaned down, intent on pasting a big kiss to her lips. When he caught the glint of fury in her eyes, Russ changed his mind and bussed her cheek with his lips. Her toes pressed hard on top of his.

He checked the expression on her face. Uh-oh. Something in those blazing sapphire eyes told him his new wife was less than besotted with his pretended ardor and would tell him all about it later.

But first they had to get past inspection from a crowd determined to glean every detail. He sucked in his breath and faced it like a man.

"Wife? But we thought you were in Green Bay getting a ring. We had no idea you were getting married!"

Russ suddenly got it. He'd blown Annie's secret, and all for nothing. He held his silly grin in place and faced them all, conscious of having just made the biggest mistake in his life. The thing was, he was glad he'd told them, even if Annie was furious.

What a way to start a marriage!

Chapter Seven

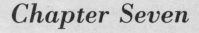

"Drew's safe at school, Annie."

"Good." Only with the utmost restraint did Annie control her anger. She pointed to the only other chair in her office. "Sit down, Russ. We have a couple of things to talk about."

She hoped he understood she would not accept the excuse he'd made last night to avoid this conversation. And surely it would be cowardly for him to run. She glared at him. He sat.

"What on this green earth possessed you to broadcast the fact that we got married?" she demanded, deliberately forcing the words out in a calm, even flow.

He glanced over his shoulder. Annie caught on immediately.

"Felicity's gone. I gave her the rest of the morning off."

"Yes, well." He fiddled with his hands. "I'd better get going, too. I've got a ton of work to do."

"It will wait." She stood directly in front of the door. "I want answers, Russ. It was supposed to be a shower for the bride and groom to be. They thought we'd been to town to get a ring, that we were *planning* to get married. Until you blabbed.''

He raked a hand through his hair, looking more like a little boy with his fingers stuck in the cookie jar than the adult he was supposed to be. Annie fought to hold on to her irritation, tried to ignore his beseeching smile.

''What does it matter?'' he demanded, taking the offensive. ''They know. Now we don't have to pretend.''

''Don't we?'' She kept her voice sweet, silky. ''Then how do you suggest we explain your *pretense* from last night?''

''We don't.'' He rose, dominating the tiny space. One hand reached out to brush her hair off her face. ''I liked your short skirt yesterday better,'' he teased.

''Can it, Russell,'' she warned. ''You were acting like a lovesick teenager.''

He snorted his indignance. ''I was not!'' She never called him Russell.

''Close enough. Now every time someone sees us, they'll expect a certain degree of, uh—'' She paused, unable to say it.

''Romance?'' He shrugged. ''So we give it to them.''

It was clear he wasn't daunted by the prospect. Annie's knees wobbled at the thought of those gentle fingers touching her face again.

''I was right that very first day.'' She stared at him, dismay filling her at the thought of remaining sane with his arm wrapped around her, his lips whispering silly things in her ear.

''Right about what?'' He wasted several staples on a hunk of paper, then, when she didn't answer, stared at her. ''Annie?''

''You are crazy. Certifiable.'' She shook her head. ''I cannot do this.''

"Think of it as a game. We act like happily married newlyweds, they get used to it and then ignore us."

"In your dreams!" How could he not realize what he'd done? "I have a Women's League meeting coming up. They'll prod and pry, want to know every detail."

He still looked unconcerned, so Annie elaborated.

"How we met, when we fell in love, what made us decide to get married so fast—on and on it will go until I'll trip over my own lies."

"So don't lie. We decided to speed up the wedding day because Pastor Burns doesn't seem to be coming back for a while and so we could get custody of Drew." He shrugged.

Annie rolled her eyes. It was the truth, but it sounded so cold. Besides, it was humiliating to put their marriage into those terms when everyone thought he'd swept her off her feet because he loved her. She'd far rather they believed that.

"Annie, believe me, I enjoy being locked up in this tiny room with you, and playing house in front of your friends will be a pleasure, but I've got to get to work. There's a lot to do before The Quest hosts its grand opening." He bent and kissed her fast and hard on the lips, pulled the door open and winked. "That's for any snoopy busybodies spying on us. I'll see you at lunchtime. Okay, honey?"

There was no point in answering. *Honey* had already left.

Annie fiddled with a few accounts, ordered some groceries and did anything else she could think of to avoid the dining room with its stack of shower gifts. She felt so guilty about that.

"Annie?"

"Hi, Nathan. You didn't come down for breakfast."

"No. I should have told you. I ate out this morning.

Couldn't sleep so I went for a walk on the beach.'' He avoided her eyes, standing awkwardly in the doorway. ''I hope you didn't mind that I stayed over a few days longer.''

''Not at all, though as the season gets busier, you might let me know first. I wouldn't want to make you sleep on the sofa.'' She smiled to show she was joking.

''I'll do that in the future. I just needed to get away, sit by the lake and think. Things kind of pile up. You know?''

''Believe me, I know.'' She smiled at him. ''I'm about to have a second cup of coffee. Want to join me?''

He grinned, his hard jaw softening. ''Second cup, Annie?''

She blushed, got up, walked into the kitchen. ''Okay, fourth. But you don't need to tell anyone.''

''I barely know anyone. Who would I tell?''

Annie carried the cups to a table, studiously avoiding the gifts stacked under the window. ''Constance?''

His head jerked up, and he peered at her. ''Why would you say that? I barely know the woman.''

''But you're getting to know her, aren't you?'' His face remained impassive, so Annie tried again. ''I saw you watching her last night. At the shower. You seem interested.''

''She's a beautiful woman.'' His face gave her no hint to his thoughts.

''Yes, Constance is lovely. A bit stubborn maybe.'' Ah, that brought a flicker of interest to his azure eyes. ''It took her forever to agree to a date with Charles Creasy, you know.''

''Police chief, right? Tall, balding?'' Nathan nodded. ''I noticed they seemed pretty friendly.''

You noticed a lot more than that, she thought, but didn't say it.

"Charles is a wonderful man and he treats Constance like a queen." Hadn't the Women's League wasted several minutes last night around the punch bowl, watching Constance put on a fresh pot of coffee while they discussed how wonderful it would be if the town matriarch found love again?

"But?" Nathan squinted at her. "I sense there's something you're not saying."

"From what she's told us, Constance loved her husband very much. He died on a missions trip, and her world fell apart. It's none of my business, of course, but I'm not sure she's ready to move on." A noise drew her attention. "Are you okay?"

"Yes." He faked a cough. "I swallowed the wrong way." He changed the subject. "Congratulations to you and Russ on your wedding. You make a lovely couple."

"Thanks." Why had she come in here? She had no desire to talk about her marriage—not to anyone.

"He seems to care for you a lot."

What could she say to that? Russ cared about his grandfather's wishes. He'd only agreed to her terms so he could fulfill his grandfather's hopes and dreams. He didn't care about her personally. It was a business proposition.

"Are you happy, Annie?"

She stared at him, wondering what he'd say if she told him she dithered between a strange kind of joy whenever Russ touched or spoke to her and an overwhelming guilt that she'd taken her marriage vows for the wrong reason.

"I don't know," she admitted at last. There was something about Nathan's quiet interest that drew her confidence. "Everything is so mixed up. Are you married?" She glanced up in time to surprise a look of radiance in his eyes. A moment later it was gone.

"I was," he murmured. "Once, a long time ago."

"Then maybe you can understand. Everything has changed, and yet everything is kind of the same. I feel off balance, as if I might step too far one way and fall off." She shook her head at the fanciful words. "Does that make any sense?"

"Perfect sense to me." He reached out to pat her hand, eyes widening at the flashing band. "Nobody goes through life with all the answers, Annie. Sometimes you just have to take it on faith that God is leading you, that He will keep you on the right path, and you just keep walking, trusting Him to catch you when you fall."

Tears welled in her eyes, tears she hadn't dared shed for fear they'd never stop.

"Thank you, Nathan," she whispered. "I needed to be reminded of that."

"Drew is a very special little boy. I think it's so great that God gave him a new mother in you. I pray the adoption goes through without a hitch. You have a lot of love to give, Annie. Never be afraid to share that." He stood, patted her shoulder. "I'd better get moving. I promised Russ I'd give him a hand with some shelving."

"That was kind of you, but you don't have to spend your free time working, especially when you came to town for a break. Don't let him talk you into anything. Sometimes Russ tends to steamroller over everyone else."

Nathan chuckled. "Yes, that describes him rather well. But truly, I want to help. He does magnificent work, Annie. Have you seen it?"

Her mouth dropped open in shock. "You know, I haven't. Somehow I just never got around to it."

"It would be nice if you were to drop by, say ten o'clock, with some coffee and, oh, a dozen of those chocolate chip cookies I smelled this morning." His eyes twinkled. "I think a few sweets might earn the right to look over his work."

"Hmm. Russ isn't the only manipulator, I see." She nodded, enjoying his not so subtle hint. "Good idea. Maybe I'll do that, Nathan. Thanks."

"My pleasure." He leaned down and whispered, "Personally, I'm partial to chocolate cake."

She laughed. "Maybe I could make that for dinner. You're welcome to join us."

He shook his head. "Not tonight, thanks. I might have a date."

"Oh." Annie tried, but she could find no hints in his bland look, and after the inquisition she'd endured last night, she refused to ask about anyone else's love life. "Well, have fun."

"You know, I think I just might. Around ten, then?" With a wave, he was gone, and the house stood silent.

Annie sighed, grabbed the laundry basket and headed upstairs. She'd slacked off yesterday, her wedding day. Today she'd have to dig in and make the place sparkle again.

She started with Nathan's room, then remembered his comments and checked her watch. An hour and a quarter until coffee time. A person could accomplish a lot in that time. Suddenly the day seemed brighter.

"I have never seen anything like this." Annie let her fingers trail over the cool sheen of silver wings that formed the base of Russ's most spectacular piece. "It's gorgeous. Reminds me of something in the Bible about cherubim. The wings are so intricate."

Russ took her hand, kissed her fingertips, then bowed at the waist. "Thank you, milady."

"How on earth do you make something like this?"

"It's a long, boring process." Russ shrugged. "You don't want to know."

Nathan glanced up from dunking his cookie into his coffee cup. "She asked, didn't she?"

Russ glanced at him, then at Annie.

"Fair enough." He took a deep breath and launched into an explanation.

"I had to start with an inner structure that had the basic shape. Then I cut out each feather, chased it, formed and soldered it onto the interior. The cord is buried in the right-hand side, and it took forever to get the feathers layered without overheating them. Believe me, it took yards of welding cloth to keep the under parts from melting." Noting her glazed look, he shrugged, grinned. "Okay, I'll stop. But you did ask."

"Yes, I did." Annie glanced at him. "I don't have a clue what most of that means, but that doesn't change the fact that it's beautiful." She touched the rim of the silver bowl that sat atop the wings forming the shade, marveling at its fragile beauty. Then she wandered from display to display, entranced by his other creations.

"There's something about them—they don't look heavy at all." Nathan pointed out his favorite, a baseball glove with a ball in its pocket. "I'd never have expected you to have the patience for this, Russ."

"I can be patient. For the right reason." Russ glanced at Annie, his eyes full of meaning.

"I think I'll go for a little walk. I ate too many of those cookies." Nathan grabbed his jacket and slipped out the door.

"You embarrassed him." Annie walked through the shop once more. "I predict a huge success for The Quest, Russ. These are fantastic."

"Thanks." He stood where he was, watching her. "You sound surprised."

"I guess I am, a little. When you said silver, I visualized jewelry. Chains, bracelets. Rings, maybe?"

"I've never tried out that area." He shrugged. "Maybe I will one day, if I get a brain wave."

"Is that what you need?" She touched the sculpted curve of a woman's head, facing into the wind, hair and gown flowing out behind. "A brain wave to create something like this?"

"Mm, kind of a mental picture, I guess you'd call it. If I can visualize it, I can usually make it." His attention stayed focused on her.

Feeling edgy, Annie continued to look around the shop.

"I like the way you've incorporated your work with the books," she murmured, noticing Rhonda's old rolltop desk with a lamp on top and a few antique books scattered over its surface. "Everything fits."

He let her wander for several minutes. "Are you nervous around me, Annie?"

Surprised, she twisted to look at him. "A little, I guess," she admitted. "Yesterday sort of changed things."

"Not really. Basically we're the same people. We just happen to be married." He turned away, began unpacking some sort of tool from its box.

"I hate it when you do that," she blurted.

"What?" He straightened, stared at her. "Unpack?"

"Pretend nothing's happened. Maybe marriage means nothing to you, but I happen to have certain beliefs about marriage. I don't think anyone can be married and remain the same." She marched over and began stuffing things into the picnic basket she'd carried over twenty minutes earlier.

"I'm sorry."

She ignored his quiet apology, continued what she was doing.

"Annie, I really am sorry if I offended you. I wasn't putting marriage down." His hands came over hers, held them still. One finger forced up her chin so she had to look at him. "You know that I'm not the marrying sort. I'm just not the type for hearth and home. I guess I look at our marriage more as a business arrangement."

Fury put her thoughts into words.

"You think of me as your business partner?" she demanded, slamming the lid closed and snatching the basket in her arms. "You think those vows we spoke are some kind of clauses in a contract?" She glared at him. "Why is that, Russ? Because it leaves you free, with no responsibility toward me or Drew?" She strode to the door and yanked it open.

"No! Annie, wait—"

"Grow up, will you? Married or not, Russ, everyone has responsibilities in life. You've just chosen to ignore yours for the past thirty odd years." Clutching the basket to her chest, she walked out the door and down the street toward her bed-and-breakfast.

"Annie, wait a minute!"

She heard him call, but not for anything would she stop and let him see the tears rolling down her cheeks. Not for anything. Russ Mitchard wanted a business deal with her? Fine. That's exactly what he'd get.

The sun sent shafts of dazzling light from her ring. Her ring—the ring blazing with diamonds that everyone assumed signified how much he cared. What a joke!

"Oh, good. You're back. I was just checking my hours before I left and—" Felicity took one look at her face, closed the time sheet folder. "Never mind," she mumbled and fled out the door.

"I'd like to throw this ring in the lake," Annie muttered, stomping into her kitchen. Her usual joy in the place had dissipated, leaving only a deep longing for something more, something personal, meant only for her, to fill the aching hole in her heart.

"I goofed, Lord. I knew a pretend wedding wouldn't be enough, but I wanted to keep Drew. And instead of waiting for Your timing, I took things into my own hands. I am such a fool."

She set the basket on the floor, stormed up the stairs to her room, then pulled the beautiful ring off her finger. Whatever hope she'd secretly nurtured for some fairy-tale future fizzled away. These beautiful diamonds meant nothing to him, other than a mask to hide behind while he got what he wanted. She would never wear her wedding ring again. She buried the ring at the very bottom of her jewelry box and snapped the lid closed.

"It's not a marriage to last, stupid. It's a temporary agreement, a mutually beneficial contract to get custody of Drew. How could you have forgotten that?" she asked her reflection.

But she hadn't forgotten. She'd just wanted to believe that for once in her life something special would happen to her. Annie grimaced. Mom had wanted the same thing, and that was the basis of all her problems.

With a past like Annie's, how dumb was it to believe in love?

"All right, ladies. Let's get this meeting underway." Constance rapped her knuckles on the table in front of her. "I suggest our first business is to congratulate Annie on her recent marriage. I know we all wish her and Russ the best.''

Annie fidgeted in her chair, her eyes stuck on the hearth rug in front of the stone fireplace. She knew her cheeks were red and that they'd think it was shyness or embarrassment. Really, she was ashamed that she'd perpetrated such a lie on her friends. They'd encouraged her after her mother's death, provided quilts for the bed-and-breakfast, been there through the first rough weeks when Annie had taken Drew in.

She'd repaid their kindness with lies.

''We're all very excited for you, Annie.'' Gracie Adam's eyes shone with excitement.

''Thanks,'' she murmured, then forced herself to face them all. ''And thank you all for the wonderful shower. You really shouldn't have.''

A great discussion ensued about the ways and means the shower had been organized.

''With any luck, we might get to do it again,'' Gracie whispered as she nudged Annie in the ribs.

''Another shower?'' Annie stared. ''What do you mean?''

''Constance,'' Wendy Maguire hissed from the other side, jerking her head to the right, toward their founder.

''Constance is getting married?'' She'd really been out of it to have missed this news, Annie decided.

''No, silly! But there's something going on between her and that man who's been staying with you. Nathan, isn't it?'' Gracie's red hair glowed in a shaft of sunlight. ''She was pretty tight with Charles for a while, but that seems to have slowed down a little. She and Nathan have been together several times.''

''I saw them myself, walking on the beach around eleven-thirty this morning,'' Wendy whispered.

"And you're not the only one." Gracie winked at Annie.

"Ladies, I'd like to introduce Justine Clemens. I'm assuming from Gracie's comments that you all know she'll be helping us out since Pastor Burns's rather unfortunate accident has rendered him inactive."

Everyone nodded, their mood sobering as they considered their pastor and his upcoming surgery.

"Justine, I'd like you to meet our Women's League members." Constance went around the table, introducing each woman.

"Thank you, Constance. I'm glad to be here. Pastor Burns has told me many things about Safe Harbor. He's even mentioned your Women's League. Apparently he's felt for some time that he'd lost touch with you ladies and thought I might be of some help. Please feel free to contact me with anything. I'll do what I can. And I'll be counting on you to tell me when I goof. Pastor Burns's shoes are pretty big to step into."

Again, discussion broke out around the room.

"Ladies, please." Constance cleared her throat. "Thank you. Now Elizabeth is going to give us her financial report."

Annie forced herself to sit through the business part of the meeting, though she wanted to run as far and as fast as she could. That would only cause more questions, and enough people were already speculating about her.

She glanced at Holly, wishing she could talk to her. But how could Holly possibly understand her situation? Holly loved Alex Wilkins. Their relationship wasn't based on anything but honest love and affection.

Wendy Maguire would try to understand, but she was totally involved with her little family, two kids and another on the way. Wendy, too, was head-over-heels in love with Robert. Hardly the same thing.

Gracie? No, Gracie was everything Annie wanted to be and never could. She was strong, confident, outspoken. She held an important job and she did it with elegance, grace and panache. How could she possibly relate to Annie's need to be a mother to Drew, her fear that she would never know the feel of a new baby cuddled in her arms?

Justine. Annie swerved her eyes away from their stand-in minister, a flush of guilt filling her. Justine would tell her she'd messed up, that marriage was for people who loved each other. She could imagine Justine's response if Annie reminded her of all those Biblical characters who'd married for other reasons than love. Annie closed her eyes, sighed. She'd better forget about talking to Justine. Once again she was on her own.

One by one, Annie ticked off the other Safe Harbor women she'd known for years. Elizabeth was seventy years old. When her sweetheart died in the Korean War, she'd given up on marriage to concentrate on her job as postmistress. Technically, Kit Peters wasn't even a member of the League, and anyway, she was too young. How could she possibly understand how desperately Annie wanted a child of her own? Felicity was too close to the situation. Though she might guess that Annie and Russ's relationship wasn't all it seemed, she was busy trying to get her own life back on track after a misspent youth. She didn't need anyone else's problems.

That left Constance. The idea was laughable. Constance had lost her beloved husband during a rebel uprising in Central America. Though the older woman would certainly understand her desire to be a mother, Annie knew she wouldn't approve of her means to adopt Drew. Constance had known a deep, rich, fulfilling love. She wouldn't be easily swayed, no matter what argument Annie chose. Besides, Annie felt far too timid to tell Constance anything. The woman was the town matriarch. Annie couldn't discuss her mistakes with someone like that.

No, Annie had taken on this marriage on her own terms and she'd have to learn to deal with these feelings. She couldn't tell the league her reasons for her marriage, nor the terms of it. And they didn't need to know. They were happy for her. Why not leave it that way?

Finally Constance called a halt for coffee. Weary of maintaining her mask, Annie searched for a way to escape. It was not to be.

"Annie, that husband of yours is a dish. No other word. But how can you ever tell what's going on behind those silver-cloud eyes?" Wendy grinned from ear to ear. "He's such a charmer."

Wendy sighed. "Kind of makes you jealous, doesn't it, Gracie? A guy like that, with everything any girl could want. How did you find him, Annie?"

"He found her. His grandfather was her mother's lawyer. Didn't you know?" Gracie sipped her coffee. "He is good-looking, I'll grant you that. And I do think Annie is very lucky. I'm just glad there's more than one fish in the ocean."

Wendy giggled at Gracie's wink and raised eyebrow. "What's that mean?"

"Have you taken a good look at our new doctor, my dear? He's gorgeous."

"Kyle came for dinner yesterday." Wendy sighed, closed her eyes and tilted her head back. "I know what you mean, Gracie. Robert used to look like that."

"What?" Annie couldn't believe her ears. "Robert never looked like that." As soon as she blurted the words out, shock covered their faces. "Oh, no." She clapped a hand over her mouth. "I'm sorry, Wendy. I didn't mean—" Wendy looked at Gracie, who stared at her. Then the two women burst out laughing.

"I can dream, can't I?" Wendy grumbled.

"Me, too." Gracie winked at Wendy, then glanced at Annie. "Not all of us get a chance to meet a successful lawyer turned silversmith who plays the organ like a master and looks like he stepped out of an advertisement, honey." She tapped her forefinger against her bottom lip. "Your Russ is a great catch. But Dr. Kyle Evans, now there's someone for me to think about. Those eyes of his give me shivers."

Russ—a lawyer? Annie froze. The two kept chatting, but Russ wasn't part of the conversation. Finally Annie had to ask.

"What made you mention Russ being a lawyer?" she asked, trying to pretend a casualness she did not feel.

"Why, I remember the hoopla when he walked out on his grandfather, of course. I was living in the city then, and the news was in every paper. Wharton Willoughby Loses." Gracie shook her head. "I'll never forget that caption. I think it was the first time the old man ever lost anything. Must have been quite a blow, considering Russ was a full partner with his dad and his grandfather."

"All part of God's plan," Wendy murmured, watching Constance resume her seat. "Bring Russ here, and the two of you marry. A match hatched in heaven. Love—God's style." Her soft voice faded away, eyes focused on something no one else could see. "Who can know the ways of God?"

Annie couldn't stand it a moment longer. They thought God had arranged this? If they only knew! She'd been so certain this could work, so positive that Russ wouldn't try to pull anything or keep her in the dark.

It just went to show how little she really knew the man she'd married.

Russell Mitchard, her husband, was an attorney-at-law, a former partner in a law firm with his father and grandfather—and she hadn't even known it.

Annie couldn't help wondering what else hadn't her *husband* told her, and why.

Chapter Eight

"Annie, please. You've burned yourself three times in five minutes."

Her rigid body language translated into *Mind your own business, Mitchard!* Russ ignored that, tried again.

"Will you just sit down and tell me what's wrong?"

"I can't sit down. I'm too busy. I have work to do."

Unlike some people. The unspoken comment was implicit in the look she slanted at him before turning to peer through the black oven glass as if it held the secret of life. "I have to take these out."

"I'll do it." Russ snatched up the pot holders, edged her out of the way and removed the slightly charred cinnamon buns from the oven. In one fluid motion, he tipped them upside down on her cooling rack. "All right?" He glared at her in frustration.

"I suppose." Annie shrugged, glaring at the blackened spots as if she could make them disappear with a look. "Now look what you've done. They're burned. I never burn things."

"What I did?" He shook his head. "They're fine, Annie.'' He lifted her hand, smoothed salve over her blistered finger. ''There, that should take the pain out.''

''Thank you.'' She yanked her hands from his, shoved them behind her back.

Russ sighed. Whatever he'd done to cause this wasn't going to be cured with ointment.

''Please, Annie, let's talk about whatever has you so annoyed.'' He wrapped his fingers around her elbow and drew her out of the kitchen and into the small sitting room at the back of the house, which she kept for private use.

For once he was glad Annie's guests were all out attending a local dinner theater. They needed time—*he* needed time to settle things between them. When better than now? Drew was tucked up in bed at a friend's house, and they were alone.

''Come over here and sit down.'' In a moment Russ had a small fire burning. ''Your hands are freezing.'' He chafed them between his.

''Probably. I went fishing before supper and forgot my gloves. The water hasn't warmed much yet.''

''Fishing? But it's been raining all afternoon.'' He frowned at her. ''Why fishing?''

Her eyes froze into blue ice chips just as her voice iced over.

''Because someone promised Drew they'd take him fishing this afternoon, Russ. Remember?''

He squeezed his eyes closed, groaned. Oops.

''I'm really sorry, Annie. I got busy working on something and I forgot.'' He checked her face, swallowed a sigh at her grim look.

Annie was a sweet, loving woman who really cared about the people in her life. She hadn't pushed him into any commitment after the wedding and that crazy shower, she'd endured his embraces and affectionate remarks, even pretended she liked them. In fact, Annie had managed the whole uncomfortable situation with a grace and panache that made him admire her all the more. He hated to be the cause of her distress because he'd forgotten something.

For Annie's sake, he had to get a handle on this responsibility thing. It had plagued him for long enough.

She wasn't giving him any points for that apology. His conscience kicked in, reminded him it wasn't the first time he'd let someone down. Russ ignored it.

"I know it's no excuse, but I really am sorry, Annie. I promise I'll make it up to him." How many times had he tried to make it up before?

"Don't make any more promises you can't keep, okay, Russ? I can only do so much to cover for you." She tugged her hands from his and sat on them. Her words stung, reminded him that she'd asked him for nothing in this marriage, nothing but his signature on a piece of paper that would give her permanent guardianship of Drew. When had he begun to want more than that from his marriage to this quiet, controlled woman?

Annie had been furious at him ever since that women's meeting after lunch. Wendy Maguire had hinted as to the reason, but Russ hadn't understood her any more than he understood Annie's anger. He sensed his wife's present hurt didn't really stem from the canceled fishing expedition. Russ was pretty sure Drew hadn't expected to fish in the rain, anyway.

No, this anger had to do with something else. The reason for it went far deeper than fishing. Whatever reason she gave, the underlying reason probably had something to do with the father she couldn't or wouldn't forgive. How many times in the last couple of days had she compared Russ to him, drawn parallels between their behaviors? But he wasn't like that! He had no intention of abandoning

Drew or her. In fact, he liked the life they were beginning to build together. He'd tell her that if he could just get her past the anger, get her to open up to him.

"Okay, I'm pretty sure you're upset because I didn't tell you about being a lawyer." Shards of ice formed in her eyes, dared him to continue. "Wendy told me you didn't even notice her when she passed by earlier. She stopped in to ask me if something was wrong and related your conversation from this afternoon."

"Did she? How nice." Annie stared into the fire, lips pinched tight. She was hurting. He knew it from the way she closed herself off, as if afraid to believe him.

"Is this about my past?" Her head jerked, and he knew he'd hit the target. Russ frowned. "Annie, I didn't tell you about my past because it didn't matter. Not to us. Not now—today."

No thawing was visible in her rigid posture or masklike face. He reached up, brushed his hand over her hair, cupped her chin in his palm.

"Come on, honey," he pleaded. "Cut me a little slack. I forgot about it because it doesn't matter to us."

She jerked her chin away.

Russ refused to quit. Her doubts about him he could deal with, he hoped. But this fear that made her afraid to open up, that had to be tackled. He wanted Annie to relax with him. He wanted them to find common ground in this marriage of theirs. He wanted her to trust him.

"Annie, just think for a minute. Have you told me every single thing in your past?" She frowned, but at least she was looking at him.

"You've been over to that house of yours ten times, trying to figure something out for the Wilkinsons, and every time you come back with red puffy eyes. But you don't explain what there is about that place that sets you off on a crying jag.''

Her head jerked up, eyes flashing. ''I do not conduct crying jags, Russell Mitchard.'' Her teeth were clenched tight. ''I also explained—''

''You said your parents weren't happy.'' He nodded. ''Okay. I accept that. But I know it isn't the whole story. Something about that place gets to you still—and your father's been dead ten years. You don't want to tell me?'' He waited, then shrugged at her continued silence. ''Fine. I can understand that.''

''Good.'' She huffed. ''Then you can stop asking questions.''

''Annie, my point is that no one can completely know someone else. No matter how close they are, how much they know, there will always be things that—''

''You promised me no secrets,'' she hissed. Another glare. ''You promised that we'd be open with each other.'' Condemnation laced her voice.

Russ shook his head. ''Annie girl, my being a lawyer in my grandfather's firm wasn't a secret.'' She twisted her head, her eyes blazing with disbelief. He searched for a way to prove it. ''Gracie knew about it.''

''News flash! Gracie isn't married to you. I am. I didn't know and I felt like an idiot trying to understand what they were talking about.''

He saw the shield of tears in her eyes and decided to give up. No way would he ever win this argument. Annie figured she'd been slighted, and maybe she had. Maybe he should have told her. But how much, and when? They'd only been married two days!

Russ felt he was walking on eggshells. He didn't want to hurt her, would never deliberately not tell her something. He needed time to figure this marriage thing out, find some balance, get to know the rules. But he'd have to do that later.

At the moment, Russ was pretty sure abject apology was the only avenue open to breaking this barrier between them. He hunkered down in front of her, used the tip of his finger to catch the tear dangling from the end of her lashes, then enclosed her hands in his.

"Listen, Annie, I'm truly sorry for not telling you I was once a lawyer," he murmured, squeezing her fingers. "I apologize."

She studied him, blue eyes dubious.

"I mean it, Annie girl. I'm sorry I didn't tell you. I never even think about that time in my life anymore, so I guess I figured it wasn't important."

"Why don't you think about it?" She fiddled with his hands, her fingers tracing the path of his wedding ring.

"That's a tough question." Russ shrugged, tugged her down to sit beside him on the carpet, backs propped against the sofa. He stared into the fire, his mind winging to the past. "It's a part of my life that was very painful. I was unhappy, I felt trapped in those offices, yet I was trying to do what was right, what was expected of me. When I finally realized that me being a lawyer was never going to be enough for either my family or myself, I walked."

"Enough? I don't understand." She frowned, peered at him. "Weren't you any good at it?"

She'd forgiven him. Russ heaved a sigh of relief. So far, so good. Some of that heart-wrenching sadness had left her face. Curiosity replaced it.

"You'd better tell me. What happened? Did you lose all your cases or something?"

Russ tilted her chin, stared into her eyes.

"Annie Simmons Mitchard," he chided softly. "You

might not know some things about me, but surely you know me better than that.'' He watched the red rise in her cheeks, felt a rush of tenderness bloom in his heart. He leaned across to brush his lips against her forehead and grinned. ''Don't you?''

''Well, I know enough about you to expect you were a great lawyer. I hate to admit it, but you're great at everything.'' She sighed, rested her head on his shoulder, relaxing beside him in a way she never had before. ''You're quite intimidating, Russ.''

''I am? Intimidating?'' He blinked. Was that what always went wrong between them—he overpowered her? Russ shook his head, remembering his many faux pas. He'd have to correct her impression, and fast.

''Hardly intimidating, wife! You didn't see me during my waiter phase. I sucked swamp water.''

She considered that, head tipped to one side, hair shimmering in the firelight. ''Maybe. But I bet you looked great in your little waiter uniform.''

To his utter surprise, his wife winked at him, then giggled.

He pinched her cheek. ''Now you're laughing at me.'' He waited a minute, then took the plunge. ''Am I forgiven for my omission?''

''I'm thinking about it.'' She smiled at him, the shadows that had clouded her blue eyes completely gone. ''What else have you done in your life, Russ? A wife should know these things.''

''Yes, I suppose she should.'' He took a deep breath. ''Truck driver.'' He saw her skepticism. ''Really. But only for two days. I got fired.''

''Someone dared to fire you?'' she teased. ''The mind boggles. Why?''

Somehow Annie always made him feel competent, in

charge, as if she truly believed he could do anything. Russ tried to remember the last time he'd felt such assurance from another, but no one came to mind. Annie was unique in her championing. Her faith made him feel ten feet tall, as if he hadn't wasted years of his life.

A sharp elbow reminded him there was a question on the table.

"Why did I get fired?" He pretended to stare at the fire. "The owner and I didn't agree."

"About what?" Her question snapped at him.

"You don't give up until you have the answer, do you, Annie?" He laid his arm across her shoulders and hugged her, breathed in the soft lemony scent of her hair. "I like that about you. You head straight for what you want."

"Uh-huh. And flattery will not alter my course." Her eyes flashed a warning. "Why, Russ?"

"Patience is a virtue, you know. You should practice it." Her stare never lost its intensity. Russ sighed, winced mentally as he admitted the truth behind another goof up. "My boss and I disagreed about the speed limit."

"Ah." She waited, tapping one finger against her thigh.

"He thought I drove his trucks too fast. I thought the idea was to get the stuff to its destination as fast as possible." He lifted his hand, palm up. "Problem."

"Yes, I can imagine."

She was laughing. He could feel her whole body shaking in amusement.

"I don't think it's nice to laugh at another's failures," he lectured. But in truth he enjoyed that laughter very much. It was the kind of chortle that shared the sting still hidden inside him. Only Annie could bring out the amusement in a situation so he forgot the hurt.

"S-sorry, Russ," she sputtered. "But I have this mental picture of you, pedal to the metal, racing past everything on a twelve-lane freeway, radio going full tilt on some country station. And you're wearing a cap. Backward.''

Russ pretended disdain, ignored her gibe. He was having too much fun to stop. Those wasted years suddenly seemed worthwhile if he could share them with Annie.

''Do you want to hear about the job I had in a bakery?''

She did laugh then, loud and long. ''You, in a bakery? As what? A taste tester? Gimme a break.''

''You slander me, wife. I rose every morning at three-thirty a.m. to make the bread.'' Russ preened, playing the role for all it was worth. Anything to keep Annie laughing. He loved the sound of it, full-bodied, rich, bubbling over him like a warm blanket they shared—just the two of them.

''Up at three-thirty? In the morning?'' She shook her head. ''We can't be talking about you, Russ. It's impossible. Drew can barely waken you before he leaves for school.''

''Despite your doubts, I did it. For two whole weeks.''

''That long?'' She marveled, giggling again.

''Uh-huh.'' He wound his finger in a delicate golden loop of hair that had escaped the lopsided ponytail and grazed her neck. ''Then I had an accident.''

''What kind of accident?'' She sounded worried.

He grinned. ''I used too much yeast.'' He stopped, realizing how right it felt to tell Annie all his failures. She made them seem normal, part of life. Not stupid mistakes he should have controlled.

''Nobody appreciated that my buns were fluffier than anyone else's,'' he mourned.

She peeked at him through her lashes, then slanted her eyes over her shoulder, one eyebrow tilted as she glanced down his back. Seconds later they were both howling like fools.

"I th-think your buns are j-just fine," she managed, then clenched her stomach as laughter burst free.

Russ couldn't smother his chuckles, but most of his amusement came from watching Annie lose all her inhibitions. Eventually she stopped laughing, wiped the tears from her eyes.

"You tell good bedtime stories, Russ."

"That was not a story." He rubbed his shoulder against hers. "It's the truth about my past. You wanted to hear it, now you know."

And it didn't sting nearly as much. She'd given him the gift of release, and though she'd never guess, that was very precious to him. For the first time in many months he felt unfettered by the past, almost free of the guilt. He'd done what he had. It was time to let it go.

Clearly Annie had.

"Seriously, Russ. You are a little overwhelming. All the women in town think I'm the luckiest girl around to have snagged someone like you."

"Only a little overwhelming?" He frowned. "Wait a minute—snagged?"

"It's a fishing term women use." She grinned. "A compliment, actually."

"Really." He supposed it was flattering in a way, but right now it seemed more important to hear Annie's thoughts on the matter. "What do you think?"

A long silence stretched out between them as she stared at him. Slowly that silence filled with unspoken thoughts, swelled with a rich undercurrent of meaning that he couldn't quite decipher.

Her fingers brushed his cheek, then rested on his chest in a featherlight caress. Her words whispered through the air.

"I think you're a very nice man who is much more

suited to working with silver than wasting his energy in some musty law library.''

For that he leaned down and kissed her.

''Thank you, Annie,'' he murmured. ''That means a lot to me.''

''You're welcome.''

They sat side by side, watching the flames flicker down until only a soft bed of coals remained. In the main living room, the fireplace was gas. This wood-burning one seemed much more intimate.

''How did the fishing go?'' he asked eventually.

''Not well.'' She met his gaze, blushed, then looked away. ''I fell in.''

''What?'' He stared at her, his entire body growing cold. ''Annie, you could have drowned!'' Shades of the past bubbled up, blurred his vision.

''In six inches of water? Not hardly, Russ.'' She snorted. ''Besides, it did me good. Cooled off my temper and knocked my pride for a loop. It's fairly embarrassing to walk through town soaking wet, you know.''

He hid his chuckle in her hair. Annie pulled away, frowned.

''You're laughing at me.'' She sighed. ''Drew laughed, too. Said I looked like a drowned cat.''

From her perch on the mantel, Marmalade lifted her head off her paws to blink at them. She howled a mournful wail, then closed her eyes and resumed her nap.

''That's her opinion on the matter, I guess.'' Russ decided to change the subject before she asked him any questions. ''Are you happy with the kids' rehearsals?'' He held her hand in his, knotted his fingers with hers. ''Nothing you want to change tomorrow?''

''No, they're great. If they could just keep it like that until Easter, it would be perfect.'' She closed her eyes, remembered the beauty of the songs. "It's so touching when it finally comes together, isn't it? Glorious and up-lifting. All the things I want Easter morning to be."

"You've done a great job, Annie. You've got a gift with kids. They respect your vision of the music and try their hardest to interpret it." He smoothed her hair, remembering the way Annie dealt with the petty squabbles that always arose. "You're a born mother."

He held his breath, wondering if he should have said that.

"Thank you." Annie smiled, eyes soft in the flickering firelight. "I love kids. I don't know why. I was an only child and I never had a lot to do with other kids, but somehow I seem drawn to them." She grinned at him. "You weren't so bad yourself. I noticed how quickly you patched up that hurt knee."

"Wasn't she an angel? Emma, that's her name. All that fair hair fanning around her head tugged at something in me." In truth, the tiny child had made him think of Annie, of what a daughter of hers might look like. The image staggered him.

In his mind's eye, Russ could see Annie kneeling in front of the fire, reading stories from that huge book she used in her Sunday school class. He'd caught a glimpse of Annie at work last Sunday morning when he'd tracked her down in her Sunday school room to hand over the parcel of cookies she'd left in his truck. The kids were crowded around her, vying for the spot nearest her gentle hands, hanging on every word she spoke. Two or twenty kids, it didn't matter to Annie. She never lost that soft, gentle tone, never bruised a fragile ego. More important, she accepted each one exactly as they were. If ever a woman deserved to be a mother, Annie did.

He'd cheated her of that.

Russ sucked in a breath as the realization hit him. Married to him, stuck in a marriage that wasn't really a marriage, Annie would only have Drew to love. The full impact of their hasty decision hit him squarely between the eyes, silencing Russ. He'd wanted to protect her, to be there to care for her so she'd forget her painful past with her father and share that well of love he knew bubbled inside her. He thought he might even want to be a part of it.

But maybe he'd ruined everything. Again. How could he be a part of her future? He'd promised he wouldn't ask anything of her.

Eventually Annie shifted against him, wiggling to get more comfortable.

"What's so great about this floor?" she grumbled. "I spent a small fortune on furniture for this room. The least we could do is use it."

"This is more fun." For some reason, Russ didn't want her to move away, didn't want to break the camaraderie between them. If he closed his eyes, let himself pretend, just for a minute, he could almost see himself here, beside Annie, among their family—

"You haven't forgotten Mrs. Yancey is coming tomorrow, have you, Russ?" Annie stared into the fire. "She has to make a home inspection, see us here, with Drew, and then file a report."

Like water on a bed of coals, the dream dissipated. Cold, stark reality moved in. The only kind of family Russ Mitchard could ever know was the temporary one he shared with Annie. After all, he wasn't daddy material, couldn't be depended on. He'd learned a lot of lessons over the years, but that one was unforgettable.

"I haven't forgotten Mrs. Yancey, Annie." But Russ didn't want to talk about tomorrow. He wanted to sit here and listen to her laugh, to hear about her dreams, to share the future. Was that so impossible?

"You can't miss it, Russ. You can't even be late. We've got to make the best impression on her if we expect to get Drew. Please don't let me down."

Russ nodded, squeezed her hand. But his mind returned to their marriage.

"Annie, this marriage thing—are you sure it was the right step?" How could he put his hopes into words?

"I—I don't know what you mean. Don't you want to adopt Drew?" Her voice brimmed with fear, barely a whisper in the silent house. "Do you want to call everything off?"

"Of course not! It's not that. I'm thinking beyond that. What about—after?"

"After?" She shook her head, confusion written all over her face. "After what? I don't understand what you're talking about, Russ."

"Don't you want more?" It seemed important that he know, that he understand exactly what she expected of him. He couldn't bear to disappoint her, and yet neither could he walk away. He wanted something from this marriage. He wanted Annie to see him as more than a means to an end. He wanted to be wanted for who he was inside.

Where had that come from?

"I'll do my best not to bother you with details, Russ," she murmured, eyes downcast. "I know the terms of our deal. Nothing's changed."

"Everything's changed, Annie. Everything!" He raked a hand through his hair, then rose and stalked around the room. "We're married. I know why we did it, but the fact is that we are. I'd like to know what you expect from me."

"What I expect?" Annie rose also, her eyes avoiding

his as she stepped over to the love seat and perched on the edge of it.

"Yes." He didn't know how to say it without begging her to give him some hope. For the first time in his life, Russ wanted to live up to what someone else expected. To what Annie expected. But what was that? "Expect as your husband," he added, unable to look at her.

She sighed.

"Sit down, Russ. Maybe I was right in the first place. Maybe our not sharing something of our pasts was a mistake."

He didn't think so. He didn't really care about her past. What he was concerned about was Annie's future. He couldn't bear to think of her wasting her life alone, without someone to hear her giggles, to see the way her eyes sparkled when she had a secret, to hear her voice swell on those high notes when she was vacuuming and thought no one could hear her singing.

"Sit down. We'll talk."

Russ flopped on the sofa.

"I told you about my parents' marriage, about my mother's unhappiness."

He nodded.

"But I didn't tell you that watching them, seeing my mother pine for him, helped me decide something for myself."

Russ frowned. "Decide? Decide what?"

"I've known for years that I would never get married, Russ. I never intended to tie myself to someone, to look for or expect love."

He couldn't believe she'd said it. Annie was made for love. She radiated it in everything she did, from watering her precious flowers to the way she smoothed those handmade quilts over the beds. She was a giver, sharing from the abundance of her heart. She would need someone who could give back. To deliberately shut herself off from letting someone take care of her was unthinkable.

Russ couldn't sit still. He got up, moved to sit beside her, grasped her shoulders.

"Annie, that's ridiculous! You can't shut down like that."

She shook her head, eased away from him.

"It's not shutting down, Russ. It's facing reality. I'm not really good with trusting other people. I like to depend on myself."

"Are you kidding me?"

Her head jerked up. Her eyes flashed a warning.

"You're serious. You really believe that." He leaned back, studied her. "Annie, you trust everyone. You trusted me enough to marry, and we barely knew each other."

"I felt I knew the real you." Her palm brushed against his chest. "The heart part inside, where nobody sees."

His heart skipped a beat, but he ignored it. "That's because you believe in people. All people."

"But my father—"

"Your parents' marriage didn't work, Annie. But for your mother's sake, you wanted it to. You even felt responsible, felt you had to take her side, learn from her example and never get hurt." Russ knew he was on the right track by the way she winced. He hated hurting her, but it was time she lived in the present.

"Did you never wonder why your mother didn't pack her bags and follow your father, Annie? Why she didn't just leave and go after him?"

"No." Annie frowned. "This was her home."

"Her home? Without him? How could it have been a home if she loved him so much, yet he wasn't there?" He shook his head. "Maybe it would have been a struggle, but at least if she'd left, they would have been together."

She stared at him, digesting his words.

"It wasn't your fault, honey." He caressed her shoulder, soothing away the tension. "You weren't responsible for her remaining in that house. That's what you thought, isn't it? Deep down, you believed you were the reason for her unhappiness, that she had to stay behind because of you."

Annie finally nodded, tears rolling down her cheeks.

He pulled her into his arms, pressed her head against his shoulder.

"Oh, Annie girl, it just isn't true. Your mother made the choice she was most comfortable with. I think it was easier for her to stay here and face the boring routine of every day than it was to risk the unknown. I don't know if you'll ever truly know why she did it, but that decision was not something you had any power over. Children are not responsible for their parents' happiness. If there's one thing I've learned, it's that."

He shifted, held her head so he could kiss her cheeks, soothe some of the pain he knew she felt.

"Stop living in the shadow of your parents' misery, Annie. You deserve so much more. A life of your own. A future." He smoothed his thumbs over her face, relished the silken softness of her skin. "You can't give up your life for them anymore. You have to be true to yourself." He pressed a kiss against her lips.

For a long time, Annie sat motionless. When she looked at him, her blue eyes were huge, shiny with tears but minus the shadows that had always been there. She lifted her arms, draped them around his neck.

"Thank you, Russ," she whispered, so softly he barely caught the words before she leaned forward and kissed him. "Thank you for seeing what I couldn't. For showing it to me."

When she finally drew away, Russ knew they could never go back to being strangers. Not his Annie. She could never be a stranger. He shifted, kissed her again.

"Russ." She stared at him, her blue eyes wide with confusion. "What are we doing?"

"I'm kissing my wife." He did it again, thrilled by her response. "Don't you like it?"

Annie snuggled a little closer, rifled her fingers through his hair, then dropped them as if memorizing each feature.

"A smart man like you asking such a stupid question." She touched his cheeks, his chin, his forehead. Everywhere but his lips.

Finally, out of frustration, he grasped her chin and aimed it correctly. After a long time, Annie sighed.

"I like it very much," she whispered, ducking away when he tried to see her eyes.

Could he be content with that? Russ didn't think so, but neither did he want to spoil the moment they'd just shared.

"Annie?" Russ caressed her neck, her earlobe, the curve of her jaw.

"Yes?" She leaned back to study him, perhaps sensing something in his voice.

Russ shifted a fraction so he could look into her eyes, see the truth for himself. He took a deep breath.

"I want us to have the kind of marriage my grandparents had."

The blue orbs blazed, then as quickly dimmed.

"But—"

"No, don't say anything for a minute. Just hear me out. I want us to work at this, to be partners in the truest sense. I want to be there when you're hurting, to help ease the pain the way you do for me. I want to go back to that old house with you and show you that it's only the memories that hurt, and if you'll let them go, we can build new ones.''

She touched his shirt, one nail tracing a pattern he could only feel.

''Think about this, Russ,'' she whispered, watching him half fearfully. ''Think hard. What you're talking about is a permanent contract between us, something that can't be torn up and thrown away when we argue and I do something you don't like. That kind of marriage is binding. If we agree it's permanent, I can't walk away. Neither can you.''

''I know. If we could just get what Gramps had, I don't think I would want to.'' He studied the soft curve of her cheek, the gentle caress of her hands, watched the light in her eyes flicker to life. ''I want to fit in, to belong somewhere. I watched my grandparents grow closer to each other the longer they spent together. He could read her thoughts before she said a word. She knew, usually before he did, when the job was too much and he needed to get away.''

She nodded. ''I remember what he said. 'We were like two halves.' It was so beautiful.''

''That's what I want for us. I want the give and take of a real marriage, Annie. We're not teenagers. We know the risks. I think we can face them, if we do it together.'' He stuffed down his doubts. How could staying with Annie be wrong?

''You're sure?'' Doubt caused tiny furrows of worry to criss-cross her forehead.

''No. I'm not sure at all.'' Russ frowned. ''I'll mess up, Annie. I always do. I'll probably drive you crazy, and you'll wish you'd never seen me. I'll make so many mistakes, you'll wonder how I ever got out of grade school.''

The warm light of hope, of knowing this was the right decision, spread inside and burned brighter.

"But yes, I want to try to be your husband. I want you to be my wife."

"And Drew?" She laced her hand through his, smiled when he kissed her knuckles. "What about Drew?"

"Drew is already part of this. That won't change. We will both take care of Drew." He ignored the doubting little voice inside that reminded him he was lousy at responsibility. Maybe if he really tried— "But beyond that, this is your decision. You have to say."

"I don't know what to say. I haven't gotten used to being married yet. Now you want to take the next step. I told you, I'm not good at trust."

He picked up her hand, frowned. "Annie, where's your ring?"

She blushed, pulled her hand free. "Upstairs. In my jewel box."

He could feel the change in her, see the way she withdrew inside herself, like a snail drawing a protective shell over herself.

"Why?" Of all the things he'd considered, Russ had never imagined that Annie would hate that ring so much she'd hide it. Embarrassment shamed him. As usual, he hadn't stopped to consider everything, including her tastes.

"I do a lot of household chores," she whispered, her eyes focused on the floor. "I mix dough, scrub floors. It gets in the way." Something like guilt passed through her blue eyes.

"They're diamonds. They can take whatever you dish out. Tell the truth, Annie," he ordered quietly. "Why don't you wear that ring?"

"Because it makes me feel like I've been bought!

Okay?'' She was looking at him, her cheeks burning as she dared him to press her.

"Bought? I don't understand. What do you mean?" Russ frowned.

"It's gaudy, show-off stuff. That's why you bought it, isn't it? So people would look at it and assume—" Her cheeks blazed a painful red.

"That it symbolized love." He understood. She thought he'd bought it to stop local tongues.

"Yes." There were tears in her eyes.

Russ sighed. Would he ever do things right?

"It did symbolize love," he whispered.

"That ring has nothing to do with love!" She was furious and she didn't bother to hide it. "You bought it to show everyone in Safe Harbor that you're a big man, that you come from money. What's worse, you were using me to project your image."

Russ sighed. "Go get the ring, Annie. I want to show you something."

She stalled, glared at him, but when he continued to stand there waiting, Annie finally climbed the stairs to her room. She returned moments later with the glittering circlet clutched in her fist. She thrust it toward him.

"Here. Take it. I don't want it."

Russ took her hand instead, drew her toward him.

"I should have explained, Annie. I apologize." He picked up the circlet. "This was my grandmother's ring. Gramps left it with his in the letter he wrote to me before he died. He told me what he'd done with the will, then said I should use these rings when I married you." He held the gleaming ring up to the light so Annie could read the tiny letters etched inside. "He had it engraved. See?"

Annie squinted. "For A.M. Always." She peered at him. "She had the same name as me?"

"Anne Marie, that was my grandmother's name." He tugged his grandfather's gold band off his finger. "This is what she wrote for him."

"For my inner harbor. Love always, A.M." Annie stood still, her eyes wide. "Her inner harbor. Like they shared secrets, anchored each other. It's a lovely thought. She must have loved him very much."

"It was mutual. They exchanged these on their twenty-fifth anniversary." He lifted the diamonds, raised one eyebrow. "Will you wear her ring, Annie? I promise, it isn't meant to convince anyone of anything. It's the dearest thing Gramps left me, and I wanted you to have it to remember him."

Annie swallowed. Her eyes remained on him as she lifted her left hand, then stretched out her fingers. Russ slowly slid the glittering ring onto her finger, then kissed it into place. Annie hesitated only a moment, then picked up the gold band, took his hand and pushed it into place.

He put his hands on her shoulders. Squeezed.

"We can do it, Annie. We can make it work, if we try. That's what Gramps wanted. That's why he put us together."

She nodded, her eyes never leaving his. "I'll try, Russ," she whispered.

Russ stood silent, imprinted the picture on his mind. Golden hair, barely lit by the fading fire, soft flowered skirt hiding her toes. Eyes, velvet dark, watching him.

"I'll truly try. But it's going to take me some time. Is that okay?"

He nodded, smiled.

"Yes. After all, we have all the time in the world, Annie."

Then he kissed her, stating his commitment to her in

the only way he knew. So why didn't that commitment bother him?

At the moment, Russ didn't care. God and Gramps had given him the chance to be part of this special woman's life. How could he possibly wreck that?

Chapter Nine

"Annie, these pants make me itchy!" Drew squirmed in his chair, his sad little face begging her to release him from his misery

"Let him go change, Annie. I think we've waited for Russ long enough." Mrs. Yancey nodded at Drew. "Go and play, son."

Drew waited for Annie's acquiescence, then raced upstairs to change into his jeans before he scurried outside into the sunshine that waited.

"I apologize again, Mrs. Yancey. Russ promised me he'd be here." Annie could barely squeeze the words out. Why? Why had he done it?

"He knew about the change?" Mrs. Yancey waited for her nod. "I know I messed things up by changing the time, but sometimes in social work, you aren't in charge of all the timing details. Saturday was just such a struggle, I had to switch to Monday. I don't usually work after five, but I know how anxious you are to proceed."

"I appreciate it. Russ does, too. Something must have come up, otherwise I know he'd be here."

Even to her own ears, it sounded lame.

"You can't excuse him, Annie." Mrs. Yancey moved near her, patted Annie's knee. "I know you want Drew, but Russ has to want this adoption, too, or it won't benefit Drew in the least. I suspect he has doubts about the whole thing, that's why he isn't here."

Annie rushed to reassure her, trying desperately to salvage what was left of her dignity.

"Oh, no, I'm sure he wants to adopt Drew. We both do. We've talked it over quite a lot and both of us—"

"Never mind, dear." Mrs. Yancey rose, straightened her suit jacket. "I have to get home. I'm afraid I just can't wait any longer. You have Russ give me a call when he gets in. I'll try to reschedule."

As Annie ushered the woman out, she fought to quash the worry. The adoption would go through, Mrs. Yancey hadn't changed her mind on it. She was just preoccupied. And frustrated by Russ's no-show.

Annie shared that emotion. Friday night in front of the fire had been a turning point in their relationship. Or so she'd thought. Russ had been so sweet and tender these past few days. He'd brought her daisies yesterday, picked fresh from the park. They'd gone for a walk last night and talked nonstop the entire time. There was so much to share. For the first time Annie felt an abundance of hope that her marriage might work.

And then this.

Where was he? Why would he deliberately jeopardize her opportunity to adopt Drew? Had he changed his mind? To do this, today, when he knew she'd counted on the meeting, it was too callous.

Fear niggled a path up her spine and settled in below her skull with a dull, steady throb. Had she said too much, shared too much? Was he worried that she'd try to make him into something he wasn't? What was wrong?

Half an hour later she and Drew sat at the table, neither one of them eating the roast chicken she'd prepared. Drew seemed to sense her fear.

"Where did Russ go?" he asked, mashing his potatoes with a fierceness that sent them across his plate.

"I don't know, honey. I expect he got busy at something and just simply forgot." Annie pushed her plate away, lifted her mug and sipped her favorite peppermint tea, waiting for the soothing rush it was supposed to provide.

"He isn't at The Quest." Drew stopped, blinked at her from under his eyelashes. "I wasn't going to bother him." He rushed to explain. "I just wanted him to explain something. But he was on the phone." He looked at her, his cheeks burning with shame. "I listened under the window."

"Drew, we do not listen in on people's conversations. It's not very nice and it's none of our business."

"He was talking to his dad." Drew's bottom lip jutted out. "They were arguing, then Russ got all quiet. The phone rang again, he talked for a minute, hung up the phone and left. He didn't even see me."

She should have remonstrated with him, insisted he prepare an apology. But all Annie could think of was that Russ had spoken to his father. What had gone wrong?

"Annie?" Elizabeth Neal burst through the doorway, white hair askew. "Oh, there you are."

"Hello, Elizabeth." Annie rose, moved toward the older woman, noting her flustered state. "Is something wrong? Can I help you?"

"Wrong?" Elizabeth sniffed. "Very wrong. My car's conked out, and it won't start. That's what's wrong."

"I'm sorry. Shall I call a tow truck for you?" Annie

moved to walk through the room to the phone at the front desk, but Elizabeth's hand on her arm stopped her.

"Already did. Don't bother. They've got some kind of pileup out on Route Seven. They're going to be a while. If you don't mind, I'll join you. Is that tea?" She moved to the table, bent over the teapot and sniffed. "Ah, peppermint. Just the thing to settle me down."

"An accident?" Annie gulped, her mind busy with several images, none of them pleasant. "Do you—" She swallowed and tried again. "Do you know who was involved?"

"Nope. Not a clue. Don't like to keep people on the line with a lot of foolish questions. Might be someone trying to call." Elizabeth sat across from Drew, and the two were soon deep in conversation.

Was that why Russ hadn't arrived on time? Had he been in an accident?

No! Annie refused to consider it, not when they'd only begun their marriage. There had to be another reason for his absence.

"Elizabeth, I wonder if you could do me a favor." The more she considered it, the more Annie knew this was the right move. "I wonder if you could stay with Drew for a while. I have something I have to do." *I have to find my husband.* No, she couldn't say that, no matter how true it was.

"Of course I'll stay. The boy and I haven't had a good visit since—" She winked at Drew. "I can't remember when." Elizabeth often feigned forgetfulness, but at the moment her deep green eyes flared with interest. "What have you been up to, Drew?"

In seconds she had him telling her all about the kite he wanted to build.

"Thanks, Elizabeth," Annie whispered when Drew left

the room to get the materials he wanted to use. "I shouldn't be long."

"Don't worry about us. We can gab all night. You go on now." Kindness glimmered in her face. She reached out and patted Annie's hand. "Young love always experiences these quarrels. Just have faith, and it'll all work out."

Would it? Annie wasn't so sure as she rode her bike down Lake Drive to The Quest. But the old bookstore was dark and shuttered. Big sheets of paper giving the date of his grand opening allowed no curious glimpse inside. She kept going, as far as the movie house, then rode back. There was no sign of Russ anywhere. She didn't know what to do next.

Safe Harbor Park lay ahead, the gazebo glowing with tiny white lights the town put up every Christmas and forgot to take down until long after the Fourth of July. They twinkled through the spring evening, beckoning her on. Annie wheeled into the parking area and coasted to a stop. Cedar signs marking the various wilderness trails fanned out in front of her. Surely Russ wouldn't have gone for a walk?

A flicker of something white floating over the lake caught her eye. A bright red sailboat floated over the blue water, its white sail full, catching all the available wind and using it to press through the waves toward the dock. Big black letters sprawled across the stern. *Lady Fair.* Her captain stood at the wheel, black head bare, shirt billowing around him as he leaned into the wind.

Annie stared. Russ? He'd missed their appointment to go sailing?

She clenched her teeth, reversed her bike, left the parking lot and pedaled to the dock area in the cove beyond her bed-and-breakfast, tossing out possible excuses as fast as her brain concocted them.

"Let him explain," she ordered her fuming emotions. "No doubt he has a rational, perfectly logical reason for missing that meeting. Just calm down and listen."

But Russ didn't explain after he'd docked the sailboat, fastened her down and pulled the tarp over her freshly painted wood. He didn't intersperse his bubbling enthusiasm with any kind of justification Annie could accept as he strolled beside her, pushing her bike as they walked side by side.

"I couldn't resist. She's such a marvelous vessel and she sails like a dove. The maneuverability, Annie! It's awesome."

"Really?" Annie sped up, her heels banging the cement as she silently fumed.

"Just wait till I show you." He grinned. "I'm calling it part of Gramp's wedding gift to us. When do you want to go for your first sail?"

Annie considered a thousand answers to that. But before she'd settled on one, they were at home. He parked her bike and locked it while she went inside.

"Elizabeth, I want to thank you so much." She ignored the older woman's perspicacious gaze and shooed Drew up to bed.

"Is everything all right?" Elizabeth frowned.

"Hey, Miz Neal. Everything's perfect here. How about you?" Russ strolled into the kitchen, slid an arm around Annie's waist and grinned.

"I'm fine as frog's hair, son. Just had a little car trouble. But it's been fixed, so I'll be on my way." She gathered her purse and her scarf, took one last look at Annie and shrugged. "If you're sure?"

"Yes, I'm sure. Thank you so much for watching Drew.

I really appreciate it.'' Annie shifted away from Russ's arm and followed her to the front door. "I hope he didn't cause you any problems.''

"That sweet thing?'' Elizabeth shook her head. "Not a chance. You're doing a good job with him, Annie. A great job.''

"Thanks. I love him, so it's a pleasure.''

Miss Neal stepped outside, clicked her remote starter, then turned.

"How'd the interview go?'' She glanced over Annie's shoulder at Russ, clicked her teeth. "Didn't show up wearing that, did you, boy? Torn jeans like that, and the Yancey woman will think you can't afford to feed yourself, let alone a child.'' Chuckling mightily at her own wit, Elizabeth scurried across the street to her vehicle, climbed in and drove away.

"The interview?'' Russ clapped a hand to his head, closed his eyes and sighed. "Oh, Annie, I'm so sorry.''

Annie ignored him, walked inside. She tidied up the kitchen, knowing he was watching her, trying to gauge her mood.

Well, if he thought she was going to behave like some kind of fishwife, Russ Mitchard had another think coming.

"Annie, I truly am sorry. My dad called and we argued—''

"About what?'' Annie snapped the cutlery into the dishwasher and started it. There was no point in getting anything special ready for breakfast. This was another day without clients. It was a good thing she'd married a wealthy man, she mused bitterly. If things kept going like this at her bed-and-breakfast, she knew where to go for a loan.

"The same thing we always argue over. Responsibility and my lack of it. I told him we were married.'' He stopped, took her arm and forced her to face him. "You might want to join his camp," he muttered. "At least you'd have something in common."

"I don't want to join anyone's camp. If you don't want to adopt Drew, that's up to you, and you'll have to tell him so. If you do want to adopt him, you're going to have to arrange another meeting with Mrs. Yancey. You might want to get to that soon, since she's getting ready to take a month's vacation to be with her sick mother in Texas."

She turned to leave, but his words stopped her.

"I didn't forget on purpose, Annie. A man in Market Square told me a friend of his was selling his sailboat and that the ad was going in the paper tomorrow. I got so involved in that, I forgot about the meeting. It wasn't intended. I didn't deliberately miss it."

"I didn't say you did. I'm simply saying that if you do intend to adopt Drew, you'd better make your intentions clear to Mrs. Yancey. I'm not forcing you into anything, Russ. It has to be your decision." She walked to the doorway, then stopped. "By the way, we're having choir practice Saturday morning because Drew's having a birthday party here on Saturday afternoon. It would be nice if you could phone your parents and invite them to come. I think its about time we all met, don't you?"

Annie walked to her room, closed the door, then sank onto the window seat that overlooked the lake.

She'd had so much hope, been so certain Russ was ready to really get involved in this marriage. But now she was back to wondering and worrying whether she'd been living in a fool's paradise. She picked up her Bible and leafed through, looking for one verse among the many she'd highlighted in the past, that would give her hope for the future.

Much later Annie stopped at the sixty-first Psalm, the words rolling over her like waves on an ocean.

"I long to dwell in your tent forever and take refuge in the shelter of your wings."

Certainly the words were referring to God, and she'd always thought of Him as her protector, a shelter she could run to. But as Annie stared at the passage, new meaning sifted through.

The words echoed the relationship she wanted to have in this marriage with Russ. She wanted to feel safe, secure, knowing he would never let her down, never disappoint her, that if the worst happened, she could run to him and be secure. But her security lay in God, not in Russ.

The knowledge descended like an eiderdown quilt. Today's broken promise had stung so deeply because Annie Mitchard wanted to be just like Wharton Willoughby's Anne Marie. She wanted Russ to be her inner harbor, her anchor, her shelter.

What did that mean?

"It's unconventional, but who says that's bad?" Mrs. Yancey fit herself into the church pew and snapped open her briefcase. "Your husband wanted to get things on the road as soon as possible, and I agree. He's explained about missing the last meeting, but I certainly hope it doesn't happen again."

"Me, neither."

Russ watched from the foyer as Annie glanced around First Peninsula Church. Probably wondering why he'd insisted they meet here before practice. He hadn't told her exactly how he'd persuaded the social worker to set another meeting after stupidly missing the last one and he didn't intend to. It was enough that she know he wanted to get this done.

He also hadn't explained the projects that kept him so furiously busy every day this week so he barely managed to make it home at night to spend a few minutes with Drew before he returned to his shop. And he didn't intend to. How could he explain that he had to prove himself to her, longed to see that light of approval glimmering in those sky-blue eyes, that he was afraid to be around her too much, afraid she'd glimpse his doubts to be what she needed?

He stepped into the sanctuary, walked toward them.

"Sorry. A shipment arrived just as I was leaving. I had to unload it." Russ bent to brush Annie's cheek with his lips and accidentally on purpose kissed her lips instead. He was delighted when she didn't try to move away.

"Hi, honey. Mrs. Yancey." He unzipped his windbreaker, then flopped down beside Annie, fingers lacing through hers as they always seemed to. "We've got a bit more than half an hour before the kids will start arriving. Is that long enough?"

"I suppose." Mrs. Yancey looked a bit ruffled. "Why is there such a rush, Mr. Mitchard? Surely next week would have done as well?"

He shook his head, then glanced at Annie.

"I've scheduled my grand opening for next week. I'll be working hot and heavy after that to fill orders. I hope you'll come to The Quest, Mrs. Yancey. Shall I send you an invitation?"

"Thank you." She stared at him for a few minutes, then launched into the explanation of procedure. "I've already taken the liberty of contacting a judge in Green Bay. He's agreed to expedite the matter so long as I am satisfied that this is the best thing for Drew. He will approve the adoption and send you the papers. In the meantime, I have a list of questions I need answered, Mr. Mitchard."

"Russ. And please, ask anything you want." He smiled, letting her see he had nothing to hide when the truth was that he still felt very nervous about this responsibility. But Annie's words had forced him to assess his way of dealing with things. He'd made her a promise, and he intended to keep it by taking this first step.

He knew he'd scared her badly when he hadn't shown up for the interview. But in typical Annie style, she'd focused on his situation, been there for him. The more he got to know her, the more Russ appreciated her willingness to give.

Mrs. Yancey fired her questions, jotting down his answers on a yellow legal pad in some kind of hieroglyphic scribble that he couldn't decipher.

"And your parents would be able to step in, help Annie with the boy, if something happened to you?"

Russ forced his face to maintain its smile while he considered her words. His parents? Did he want them involved in this? But how could he possibly leave them out? He was married to Annie. He should have made the first move, invited them down here to meet her immediately. As Annie had said, it was time to start looking ahead.

Russ nodded. "I'm sure my parents would be pleased to help out however they could, Mrs. Yancey," he murmured. "They love children."

"Have they seen your new business? Met Annie?" Mrs. Yancey looked faintly worried.

"Not yet." Russ would have far preferred to tell Annie in private, but there was no help for that now. He turned to her. "Dad phoned this afternoon. They'll be here for the birthday party. Have we got room for them to stay over?"

She smiled, really smiled, that beaming, heart-cheering grin that told him everything would be okay.

"Of course we have room." Her eyebrows rose. "I run a bed-and-breakfast. I can sleep a lot of people."

Mrs. Yancey scribbled on her yellow pad, biting her bottom lip.

Russ squeezed Annie's hand. "Thanks," he whispered, a little jig of nervousness dancing in his stomach. He knew he could count on Annie, but he had no idea what his parents' response to either her or his business would be. He'd made a deliberate effort to stay clear of them while he worked out his start-up plans. If he knew Annie, she would go all out to include them.

Somehow it didn't scare him as it should have.

"As rehearsals go, that was not one of our finer moments." Russ gathered the music and nudged Annie from her seat on the front pew. "Come on, woman. We've got a birthday party, remember?"

"As if I could forget." She stood, stretched her back just as Marmalade did, then sighed. Disaster. He should have said it was a disaster. "Okay, onward and upward. We'll chalk that one up to their excitement about Drew's party."

"Uh-huh." He laughed at the way she poised her heel over his toe. "Forget it, Annie. I'm bigger and stronger and I don't fight fair." He placed the sheaf of music in her portfolio and handed the leather case to her, brushing the tip of her nose with his lips.

"There could be children running around here," she whispered, remaining exactly where she was.

"Nope. They've all run home to get ready for the party." He kissed her again.

"Well, Drew's here." She glanced over his shoulder but didn't see her soon-to-be-adopted son anywhere.

"Wrong again. He went home with Billy." Russ

pressed a finger over her lips. "I said he could. He wants to look at Billy's new bike before the party."

"Ah." Annie grinned. "Whetting his appetite, are we?" She shook her head. "You're bad."

"Not true, and stop tempting me like this." He pressed one quick kiss on her lips, then freed her. "I still have the things on the handlebars to put on. You had to get the bike with the most gizmos possible, didn't you?"

Annie nodded. "Yes." She looked around for her jacket, remembered the warm balmy afternoon and shook her head. "Okay, I'm ready. I've got a couple of things to do myself."

"You're not doing any more to that cake," Russ warned, holding the door open so she could walk through. He followed her down the church stairs and matched her step as they headed toward the bed-and-breakfast. "I heard you come upstairs at quarter to three last night, Annie. What were you doing?"

"Putting gumdrops on the train." And praying they stayed there, she could have added.

He shook his head, but tenderness shone in his silvery eyes. "The little mother."

"I want this birthday to be wonderful—the first of many we'll share with him."

Russ folded her hand in his. "Let's get to work, then."

"It's a little like a zoo," Russ muttered, gazing at the pandemonium surrounding them. "Let's go outside for a bit." He led his father through the garden doors of the dining room to the small flagstone terrace that overlooked the lake. With the doors closed behind them, something like peace settled on him.

"You've adjusted very well," his father murmured, sitting on the low stone wall that surrounded the space.

"Taking on a child and a wife would daunt anyone. Don't let yourself get overwhelmed by everything now."

"Sixteen kids would overwhelm anyone with a coffee cup of brains."

His father chuckled. "You scare too easily."

Funny, Russ mused. He thought he'd handled everything fairly well for someone who'd gone to great pains to avoid responsibility. Those words from his father sparked a whole new flood of doubts. Anger surged.

"You had to say it, didn't you? You just couldn't accept that I'm capable of managing my life in my own way." He gulped down the burning coffee, resentment coiling like a spring inside him.

"Son, I wasn't criticizing. I was trying to encourage you. Your mother and I are very proud of you. We love Annie. And Drew—" His father stopped, choked down his emotion long enough for a shaky smile to emerge. "He's so much like Adam, isn't he? Funny, they even have the same birthday."

Russ froze, every nerve in his body clenching tight.

"You didn't realize?"

"I knew."

He watched as the glow of sadness in his father's eyes seemed to magnify, condemning him for abandoning his brother so easily.

"Drew's actual birthday is next week. Because it's a school day, we decided to have the party today. Anyway, I haven't even thought about the date. Annie bought that bike unassembled, and I've spent hours trying to put the thing together. Mechanics have never been my strength."

"That much hasn't changed." His father tried to hide his smile. "I snuck it outside when the kids were busy with the treasure hunt and exchanged front and back wheels. He should be able to ride it now."

Russ groaned, turned his back. "I guess I blew it again," he muttered.

"Blew it? Hardly." James Mitchard shook his head. "I think you've made a huge success of things."

"You do?" Russ turned, stared.

"Of course." James waved a hand at the bed-and-breakfast. "Look at your life, son. You've got a wife who clearly cares about you, you're adopting a child who adores you and you're opening a brand-new store. What a lot you've achieved in a year." He chuckled. "I'll admit I was a little skeptical when Wharton imposed those conditions on your inheritance, but now that I've met Annie, I understand what he saw in her for you."

"You do?"

"Don't you? Her nature compliments yours, she obviously pushes you to achieve, and you somehow help her stop trying so hard. It's quite amazing to watch."

Russ got caught on the first comment. "Annie doesn't push me. She doesn't have to. I'm doing what I love, and she appreciates that."

James nodded. "I know. That's what I meant. You sort of grow taller when you're with her." He faced Russ, his face serious. "You've always thought I was criticizing you, haven't you?" He shrugged. "I suppose in a way I was. But not because I thought you wouldn't measure up, not because I didn't love you."

Russ wanted to answer, to remind him of all the times he'd hit hard with cruel words. But something about his father's face kept him silent.

"I think I loved you too much, Russ. After Adam died, I heaped all my hopes and dreams on your head. I thought you'd fulfill every one of my expectations, and when you wouldn't fit the mold, I got scared."

Scared? His father? Russ blinked, trying to absorb the meaning.

"You were so cavalier, Russ. You glided through life without letting it touch you. I was afraid you'd get mowed over when you least expected it. You pretended to get by on your natural talents and good looks, and I knew you were capable of so much more. All I could think of was that if I didn't warn you, didn't keep you on your toes, I'd lose you, just as surely as we lost Adam."

"I tried to be what you wanted, Dad." How many times had he dreamed of having this conversation? How often had he wished to dump all the frustration and anger of those hurting years on his father's head and make him see his pain? But more than a year of anger and hurt had kept them apart, a year he should have been near home, near his grandfather. Suddenly, Russ didn't want to keep it going. It was time to heal.

"I couldn't be the lawyer you wanted, Dad. I'm sorry. I tried, but it stifled something inside of me."

"I know." Tears flooded his father's eyes. "I watched it happen." He smiled sadly. "Not that you weren't good at it. Your quick thinking saved us on several cases. I've never seen anyone empathize with a jury the way you did. But your heart wasn't there. It was just playacting for you, and it was serious—a life's work—to me. I was wrong to foist my life onto yours."

Russ took a deep breath. For the first time in his life, he felt as if his father accepted him, faults and all.

"I'm sorry about Adam, too, Dad."

His father frowned. "Son, Adam is dead. You're alive. You have to get on with your life, not waste it rehashing the past."

"But I'm the reason he's dead. It's my fault." The words were whispered on a breath of pure pain. Russ felt the crushing load of guilt descend on him once more and fought to break free of it.

"Russ, I didn't mean to blame—"

"Hey, you two. We're going to have that birthday cake now. Want to join us?" Annie stood in the doorway, glanced from Russ to his father and back again, her eyes widening as she realized she'd interrupted. "I'm sorry," she whispered, eyes pleading with Russ to understand. "Excuse me."

Russ jerked to his feet, strode across the patio and wrapped his arm around her waist. Maybe his dad was right, maybe Annie was his other half, because immediately, as soon as he touched her, he felt some of the hurt recede.

"It's okay, honey," he murmured. "We're coming."

He laughed with the rest of them when Drew couldn't blow out all the candles. He poured juice, cleaned up spills and chatted with parents who came to pick up their kids. When Nathan suggested they take everyone for an evening sail on his new boat, he persuaded Annie to agree and then ferried them all along the coastline to see the beauty of the peninsula in the evening sun.

But later, after the kids had been picked up and his parents had traipsed upstairs to their room, while Annie was putting Drew to bed, Russ couldn't settle down, couldn't relax. Adam's birthday. The day he'd died. How could he ever forget that? Grabbing a light jacket, he scribbled a note to Annie, then left.

And in the caverns of his mind, the old mantra echoed over and over again, like the sentence a jury had handed down.

Guilty.

Guilty.

Guilty.

Chapter Ten

Annie walked over the pavement, breathing deeply of the night air. She was tired, but it was a good kind of tired. Delighted with his birthday party and the sailing afterward, Drew had fallen asleep before she'd finished the first page of his usual bedtime story. With the other kids he'd been so excited she wasn't certain Drew even realized he was on the lake. Apparently he'd accepted his parents' deaths, and when the right moment came, Annie would help him talk about them. A moment ago Nathan had found her reading Russ's note and suggested she take a walk, also.

"You need a break, Annie. I'm going to read down here for a while. I'll listen for Drew and the phone."

"Thanks, Nathan. I feel like I should pay you. You're always working."

He'd brushed off her thanks and settled into the big wing chair.

Annie automatically headed for the park, a favorite haven where she could sit on a bench, stare at the stars and think. One thing about Safe Harbor—before the tourist season got going, you could walk outside and find a nice quiet spot almost anywhere in town. She found a comfy seat on a cedar bench under a towering pine tree and closed her eyes, breathing in the scent of spring buds and newly worked earth from nearby flower beds.

After a while, a noise drew her attention. Someone was in the cemetery. But who would visit now? Annie hesitated, then stepped across the grass. Perhaps they needed help. She walked forward slowly, trying to discern the identity of that kneeling figure.

"Russ?"

He never moved. His attention was focused on something. Annie stepped nearer, watched as he brushed a hand over a small white stone, his finger tracing the words upon it.

"I'm so sorry I failed you, Adam." The grief in his tortured voice made her move closer, stretch out a hand.

It was obvious he hadn't heard her. Otherwise he would never have continued.

"I wanted to be your big brother. I wanted to protect you, make sure you never went through the things I had. But I failed you, just like I failed everyone else. And now I'm afraid I'm going to fail Annie and Drew."

Somebody did need help. Russ did. She stepped behind him, laid her hand on his shoulder.

"You won't fail us, Russ." The steady assurance in her voice surprised even Annie, but she didn't stop. "You're very important to us. We need you as much as you need us. Individually we're weak, but together we make a good team, don't you think?"

Although she startled him, Russ smiled at her, but only his mouth moved. His eyes were filled with a grief she'd never glimpsed before. His fingers threaded through hers.

"Hi, Annie."

"Hi." She glanced down, read the words. *Adam Mit-*

chard, beloved son and brother. "What are you doing here, Russ?" she whispered, her heart sinking to her shoes as she realized that this was the brother he'd once spoken of.

"I want you to meet someone." He nudged her, so Annie knelt beside him. "Annie, this is my brother, Adam."

So many things were explained by that simple statement.

"Hi, Adam." She stayed where she was, staring at the white granite, her fingers entwined with Russ's.

"My dad reminded me that today would have been his birthday. Today was also the day he died. As if I could forget." The words seemed to be dragged out of him, as if he didn't want to say them but couldn't stop them, either.

"I'm sorry, Russ. I wish I'd known him."

"He wasn't like me. He was two years younger and very quiet, not introverted, really, just caught up in his own world. He liked to explore. Every summer we'd spend hours collecting stuff, and he'd take it back to the cottage and study it, he and Dad, under an old microscope Dad bought."

There was nothing to say, nothing that would ease his memory. So Annie sat silent and listened.

"He was the son they wanted. He was obedient, he did what Dad expected. They shared the same interests. Adam didn't care about sports, never really enjoyed sailing as much as I did." Russ smiled, brushed a few spears of dried grass off her skirt. "He didn't like swimming. He was going to be a lawyer, just like Dad and Gramps."

The words shocked her. She stared at him, trying to sort out the pieces of information he'd given. Was that the problem, the reason Russ had taken law in the first place, only to find it didn't suit him? Was he trying to take his brother's place?

"He was going to do environmental work, save the water, protect the planet, that kind of thing. He was only eight, but Adam knew exactly what the future held for him." His voice caught, died away, then returned. "He loved fishing, but he'd never keep the fish. We always had to throw them back."

"Russ—" She stopped, aching at the ravages his grief had etched into that handsome face.

"That's how he died, you know. We'd been fishing off the dock, and I'd caught this huge one. I was teasing him, telling him I was going to cook it for supper. I waved it around and then dropped my rod in the water." His hand moved, brushed against the granite marker. "Adam couldn't let it go. He wasn't worried about the rod and reel, of course. He died trying to save a stupid fish. Drew reminds me of him, the way he fusses over that cat."

"It was an accident, Russ. No one blames you." She hoped that was true, but having only just met his family, Annie wasn't entirely sure.

"Don't they?" Russ shrugged. "Doesn't matter. I blame me. I told him not to jump in the water, that it was too cold, but he wouldn't listen. The fish splashed around for a minute, and that decided him. He jumped in, hit his head on a beam."

She wanted him to stop reliving it, wanted to have the old, carefree Russ back, the one who made her think of her cavalier father. It didn't matter that she hadn't liked that side of him. She'd gladly go back if only he could be free of this awful memory.

"I yelled and yelled for someone to help. But it was too early in the season, and no one was on the dock that day. So I jumped in and tried to drag Adam out of the water myself. But I couldn't get him onto the dock. I was only ten, and he was too big for me." His eyes glazed over, his face whitening with every detail of this nightmare description. "I don't remember how I got out. All I can remember is my mother holding Adam, crying. I didn't understand he was dead, I just wanted him to wake up. But he never did."

The moonlight dimmed as clouds moved across the night sky, the evening gloomy with eerie shadows and a faint wind that pushed through the cemetery. Annie shivered, wondered what to do. How could she possibly help him?

"Russ, we need to go home."

He stared at her, his gray eyes cold as steel. "It should have been me, Annie. I should have been the one to die. Adam was everything to them, their dreams for the future. I was the brat, the irresponsible one. It should have been me who died."

"Don't say that!" She jumped to her feet and yanked on his arm. "Get up, Russ."

"Why?" He shook his head. "I don't want to."

Annie had to do something—something that would shock him back to reality.

"Get up anyway." She grabbed his arm and pulled as if she could bodily lift him to his feet.

"What's the point?"

"The point is that you're alive."

"I shouldn't be."

"Why?" She slapped her hands on her hips and glared at him. "Because you decided?" She laughed, a harsh, biting sound. "News flash, Russ. You don't get to decide who lives or dies. God does. And He decided you should live and accomplish something with your life. Are you going to throw that away?"

Russ finally stood, dusted off his pants, looked at her with confusion.

"I'm trying not to, Annie. But it's getting harder. I make so many mistakes. What if I mess up with Drew? I'm not father material."

"You can learn. If you blow it, then you apologize to him and try again."

"You make it sound so simple," he sighed.

"Simple? You think life is supposed to be simple, Russ?" Annie shook her head. "Life is exactly what you make of it. And somehow, you never struck me as the kind of guy who'd be happy with simple. You're the fellow who thrives on a challenge, who takes a hunk of cold metal and pounds it until he gets something beautiful from it, something that lasts and adds light to people's lives."

"But I don't save animals or ecological systems. I just make lamps."

"And I provide beds. I don't do research for the cure for cancer or work at feeding the starving children of the world. I just keep making breakfast for people who want to stay in my house while they visit Safe Harbor." She lifted one finger, brushed a speck of dampness from his cheek. "God doesn't expect me to be a rocket scientist. He expects me to brighten the corner where I am. That's my job, my duty. And I enjoy it. What's wrong with that?"

He shrugged. "Nothing, I guess."

"And there's nothing wrong with what you do. It's what He suited you for."

Annie watched Russ glance at the marker one last time.

"Happy birthday, Adam," he whispered, then turned and strode across the grass, walking toward the lighthouse.

"I should have brought my car." Annie tailed along behind, watching as he adjusted his stride, waited for her, then took her hand. "But I needed some fresh air."

"Mind if I walk with you?" he asked, staring at their entwined fingers.

"Why would I mind?" She deliberately lengthened her step, forcing him to slow down while she wondered if she'd helped or harmed him by interrupting him. "Do you enjoy your work, Russ?"

"Yes." He frowned. "You already know that. Why are you asking now?"

"Because you act as if there's something wrong with enjoying what you do."

"It's not that." He raked a hand through his hair, glanced at the moon.

"What then?" She stopped, waited for his answer, ears attuned to all the sounds around them.

"Adam can't enjoy anything!" he finally blurted.

"Really?" Annie prayed for the right words to ease his troubled soul. "Russ, have you ever talked with anyone about this?"

"You mean a shrink? No." His tone advised her he wouldn't consider it.

"You should have. They could have helped you."

No answer. Russ half turned away from her, his eyes on two birds soaring through the night sky.

"Where do you think Adam is, Russ?" she asked softly.

He jerked around, glared at her. "What?"

"Do you believe in God?"

One nod. "Of course."

"Do you believe in heaven?" Another nod. "Well then, if Adam's in heaven, and I'm certain he is, what is there on this earth that could possibly compare to that?"

He frowned.

"Russ, while you've been slogging out your battles down here, Adam's been with God. He doesn't want or need a second chance here on earth because he already has everything he needs. You're wasting your time and you life trying to atone for what he's missed. The truth is, Adam hasn't missed anything. You have.''

Annie knew he found it hard to hear. His eyes flared with temper. He jerked his arm away and turned to face her.

''You're holding back from life for fear you'll make another mistake.'' Annie smiled. ''But we all make mistakes. It's called being human. So we fix them the best we can, mend our fences and move on.''

''Some mistakes are worse than others.''

She took a deep breath, moved nearer.

''Russ, it was you who challenged me to look at my mother's unhappiness in a new way. You said she chose to be unhappy, and I think you were right. It just never occurred to her to let go of the old and try something new because she was caught in the past. When I went over yesterday to look at the changes they'd made on the house, I realized that I'd only allowed myself to see the place through her eyes until you came. Then I started to think about the possibilities, and that helped me see how badly she was caught in the past. Don't do that to yourself.''

''Is that what you think? That I've been living in the past?'' His anger rippled around her in waves of tension.

Annie continued. She couldn't stop now.

''I think you're living each day looking over your shoulder. You wanted to launch out and try something different—to be a silversmith—and you reached out for it. Well, the thing is—you've made it, Russ. You're a fantastic silversmith. But with your other hand, you've been searching for a lifeline, something to make it safe to swim in unknown waters. Something you can use to get to safety if it gets too rough and you change your mind.''

''You're speaking in metaphors.'' But he was thinking about her words.

"I like metaphors," she told him with a grin. "But my point is this. You've started something here with me. Tonight you got a little deeper, and now you're looking for some guarantee that you haven't made a mistake. Tell the truth. Isn't thinking about the past part of the reason you missed our meeting with Mrs. Yancey? You were trying to recapture something. Formally adopting Drew is a big step. I think you're running scared."

"What? Me, scared?" His eyes blazed molten silver, but he didn't contradict her. "What are you, Annie? Safe Harbor's psychoanalyst?"

Heat burned her cheeks, but Annie refused to back down.

"No. What I am sick of is being afraid. I'm married to you and I intend to adopt Drew. It was an awfully big jump for someone like me who doesn't take chances without carefully planning every minute detail years ahead of time. But you know what? I think the risk is worth it. I think Drew is worth it, and I think you're worth it, too, Russ Mitchard."

She stalked down the street, stopped, waited.

When Russ didn't follow, her heart sank, but she wouldn't let him see.

"I have to get back. I left Nathan in charge, but he's a guest and he shouldn't have to do my job." She waited a moment. "Are you coming?"

He stared at her, then nodded. "I'll walk you back to the bed-and-breakfast, but then I'll walk some more." He turned, looked over one shoulder at the cemetery.

"Fine." She wanted to tell him to walk away from Adam's sad little grave, away from the hurt and pain of the past. She wanted to tell him to walk into the little space she'd carved out for him in her heart.

Annie did neither. Instead she strode down the street

beside him to the bed-and-breakfast, endured the soft brush of his lips against her cheek and watched as he sauntered away.

She thanked Nathan for his help, turned out lights, all but the one over the front door and a small wall lamp to help Russ find his way. Then she wearily climbed the stairs and prepared for bed. Only once she was there did Annie finally tug out the knowledge that had been chewing at her all through her talk with Russ.

She loved her husband. And now she was taking the biggest risk of all.

"Is there anyone who didn't come to this grand opening?" Constance surveyed the steady flow of people through the doors and smiled. "I'm very happy for Russ. With all the work he's done, it's nice to see it pay off."

"I think so, too. And I know he'll want to thank you for organizing the Women's League to supply these trays of goodies. I've been so busy lately, I couldn't possibly have managed hors d'oeuvres."

"We're just glad you let us help." Constance glanced around the room once more, then homed in on Annie. "Is everything all right, dear? You seem a little tired lately."

"Is it any wonder?" Gracie winked at Annie over Constance's left shoulder. "The woman just opened her own business, got married, is adopting a child and directs a children's choir. I'm tired just talking about it." She snatched a canapé from a passing tray and popped it into her mouth. "Yummy. I've got to get to the office, Annie. My break is over. But tell Russ I'll definitely be back. Soon."

"Thanks, Gracie." She smiled, watching the redhead dodge her way out of the store. "I think I'd better get back to my business, too. I've been spending entirely too much time away.''

''You will let me know if I can help, won't you?''

''You'll be the first.'' Annie hugged her. ''Thanks, Constance.''

''Mrs. Annie Mitchard?''

Annie glanced at Constance, shrugged and turned to the man in the brown delivery suit.

''Yes, I'm she.''

''Sign here, please.''

Annie signed, remembered the last time she'd received a courier's envelope and cringed. Uh-oh. ''Excuse me, Constance. You know how curious I am.'' She tore the letter open, lifted out the sheaf of official documents.

She held her breath, remembering that she'd felt this same wave of trepidation swamp her the day they went to court. She'd stood beside Russ, her hand wrapped around Drew's smaller one as they answered the judge's questions. And she was fine until that last question.

''You've had Drew for some time now, Mrs. Mitchard, but your marriage is new. Are you and your husband certain the boy's presence won't cause problems? Newlyweds generally like to be alone together. An active child won't allow either of you a lot of privacy and adds tremendously to your responsibilities.''

From the corner of her eye, she saw Russ's dark head jerk upward from its contemplation of the floor. Would his uncertainty about becoming a parent be as evident to the court as it was to her?

She prayed for help. The answer arrived seconds later when Russ began to speak.

''Your honor, we know there will be problems. Every marriage, every family has them. We'll try hard to resolve them, but the bottom line is that we don't have all the answers any more than any new parents do. All we can promise is that we will do our utmost to give Drew a home and a family that will care for him, protect him and prepare him for whatever challenges he meets. He is already a part of our lives.''

The judge smiled. "That kind of commitment is reassuring. It's not that common anymore."

Annie felt Constance's nudge and realized she was still holding the envelope.

If these documents said what she hoped, she was going to need every bit of Russ's commitment to her and Drew.

"Oh, praise the Lord."

"It's official." Constance grinned. "You're a mother, Annie. I've been praying Mrs. Yancey would get this done before she left on holiday."

"I've got to tell Russ. Excuse me." Annie searched through the crowd of people, barely answering those who stopped her to ask questions. Finally she found him, sitting in a corner, explaining his work to a local reporter.

"Hi, honey." He wrapped an arm around her waist, drew her close, introduced her to the reporter. "This is my wife."

"It's nice to meet you," Annie murmured. "Russ, I need to speak with you privately, please. It's important."

Russ made his apologies to the reporter, then waited until she'd left them alone before he turned to face her, a frown tipping his mouth down.

"What's wrong?"

"Nothing's wrong. Something is right," she explained and thrust out the papers.

Russ read slowly, his hands clenching a little, crackling the stiff, formal papers. "The adoption went through."

"It's official. We are Drew's legal guardians. Isn't it great?" She threw her arms around him and hugged for all she was worth. Russ hugged her back, but Annie sensed something restrained in his manner. "Aren't you happy?" she whispered.

He nodded, brushed his fist against her cheek. "I'm very glad we were able to provide a home for Drew, Annie. He's a wonderful boy and he deserves to have someone like you to love him."

"And you." She broke free of his embrace, twirled, tripped on his foot and landed in his arms. "Let's have a party."

"I thought we were." Russ's eyes crinkled in amusement.

"Another one. You can never have too many parties," she told him with a wink. "Let's see. Today's Wednesday. How about Saturday evening? We could ask our friends to the bed-and-breakfast for a potluck dinner. Your parents are coming today, aren't they?"

He nodded.

"We'll invite them for Saturday, too, so we can induct them as official grandparents. Good, they've just come through the door, I won't even have to phone. What do you think?"

"That you're very sweet." He leaned over and kissed her. "Thank you for thinking of them."

It was almost like having the old Russ back. Annie melted at that sweet kiss, took forever to regain her composure and pretended she didn't see the shadow in his eyes.

"Of course I think of your parents. They're part of our family." Suddenly she realized that she was keeping Russ from the most important moment in his career. She tugged his hand, dragging him to his feet.

"Come on. You have to mingle. These people are here to buy your beautiful creations, Russ. Send them home with something lovely, and they'll send back a friend. Before you know it, you'll be famous.''

''Uh-huh. You have a lot of faith in me, Annie.'' He smiled at her.

''Of course.'' She grinned. ''You're the best silversmith I've ever known.''

''I'm the only silversmith you've ever known.'' He burst out laughing at her surprised look and swung her around. ''Thanks, Annie. With your backing, what man would ever dare fail?'' He lifted her hand, brushed his lips across her knuckles while staring into her eyes. ''I'm very lucky.''

''You're welcome,'' she murmured automatically. He was soon drawn away into the crowd. Annie stood where she was, enjoying watching his eyes dance as he talked about his work.

''He doesn't look too upset by the news.'' Constance stood beside her, also studying Russ. ''Though with some men it's hard to tell what they're thinking.''

''I think I should have waited,'' Annie mumbled. ''After all, this is his day, the day he's waited and planned for. It should belong to only him.''

''It belongs to all of you. You're a family now.''

Constance disappeared into the crowd, leaving Annie to stare at the papers she clutched.

It would take more than a few official documents to make them a family. It would take love. Could Russ ever learn to love her?

Annie could only hope. But in the meantime, her heart soared as she left The Quest and hurried to find Drew. She could hardly wait to see his face.

Chapter Eleven

"**C**'mon, Annie. Russ 'n' me want to go sailing, but Russ says we can't go without you, 'cause you're working too hard and you need a break."

Annie looked up from the tenth list she'd written, smiled at Drew, then added a notation to get some pickles. Open-faced buns, a tray of meat, cheese straws and some pickles. That would be her contribution to the party.

"Annie?" Russ's voice interrupted her thoughts on decorations.

"Yes?" She scribbled down balloons, then glanced up. "What is it?"

"Are you ready?"

She shook her head.

"Russ, a lot of people are coming tomorrow. I've got plans to make. And besides, it's Friday night. I need to be here to check in any new guests."

She wanted to get back to her lists, but Russ was holding her arm.

"Come on, Annie. Leave the grindstone and let's go." He pulled her to the doorway of the dining room and pointed. His voice dropped. "Constance and Nathan are in there with Charles and Elizabeth, watching a video on whales. Nathan said he'll take care of anyone who comes."

"Russ, he's supposed to be a guest, not an employee! Besides, this party—"

"Will turn out just fine no matter what you do. They're coming to celebrate, Annie, not to pick holes in your hostessing." He drew her toward the front door. "Drew, have you got her jacket?"

"Uh-huh. The blue one. It's got the fuzzy insides." He huffed out the words as he lugged a small blue cooler across the floor. "Can somebody help?"

"Of course we can." Recognizing defeat, Annie took her jacket while Russ grabbed the cooler. They each grasped one of Drew's hands and swung him between them, grinning at each other as he howled with delight.

"Hey, can I bring Marm?" he asked suddenly.

Annie froze. She wasn't a very good sailor as it was. But with a cat on board?

"No, sport. Sorry. I don't think Marm is fond of boats. She'd far rather snooze by the fireplace." Russ helped them into his truck, and they took off for the boat slip. While Drew busied himself singing a little song, Russ addressed Annie. "I thought I'd never get you out of there."

"Why did I need to get out?"

"To leave Charles and Constance alone, of course."

She frowned. "Why?"

Russ fixed her with a severe look. "Think about it, Annie. Spring evening. Crocuses just beginning to bloom. What comes to mind?"

She stared at him until he pulled into a parking spot, then blushed. "Oh. But they're not alone. Elizabeth and Nathan are there."

"True." He shrugged, laughed as he helped her down, then swung Drew down behind her. "Did I tell you that I love sailing?"

"Once or twice." She wobbled over the dock behind him, wishing the butterflies dancing a jig in her stomach would settle into a nice, calm waltz.

She stopped, watched as Drew and Russ vaulted off the deck and into the boat, as surefooted as cats. Her butterflies picked up double time, and she froze.

"Annie?" Russ stood, one hand outstretched, waiting to help her aboard. "What's wrong?"

"I'm not very good with sailing, Russ," she whispered, not wanting Drew to overhear. "I've only ever been out once, with you, and it wasn't fun."

"Wasn't fun?" He sounded indignant, offended. "What do you mean it wasn't fun?"

"As in, I hated it!" She glared at him, embarrassed by the admission.

"You did not hate it." Russ lifted one hand at her glare. "Okay. Okay, I get it." He jumped onto the dock beside her, causing it to sway beneath her feet. "Were you seasick?"

She shook her head. "No. My stomach was funny but not sick. Just kind of nervous. I'd as soon sit here and wait for you both."

"No way. Annie, honey, sailing is perfectly safe. I would never have asked you to come along, or Drew, if I didn't think I could handle whatever came up." His hands took hers, squeezed. "I have navigation systems on board, if I need them, but I sailed this coast a lot when I was a teenager. I know it by heart."

"But—but what if a big wave comes up and swamps us?"

"Like Jonah, you mean?" He grinned to show he was teasing. "Annie, look at the water. It's calm as glass."

"Yes, and it can turn in a moment. I've seen it. What do we do if we're stuck out on the water then?" She glared at him, wishing she could go back to her bed-and-breakfast and forget this sailing thing. She'd only gone the first time because it was a special occasion. It would have looked odd to opt out. Russ seemed to love it so much, and she'd wanted to share that with him.

"If a storm comes up, we head for shore. We have enough provisions to last several days if we have to and a radio to call for help." He smiled. "But I checked the marine forecast, and there is no storm coming. We'll be fine. Come on, Annie girl. Get in and I'll show you."

Annie glared at him but held on tight as she clambered over the edge and into the boat. "Why couldn't you like checkers or something normal?" she groused, flopping down on the seat.

Russ laughed, a carefree, joyous sound that burst from him.

"My dear wife, checkers are for cold winter nights in front of the fire. Full moons are for sailing." He tossed her a life jacket. "Put that on. Drew?"

"Mine's already done up," the little boy assured him.

Annie stayed exactly where she was and watched the two men of her family scurry hither and yon in preparation for sailing. Finally Russ ordered Drew to sit beside Annie and tell her when to duck.

"Duck?" Annie stared at Drew, aghast.

"He's teasing." Drew grinned, eyes wide as he watched Russ steer them out of the cove and into open water. "You should never have let him know you were afraid. Now he'll tease you all the time. Russ loves teasing."

"Aren't you afraid?" She'd wondered how the little boy could manage sailing. Would he be reminded of his parents' sailing accident? But Drew seemed fine.

"Nope," he told her, grinning from ear to ear.

"How come?"

He shrugged. "'Cause I got you and Russ to look after me. I asked God for a new family, and He gave me you guys. I figure He'll keep us together."

"Oh." Out of the mouths of babes, Annie decided.

"Besides, I like sailing. I'm like my dad." He glanced at her and repeated the phrase Annie had heard so often when her friends were alive. "Give me some water and a boat, and I'm a happy man."

Annie waited, but no tears followed. No sadness crept into their lives. Drew, it seemed, had accepted his parents' deaths.

"They're not hurting, you know, honey."

He nodded. "I know. They're in heaven with Jesus. I miss them sometimes, but then I think about you and Russ, and I think that God must have left me here so's I can be your kid. I don't mind." He closed his eyes, leaned his head back and smiled. "I sure do like sailing."

Halfway through the little speech, Annie caught Russ's eye, knew he was listening.

"You see, Annie," he said, his voice carrying clearly over the water. "Drew trusts me not to get us in trouble. Can't you?"

And that was the question. Would she trust him completely, or would she cling to silly doubts and worries?

"You know, Russ, I was thinking. Do you think God asked my mom and dad to look after your little brother? They used to like kids a lot. They wouldn't let him be sad."

Russ flickered a glance at her, then nodded, his smile tender as he spoke to Drew. "I think you could be right, buddy. Thanks."

"Welcome."

Annie wiped away a tiny tear, her heart bursting as she saw the love between man and boy. Of the three of them, Drew was the bravest, unafraid to move on, trusting that God would care for each of them in His special way.

Russ wanted more from their marriage, he'd said. And she'd been afraid of that. Maybe it was time to stop being afraid. Her fingers clenched tighter, and her thumb brushed over the diamond studded band as she remembered the inscribed words.

Inner harbor. Could she ever be that to Russ? Would she let him be that for her? She already loved him. Wasn't it time to show him?

Annie got up, walked across the gently rolling deck and stood beside him.

"I trust you, Russ," she whispered. "I'll trust you."

He settled his arm across her shoulders, brushed her cheek with his lips.

"Thank you."

"Hey, what about me?" Drew wiggled between them. "Don't forget me."

"We could never do that, Drew. You're a part of our family. That's what we're celebrating tomorrow. You're our son, and we love you."

Drew grinned. "You mean I get another party? Cool."

Russ roared with laughter.

They sailed for a little longer than an hour, the billowing white fabric carrying them across the navy velvet water until the sun had almost sunk below the horizon.

"Time to get back." Russ tacked into the wind and headed for home. "That wasn't so bad, was it?" he asked Annie, grinning at her salt-sprayed cheeks.

"It was great. I can't believe that I let myself be afraid of this." She glanced at Drew, snuggled up on a bench, fast asleep.

"I think maybe it has more to do with who you were with. I'm sorry, Annie. I should have noticed your fear last time." He hugged her close. "You were so quiet tonight. What were you thinking of?" His breath knocked aside a few hairs, blew warm against her neck.

"You." She smiled at his surprise. "I was thinking of all the things you've brought to my life, things I would never have known if your grandfather hadn't sent you."

"Good things, I hope?"

She nodded. "The best. Dishwater coffee, burned toast, seasickness."

"Lies." He was silent for a moment, thinking. "He did seem to know what he was doing," Russ admitted. "You're a wonderful woman, Annie. I couldn't have asked for a better wife."

She snuggled against him, delighted to enjoy his embrace and forget everything else. After all, what else mattered?

When they got near the slip, she sat again, knowing he needed all his attention to focus on getting the boat into the dock. Once fastened to the dock, he helped her out, lifted Drew into her arms and began closing up his boat.

Then Russ took Drew from her and carefully placed him inside his truck.

"Russ?" Annie touched his sweater, searching for the right words to explain her feelings.

"Yes?"

"Thank you. Not just for tonight. For everything, I mean. You're a good husband, too." She stood on her tiptoes, placed her hands on his shoulders and pressed her lips against his mouth.

In a flash, Russ had his arms around her and was returning her kiss as if he meant it.

"Annie?"

Annie pulled away, startled to find Drew watching them. "Yes?"

"Can we go home now? I don't want to be tired for the party, and you guys can do that at home, can't you?"

Russ, chuckling under his breath, helped her inside the truck. "I guess we can, son. I guess we can."

"Good." Drew snuggled into his seat, closed his eyes and waited for them to take care of it.

Russ got in, started the engine, then turned to glance at Annie. She met his gaze, smiled.

"Our son," she whispered. "Aren't you proud of his clear thinking?"

Russ stared at her for several moments. Something dark crowded into his eyes.

"Russ?"

He nodded, once, started the truck and headed for home. Annie had a feeling she'd said something wrong. Her impression was confirmed when, after tucking Drew in, he absently kissed her good-night, then went to sit on their tiny patio.

She'd been hoping he wanted to deepen their marriage, make the commitment stronger. Now she wondered if it hadn't been simply wishful thinking. He wanted more from their marriage, he'd said.

Did he still?

"You and Annie are getting good at throwing parties." Nathan motioned toward the huge crowd that filled the bed-and-breakfast. "Every weekend, a new occasion. Though this is certainly one not to be missed."

Russ shifted uncomfortably. He didn't know what to say or how to say it without letting his insecurity show. Truth to tell, this party unnerved him more than that shower the Women's League had thrown.

"Congratulations on becoming a father." Nathan shook his hand, his whole face smiling.

Russ muttered something inane, shook his hand and picked up an empty tray. He made a beeline for the kitchen, hoping for a bit of space and enough quiet time to sort through his emotions. At the moment he felt like a creep for having second thoughts about adopting Drew. But—a father? The thought made his knees knock.

"Hey, son. Come to help me eat these cheese things your wife made?" His father held one aloft, then popped it into his mouth, groaning his appreciation. "You know, there are times when I'm delighted your mother can almost boil water. If she had stuff like this lying around, I'd spend hours at the gym."

"You have too much nervous energy to get fat, Dad. Kind of like me, I guess." Russ ignored the cheese things, poured himself a glass of water and downed it like a man dying of thirst. "Besides, Mom's a crack lawyer, and you love that."

"Yes, I do. I couldn't care less if she never boiled water." James Mitchard forgot about the cheese delicacies, focused on his son. "What's wrong?"

"Why is it that whenever you see me, you immediately assume something is wrong? Why is that, Dad? Am I such a screwup that you can't imagine me doing anything right?" Russ regretted the words as soon as he'd said them, but they could not be taken back.

It was just that suddenly everything overwhelmed him. He'd told Annie he wanted more out of this marriage, and that was the truth. It was bittersweet torture to get up every morning and play the part of her good friend. He wanted the intimacies that being a husband brought, to know she felt comfortable enough to tell him what caused that dark shadow at the back of her eyes, to hold her and comfort her however he wanted, without wondering if he'd gone too far, scared her off, offended her.

But Russ danced between longing and the fear that, once committed, he would do something stupid, irreparably damage their relationship and make her wish she'd never seen him. His father's words accentuated that fear.

"Russ, I apologize if that's the impression I've given. Nothing could be further from the truth. Your mother and I are very proud of what you've done with your life. Haven't we told you that? We think your work is outstanding. It's no wonder you had to get out of the office. Creativity like yours can't survive except by expressing itself, and we should never have ignored that."

Russ swallowed, stung by the tender praise.

"I tried to tell you this before, at Drew's party, but I don't think it came out right. We were wrong, Russ. I was wrong. I wanted to mold you into something you knew you couldn't be. A father doesn't have that right. I'm encouraged that you're not making the same mistake with Drew."

"I'm not?" Russ blinked. How could anyone tell?

"Drew is perfectly comfortable telling you his opinion. He doesn't shrink back or keep silent because he's afraid he's offended you." James shook his head, his mouth tipping down. "That's exactly what I did and I apologize. I was wrong."

"It doesn't matter."

"It matters to me. Will you forgive me, Russ?"

It took several moments for Russ to search those eyes so like his own, to see the need for forgiveness. Then he gave it gladly, wrapping his father in the hug he'd always longed to share.

"Thanks, Dad."

"Your mother and I both love you, son. But don't live your life to please us. Live it to satisfy yourself." James pulled away, turned a dark, painful red. "I'd better get back to your mother," he mumbled, then hurried out the door.

Russ leaned against the counter, stared at the lake.

Hadn't his grandfather said exactly the same thing— fulfill all your dreams. Every day with Annie was like moving a step closer to the marriage his grandparents had shared. He cared deeply for her, wanted her happiness above all. There was no one Russ wanted to be with except Annie. He could spend years telling her his dreams, sharing hers. If it wasn't for Drew.

Russ felt horribly guilty for even thinking that. But if he was completely honest, Drew wasn't at the heart of his problem. The future was. Annie was a wonderful mom to the little boy of her best friends. She'd revel in being a mother to her own babies. But that would mean he'd be a father, a daddy. He'd be responsible for yet another person.

And that was what made his palms sweat, and sent his heart rate into the red zone. To be with Annie was to get tied up in her strings—gossamer threads of silk that could bind so tight he'd never get free. She deserved to be a mother, but Russ couldn't conceive of being responsible for even more tender souls. Watching out for Drew was more than he could manage.

"Russ, I've been looking for you all over. What are you doing in here?" Annie, her cheeks flushed, took a deep breath, then leaned against the counter. "You're not making anything, are you?" she teased.

"Getting a drink of water."

"Oh." She peered at him, eyebrows furrowing with concern. "Is something wrong?"

"No, of course not. Dad was just in here. We sort of made up."

"That's wonderful. I want them to be around for Drew, and it's much nicer if there's no tension between us." She slid another tray out of the fridge, handed it to him. "Is there anything else you need to tell me?"

Suddenly he wanted to hold her, to reassure himself that he was in the right place, doing the right thing. That she'd be there if he messed up with this father thing.

"Yes." He set down the platter.

"Oh." Annie lifted a tray out of the oven, glanced at him curiously and set it down. "What?"

"This." He folded his arms around her, snuggled her close, rested his chin on her head. She fit in his arms as if he'd carved her there, her soft flowered dress floating around his feet like a benediction. It felt right, perfect, to hold her like this, to feel her weight against his arms, to sniff her sweet lilac perfume.

One hand arched over her waist, fitting itself against her curve as if it knew her shape perfectly. The other he kept on her back, brushing against the soft curve of her spine, feeling the frailness mingled with strength.

She tilted her head, peeked at him.

"Not that I'm complaining, but are you okay, Russ?"

"I'm fine," he whispered, then kissed her as he'd dreamed of kissing her for the past several nights.

"Uh-oh." Elizabeth Neal stood in the doorway with several others crowded behind her, their eyes huge as they took in the scene.

Russ felt Annie wiggle but refused to let her go.

"Can't a guy even get a few minutes in the kitchen, alone, with his wife?" he grumbled, willing them to leave.

"Oh, we're going, Russ. And we'd be happy to leave you two alone to continue—especially now that you're officially a father and will have to divide your time between being a daddy and being a husband. It's not an easy balancing act. The responsibilities of fatherhood are heavy, and we believe you deserve every chance you get to kiss your wife.'' Kit Peters elbowed her way to the front of the crowd, marched into the kitchen and grabbed the platter Russ had set down. ''Just give us more of those cheese things, and we're outta here.''

''Speak for yourself, Kit.'' Liz Neal crossed her arms over her chest, leaned against the door and grinned. ''I'm perfectly content to remain exactly where I am and watch.''

Russ groaned, winked at Annie.

''No more parties. Promise me. Not for ages. At least not until Easter. We'll have one after the cantata's over.''

She caught on immediately. What an excellent wife!

''Yes, I quite agree,'' she murmured, just loudly enough that they'd hear. ''It's getting very difficult to get a moment's privacy around here. Maybe one of them will invite Drew for a visit, but then, with our luck, we'll get a house full of guests.''

''Did they write that part into the adoption manual?'' Russ asked, only half kidding. ''The part about losing your privacy?''

''Poor babies! And you with that nice big boat, Russ.'' Nathan's voice parted the women. He strolled in, his grin stretching from ear to ear. ''I'm happy to play baby-sitter for either Drew or the bed-and-breakfast anytime you need me. You should find all the privacy you need out on the water.''

''He's right, honey. We're going to have to leave home if we want to see each other more often.'' Much as he regretted it, Russ let Annie go. He thrust away all his internal questions and concentrated on being host.

"Come on, Annie girl. Get those ovens working. This mob will start gnawing on the woodwork soon, and we'll be back to the renovation phase."

"I can't believe we went through that huge potluck a couple of hours ago and now we're eating again. There must be something about living on the water that stimulates appetites." Constance surged into the room, her hands filled with empty containers. She glanced around, puzzled by the sudden silence. "What did I say?"

"Appetites." Holly snickered. "We were just saying that living in Safe Harbor can stimulate all kinds of appetites." She snatched the platter Annie had prepared, then linked her arm through Russ's. "Come on, hon. You and I will feed the animals. I'll get Alex to help Annie. That way she'll be able to keep her mind on what she's doing."

"I could help her."

"But then we wouldn't get any more food. Come on, Russ. Take a little break."

Resigned to his fate, Russ accompanied Holly through the house, passing around food and drinks until finally the last soul had departed, his parents bid them good-night, and Drew had long since fallen asleep. He found Annie downstairs, loading the dishwasher.

"Nathan gone up?" he asked.

Annie shook her head. "Walking Constance home," she murmured, her back to him. "At least, that's what he *said* he was going to do."

"With Nathan, I have a hunch it's what he doesn't say that matters."

Russ took the cutlery out of her hands, set it down and turned her to face him.

"Let's leave all this for a moment and go watch the stars."

She stared at him, but finally nodded. Russ switched out

the lights, grabbed a display quilt off a hanger and led the way onto her patio. He'd placed two chairs side by side, and once she was seated, he wrapped his arm around her, then wrapped the quilt around them both. Just for a while he needed the reassurance of her next to him.

Facing the water, they sat together, silently watching as the night grew darker and yet more stars twinkled in the inky blackness.

"Beautiful, isn't it?" she whispered, her hand snuggled inside his.

"Exactly what I was thinking." He stared at her, wondering how to broach the subject that bothered him so deeply.

"Look, Russ, there's a falling star. Quick, make a wish." She squeezed her eyes closed, and her forehead pleated. A moment later her eyes flew open. "Oh, it's gone."

"What did you wish for?" Russ murmured.

She giggled. "You know I can't tell you or it won't come true." The phone rang. Annie sighed, eased away from him. "Sorry," she muttered and dashed inside.

Russ stayed where he was even though the night was cool without her beside him, even though loneliness swamped him. What was better? To be with Annie and risk hurting her and Drew or to be alone, dreaming of Annie?

He wished for the first, but the second was far safer.

Chapter Twelve

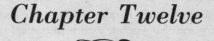

"Okay, this is our second to last practice. We'll have one more the day after tomorrow, on Saturday, but that's it. We need to nail this, kids. Nobody fools around, nobody goofs off. We all work together and we get it right. Okay?"

"Okay," they shouted.

"Let's do it." She waited for Russ to give them their entry, but when nothing happened, she turned to call out. Of course, that's when he played it, and she wasn't ready, so they had to begin again. By the fourth time, they were both getting frustrated, and the kids knew it.

Annie forced herself to control her flutter of nerves, prayed for strength.

"Okay, that was my goof up," she told them with a smile. "Now that we've all had one, let's get it right."

She held up her hand, waited for Russ's introduction, then led them through each piece. It was obvious that Russ had his mind on something else. He forgot interludes, missed entire sections and generally confused the whole issue. Annie wanted to rant and rave at him, but she couldn't. He'd been like this for days, as if he chewed on some terrible problem but made no progress toward its resolution. He refused to discuss whatever was bothering him. Annie could think of no way to help him.

"Okay, boys and girls, that's it. We're finished. I'll see you all on Saturday morning."

They hurried out, subdued, glancing from Russ to Annie and whispering among themselves. Even Drew was quiet as he asked permission to play with Billy. Annie gave it, watched him join his friend, then turn to cast them a worried glance.

She waved and he left, smiling.

"I'm going to stop by the old house. Mrs. Wilkinson is down for the weekend, and she asked me to drop in and see the place. They're almost finished renovating." Russ said nothing so Annie continued. "I thought I'd have a good look around before I headed home. Want to join me? After all, you were the one who insisted I do sketches for them."

He seemed startled by that, but eventually nodded.

They tramped along in silence, Annie because she couldn't think of a thing to say that wouldn't sound either forced or trivial. She didn't know what was bothering Russ.

Annie had to check the number twice to be sure they were at the right house. White clapboards gleamed and shone in the sunlight, glass sparkled in pristine windows that seemed glad to see them.

Mrs. Wilkinson let them in. "Annie, Russ, we haven't seen you in weeks. I'm so glad you stopped by. Please come in and take a look."

The fireplace in its marble finish glowed in the streaming sunlight. Comfortable chairs and two love seats were placed about the room exactly as Annie had drawn. The kitchen reflected Russ's vision from that long-ago day. Cherry cupboards burnished a rich, deep color welcomed them in. White marble countertops, a bank of cheery windows and a host of appliances created the aura of efficiency. Copper-bottomed pans hung from a big metal rack.

"This is even better than Russ's dream," Annie praised when it appeared Russ would say nothing.

"You'll remember the dining room," Mrs. Wilkinson said. "We didn't change much here. Just cleaned it up and added some plants."

The room invited one to sit down and partake with friends.

"You've done a wonderful job," Annie enthused. "It's a completely different place. May we see upstairs?"

"Of course. I think you're going to like the master suite. I used almost all your ideas, and they work beautifully."

Annie loved it. Gone were the dingy reminders of her stay here. Sunlight burned out the memories, flooded the house with cheer. Filmy billows of white sheer curtains let the scent of springtime flood the area. The children's bedrooms were everything Annie could have dreamed of.

"It's absolutely perfect," she told her hostess, thrilled to see her dreams alive. "You've really turned it into a home."

"Only with your help. We could never have done it without you, Annie. We knew there was something special about this place as soon as we saw it, but we just couldn't visualize it. Then you came along, and suddenly everything seemed possible. I don't know how to thank you."

"Don't thank me. Drawing those sketches, watching the changes you've made, they really helped me shed some negative memories and let some light into my own past." Annie glanced around. "I used to hate this place. But now I see that it wasn't the house, it was me. You've made it into a harbor, a place to be safe and get a fresh outlook on life. I hope you enjoy it.''

''I think we will. As soon as my husband gets some holidays, we'll come down and spend a week or two. We'd like to have you over, both of you. Maybe we could be friends?''

Russ said nothing, his eyes stuck on some far distant point. But Annie was delighted. In several of her visits during the construction phase, she'd learned Mrs. Wilkinson was a gourmet cook. Exchanging recipes would be a hoot.

''Thank you very much. We'd love it.'' Annie accepted the invitation for both of them, smiled her thanks. They chatted for a few minutes, discussing what was planned for the landscaping, then Annie and Russ left.

''It looks great, doesn't it?'' she enthused.

''Different.'' He frowned. ''No bad memories?''

She shook her head.

''Not a one. It's the way I dreamed it could be, and it will be filled with laughter and love. There's no resemblance to my past. It's as if it died.''

''You don't see your father in those rooms?''

She considered that, then laughed. ''You know, it's funny, but I could almost see him bounding in from a day of golf. He liked to be outside, loved picnics. I'd forgotten those little baskets he used to pack when he took me to the beach and we'd count the sailboats. I'd forgotten the good times I had with him.'' As they walked home she let her mind drift, remembering those happy times. ''Yes, my father would have loved that house. But I don't think my mother would have.''

Remorse gripped her, but suddenly it seemed important to speak the truth, let it out into the fresh air.

''My mother couldn't stand sunlight. She never went

with us to the beach, never allowed me to pull open the drapes in her room if the sun was shining. She said it faded floors and carpets.'' Annie glanced at Russ. ''I loved her, but she was a sad woman who needed help. I never really saw that until you made me face the truth of the past. Thank you for that.''

Russ shrugged. ''It's nice of you to say.''

''I'm not trying to be nice.'' Indignation rose. What was wrong with him? ''I'm telling you what I feel. Seeing my old home in that condition has made me realize how many things could have been different if my mother had just made an effort, hadn't allowed herself to sink into depression so deeply. You did that for me, Russ. You have a knack for helping people face reality. Drew told me he and you had talked about his parents once when he was at your shop.''

''He was just sounding off, really.''

Annie frowned. What was wrong with him? Why was he deliberately making light of his efforts to help them?

''I don't care why he talked to you,'' she told him. ''I'm just glad he did. There were some things he needed to say. I guess, since the adoption's gone through, he felt he could trust you.''

''Don't say that!'' He raked a hand through his hair.

''Say what?'' Annie didn't get it. Whatever was bothering him was obviously to do with Drew. Why didn't he explain? ''Russ, what is wrong? Don't you want Drew to trust you?''

''No, I don't.'' He bit his lip, cutting off the words as he jerked her front door open and waited for her to go through. ''I'm going to The Quest. After closing time, I'm going for a sail.''

''Alone?''

''No. Nathan's down early for the Easter weekend. He's

bringing Drew later. We're going to fish for a while, so we'll probably be late. Maybe you could send along a lunch for supper. That would save you having to cook.''

''B-but aren't you going to explain what you meant?'' Or ask me to go with you? She stood where she was, ignored the interested stare of her guests and prayed he wouldn't walk out the door. ''Tell me why you don't want Drew to trust you,'' she whispered.

''Never mind. The truth will come out soon enough anyway. It always does.'' He hesitated, then leaned forward and kissed her. ''Don't worry about it, Annie. It isn't important.''

But Annie knew he lied. It mattered a great deal.

Was Russ sorry he'd married her?

Chapter Thirteen

"It was a good idea to go out, Nathan. Thanks for suggesting it." Russ stood in front of the wheel and manipulated the craft toward shore.

"And thanks for the chicken. I was starving." Drew smacked his lips, then giggled.

"You're welcome. I think being on the water makes everyone hungry." Nathan checked Drew's life jacket once more, then settled the boy beside him, allowing Russ to concentrate on his maneuvers.

Russ focused on his job and managed a perfect slide into his berth. He fastened down the ropes, then began packing myriad items Drew had left scattered all over the deck. Drew, free of his life preserver, stood at the side rail, ready to climb out as soon as he was allowed.

"We're going to have to check you out before you come aboard," he told the little boy. "What a lot of junk!" He heard the sour note in his voice, saw Drew's face change. Russ tried to soften his censure. "Leaving your toys all over like this is dangerous. Someone could trip. And we can't bring Marmalade again, Drew. She doesn't like being on the water, and you shouldn't have snuck her here in your backpack without telling me.''

"I'm sorry, Russ. I thought she'd like it on your boat. I wanted to give her a treat. I thought she liked the water. Just like me.'' Drew turned to look over the lake.

Russ caught the glimmer of tears and knew he'd been too harsh. But how did you know? How could you tell whether or not a child listened to what you said? It was all part and parcel of this parenting thing, all tied up with responsibility, and he just wasn't good at that. He only had to look at Drew's unhappy face to know he'd blown it.

Russ turned to apologize. From the corner of his eyes he saw Marmalade's interest in a nearby bird, witnessed her sudden break for freedom. A second later she'd disappeared off the bow of the boat, and Drew was leaning over the side of the boat to get her.

Russ's heart stopped. His whole body froze as the little boy teetered on the rail.

"Drew, no!''

He shouldn't have said it. Drew jerked around, and in doing so lost his grip. He disappeared off the deck. A moment later, Russ heard a loud splash and a grunt of pain.

In slow motion his mind went back to Adam, saw him plunge under the icy water.

"Nathan, quick!'' Russ tore off his bulky sweater, slid out of his shoes.

"I'm here. I'll get a rope ready while you find him.''

Russ took a second to assess the situation. The space between the boat and the dock was too narrow. He couldn't dive. He'd have to lower himself. Why didn't Drew call out?

Russ aligned himself vertically, checked the water below, then let go of the rope. The splash of frigid water took his breath away. What must it be doing to Drew?

Where was Drew?

He searched frantically until he caught a glimpse of a red sweater near the bow. It took several desperate minutes until he had the small solid figure locked in his arms, several more before he could make his way to the ladder on the other side.

"Help me, Nathan," he called.

"I'm here." Nathan's hands reached out to grasp the boy as soon as Russ got close enough. Tenderly he lifted the unconscious child over the side rail, laid him on the deck and began to check his vitals. With grim lips, he peeled off the sopping sweater and started CPR. "We're going to need help."

"What's wrong with him?"

Drew's eyes were closed. A huge blue lump had formed on his skull just under the hank of dark brown hair that always flopped over one eye. Russ reached out a hand, touched the freckle beside his mouth. The skin was icy.

"Go call nine-one-one, Russ. Go now." Nathan continued his rhythmic pattern of pressing and blowing.

Russ jumped off the boat and raced to the nearest pay phone where he related the information, his throat pinching tighter as he explained.

"Please hurry," he whispered. "Please." Then he hung up and went back to the boat.

"Come on, Drew. Breathe. Breathe." Nathan pumped the small chest.

With every press Russ prayed for a miracle. *Don't let him be dead, God. Not another one. Not again.*

He didn't know how long they waited until the ambulance came. Then the attendants took over, pushed him and Nathan out of the way and began to bag Drew. Finally Drew's small body was loaded into the vehicle.

"Are you coming with us?" they asked Russ.

Nathan urged him forward. "Go, Russ. I'll get Annie."

Annie! Russ's heart sank to his feet. What would Annie say? Would she finally see the truth—that he was a failure at fatherhood? Would she blame him? From the corner of his eye he saw the cat perched on a post, watching.

"C'mon, guys. Make it fast. We're rolling."

"You go, Nathan. I have to tell Annie myself. That's my job. We'll meet you at the hospital." He reached out, touched Drew's forehead. "Hang on, son. Just hang on."

Seconds later the ambulance was screaming down the street, and Russ was left to face the crowd that had gathered.

He slipped on his shoes, ignored them all and grabbed the cat. Then he headed for home to say the hardest words he'd ever spoken.

"Russ?" Annie's big blue eyes widened at his sopping clothes, blinked when Marmalade dashed through the room. "A little cool to go for a swim, isn't it?" She touched his shirt, wrung out a bit of water.

He couldn't say a word, couldn't get the truth out. But he had to. Annie would want to be there when…

"It's Drew, Annie. He fell overboard. I went in after him, but—"

"But what? Is he alive? Russ, where is our son?" Her nails scraped his skin. She jerked at his arm. "Where is he?"

"They've taken him to the hospital. Nathan's with him. He—he wasn't breathing."

She froze, her face whiter than he'd ever seen it. Her hands fluttered uselessly, then dropped to her sides.

"Oh, Drew," she whispered, her eyes filling with tears. "Poor baby." She blinked at Russ. "We have to go to him."

"We're going," he told her, squeezing one hand. "Give me two seconds to get changed, and we'll be out the door."

The phone rang. Annie didn't move, so Russ turned, stepped across the room and with dread oozing from every pore picked up the receiver.

"Hello."

"It's me. They're airlifting him to Green Bay. Shall I go with him?"

"Yes." Russ felt Annie's hand slip into his, but he'd never felt more powerless to console her than he did now. "Yes, you go, Nathan. We'll meet you there." He paused a moment, then lowered his voice. "Nathan?"

"Yes?"

"Pray."

"I have been, Russ. Nonstop."

Russ hung up, then explained the situation to Annie.

"Go and change," she ordered. "I'll turn on the answering machine and get my purse."

By the time he came back she was hovering at the door. He pushed it open, but she hesitated.

"Russ, I think we should pray before we go."

He nodded and closed his eyes as Annie began to speak.

"Dear Lord, we ask You to please be with our son right now. We love him very much, and he needs Your help. Please take care of Drew. Amen."

Russ watched her scrub the tears from her face.

"Not much of a prayer, was it?"

"It said everything," he murmured, then took her arm. "Come on, let's go."

But as he locked the door, her words flooded over him. *Our son.*

Russ grimaced. He wasn't really Drew's father. He wasn't fit for that any more than he was fit to be Annie's husband. A father wouldn't have let it happen, would have known to keep the boy near him. A father would have protected him. A husband would have kept Annie's child from harm.

Annie was Drew's mother, Drew was his responsibility, and he'd failed them both in the worst possible way. Drew showed more responsibility when it came to looking after Marmalade than Russ had shown in caring for his own child.

The truth was hard to swallow.

Minutes stretched into hours. Hours seemed like days. The night darkened, deepened through the blackest hours. And yet still there was no news. People came and went through the small waiting area, and every time Russ jerked to his feet, his white face frozen.

After midnight someone told them that Drew was breathing on his own, but he still hadn't regained consciousness.

Annie glanced at Russ's tall, lean body, silhouetted by the morning sun through the windows, and wondered what she could say that would erase the pain he privately endured. How awful for him. Compassion rippled through her at the agony distorting his features.

She knew what he was thinking, could feel it as if his thought waves were visual. He was blaming himself. He was thinking of Adam, remembering, comparing his actions then and now and finding himself to blame. She loved him so much, longed to hold him, to comfort him. But she knew he wouldn't accept it. Russ believed, perhaps more strongly now than he ever had, that he didn't deserve love. She'd tried to reach him, but nothing worked.

But she would not give up. Not on Drew, and not on Russ.

Annie got up, walked across the room and threaded her fingers into his.

"It's not your fault, Russ. He's a little boy. Boys have accidents."

"Especially on boats," he muttered so quietly she almost didn't hear.

"What if he'd fallen off his bike or been hit by a car? Would you blame yourself then?" She leaned her head against his chest. "Things happen, Russ. But God is in control. He will bring something good out of this, I just know it."

Russ jerked away as if he'd been burned. His face was stretched into lines of anger.

"What good could possibly come of a little boy almost drowning?" He spat the words out.

"I don't know. I just know that all things work together for good. And I trust God to put the pieces back together."

That seemed to anger him further. "Aren't you worried, Annie? Doesn't it bother you that my carelessness caused this?"

"How? How did you cause it? Did you neglect him? Did you push him over? What?"

"I should never have taken my eyes off him. That's what a father does."

Annie shook her head. "That's what God does. Earthly fathers can't protect their children from everything."

"You didn't see him, Annie." The agony on Russ's face made her wince. "He was being so careful with that stupid cat, making sure it didn't stray too far or get in my way. He was so—diligent about his responsibility. Patient. Exactly the opposite of the way I was with him. I got mad at him for bringing that animal."

"Parents get mad sometimes, Russ. Besides, Drew's not a baby. He understood that he was to stand there and wait for you. But he didn't. He also disobeyed when he took the cat on board. Falling overboard was an accident. It's not your fault.''

But Russ wasn't listening. His head jerked up as footsteps echoed down the hall. His whole body stiffened. Sighing, Annie stepped away from him, turned toward the doctor.

''He's awake.''

''Thank God.'' Nathan slumped against the tired vinyl seat, his eyes closed in relief.

But Annie stood where she was, waiting for the rest. God had carried her this far, brought her this marriage, given her this child. Now she would learn what else He had in store for her and then she'd pray for the courage to endure and triumph.

''He has a concussion, but as far as we can tell, there doesn't seem to be any permanent injury to the brain. He doesn't have a loss of memory. The early tests have all come back negative.'' The doctor smiled. ''In fact, he's a very lucky boy. He suffered only minimal hypothermia, thanks to his father's quick reactions. We'd like to keep him the rest of today for observation. If he keeps progressing, you can take him home tonight. Tomorrow morning at the latest.''

Annie smiled, whispered a prayer of thanksgiving.

''Thank you, Doctor. My husband and I are very grateful.''

Russ's head jerked up, his eyes narrowed at the term husband, but he only repeated her thanks.

''Can we see him?'' he asked, as if he feared that very event.

The doctor nodded. ''Of course. He's been asking for his dad.'' He smiled at Russ. ''It seems your son is champing at the bit to apologize.''

Annie turned to grin at Russ, but found his expression even more strained. She took his hand and led him down the hall.

"He doesn't owe me an apology," he muttered darkly. "He doesn't owe me anything."

"Just his life." Nathan clapped him on the shoulder. "You let Drew decide what he needs to do, Russ. It will ease his mind."

Annie hurried through the door and wrapped her son in a bear hug, thrilled to hold his warm little body so close.

"Drew, you scared the daylights out of us."

"That's what you guys always say. And I still don't know what daylights are." Drew hugged her, but his eyes were on Russ. "Is Marmalade okay?"

"Marmalade is fine. She wasn't in any danger, Drew. She always falls on her feet. Cats are like that. But thank you for worrying about her so much."

Annie stood silent as the solemn words died away and Russ shuffled from one foot to the other.

"I'm sorry I disobeyed, Russ," Drew whispered. "I'm really sorry. You probably don't want me to be your son anymore, do you?" His eyes brimmed with tears, but he sat straight. Only the quiver in his bottom lip gave him away.

"Oh, Drew. You're a wonderful son." Russ enveloped the child in his big strong arms, his lips clamped shut. But Annie knew he was holding something back. His ordeal wasn't over yet, but she had no idea how to help him through whatever was keeping him prisoner.

She had a hunch it would take faith and a mountain of prayer to do that.

Chapter Fourteen

Russ stood on the church steps and watched Drew race around the lawn, chasing another child in a game of tag. The Good Friday service, he'd learned, was a community one with several of the local pastors sharing duties. Half the town had shown up.

Russ had sat through the service, Annie's shoulder brushing his, while his mind seethed with a thousand unanswered questions. He'd heard very little of the sermon.

A few moments ago Annie had told him of the prayer chain Nathan had set in motion by contacting Constance after Drew's accident. Constance had organized the whole thing. The entire town knew about Drew's mishap and Russ's carelessness. As he stood waiting for Annie to finish thanking several members of the Women's League, one person after another came to shake his hand, to commend him for his quick thinking, for his fatherly devotion.

When Russ felt he couldn't endure it a moment more, Annie returned, swinging hands with Drew.

"Russ, there are several families whose children can't

make rehearsal tomorrow. I thought perhaps we could have one this afternoon. Just a short one?''

He wanted nothing less, but Russ forced himself to nod. It was his duty, and he'd do it. But he wouldn't be volunteering again any time soon. He'd obviously taken his commitments too lightly. Only now was he realizing how tightly bound he'd become to this community and how easy it was to fail them.

''Okay.'' She smiled, squeezed his hand. ''Just give me a minute to spread the word. I can walk home if you want to leave.''

She was always so considerate. Why was that? He didn't deserve it, didn't want it, really. It made him feel beholden. Russ called himself a fool. Tired, that's what he was. A night of dreams where Drew became Adam tore across his mind, killing any hopes of sleep. If he could just get away, think for a while, figure out how to atone.

''Okay, let's go. We can have a quick bite at home and be back here soon enough to run through all the numbers. Then we'll leave it alone until Sunday morning.'' She mussed Drew's hair. ''You guys know all your parts anyway. I think you'll do a great job. We all will.'' She grinned at Russ, as confident as could be.

It was that confidence that shook him. Why did she trust him? Why did she place so much faith on his shoulders? He didn't want it, hadn't asked for it, and yet Annie acted as if he were some kind of hero. He couldn't take that.

Once the rehearsal was over, Russ made it through the rest of the day by avoiding Annie. He pretended to work at his shop, but nothing interested him. He took a walk in the park, but the hordes of families enjoying the glorious sunshine only reminded him of Annie and her gentle smile. The book he'd started last week didn't hold his interest, so he walked all over town until his feet ached and he was certain he would sleep.

But sleep proved elusive, and Russ was up with the birds the next morning. It was a beautiful day, the sun beaming down on the calm lake. Suddenly he yearned to get away and think, to sort through the mess he'd made of his life and find some answers. The lake beckoned.

He scribbled a note telling Annie he'd gone sailing, packed himself a lunch and grabbed a jacket. Tourists or not, he needed a day off.

"Leaving me another note?" Annie glanced at the paper on the counter. "That's getting to be a habit."

"I thought you were out."

She said nothing, simply stood there, waiting for him to explain. Russ couldn't do it. He didn't have the words, and anyway, she wouldn't understand.

"There's something wrong, isn't there? I can see it in your eyes, in the way you avoid me."

"It's not you, Annie."

"I know. It's you. You're afraid, aren't you, Russ?"

"Afraid?" He hated the way she probed, inflicting pain with her pointed questions.

"You said you want our marriage to be real. You wanted to take it a step further. I do, too. I've been waiting for you to make the first move, but ever since Drew's accident, even before that, you've been backing away. Why?"

"I—I don't know."

"Sure you do." She stepped closer, until her face was only inches from his. "I think this life we have together, your shop, Drew—I think it goes a long way to fulfilling your dreams." She smiled. "Mine, too."

He didn't know what to say. He wanted to grab her,

reassure her, but once he took that step, he'd be committed. "I can't—"

"You can't what? Love me? Stay with us? Be a father? All of the above?" Her blue eyes remained clear, focused. "Did you ever ask yourself why you're running scared right now, Russ? Did you ever wonder why you're denying yourself what you want?"

He shook his head. "I'm not who you think I am. I'm not dependable."

"Oh, Russ. That's garbage, an excuse, and you know it." She slapped her hands on her hips. "You're denying yourself this opportunity to be happy because the responsibility that comes with having what you want scares you to death. You feel inadequate. You're afraid that if you are put to the test and have to perform, you wouldn't live up to your own expectations. Life is about believing in yourself, trusting that God will help you make it through. And you're running away. Ask yourself why."

He sucked in his breath when her hand cupped his chin.

"You've already been put to the test and passed with flying colors. You got Drew to safety. He's fine. You did exactly what a loving father would do."

He shook his head. Annie only smiled.

"It's not others you're afraid of disappointing, Russ. It's yourself. You've told yourself a story—that you weren't strong enough to be your own man, that you failed your family. Then you bought into that story, and it's sabotaging your life."

"That's not true."

"Sure it is. Your parents are proud of your silver work. You haven't disappointed them. Your grandfather knew you'd succeed—that's why he left you the money to help you on your way. Drew trusts that whatever happens, you'll be there to see him through. He knows you'll be there for him.''

He stared at her, the whole truth waiting to be spoken. ''And you?''

''I know you, Russ. I know who you are underneath that facade you put up. I trust you completely. You will never let us down. That's not who you are.'' She brushed her lips across his cheek. ''But you have to figure the rest out for yourself. That's the only way this marriage can work. So have your sail, think through what you really want from me and be honest with yourself. I'll still be here. Waiting. You see, I have a lot of faith in R. J. Mitchard.''

Her hand, with its flash of diamonds, squeezed his, then she walked away.

Russ had been out for five hours, breezing over the placid water with a bounce that coaxed him back to life. When he grew tired, he anchored, stretched out on the deck for lunch, then dropped off to sleep.

The storm whipped him awake with unexpected fury. His anchor hadn't held. He was bobbing around the lake, tossed like a cork on the ocean. Lightning sizzled the water not fifty feet away. He had to go. But where? Oh, Lord, where could he hide?

The wind lashed the water into a fury of white foam. Rain poured down on him, cutting visibility to almost nothing. Russ reckoned his directions and adjusted his course until he saw land. He kept as near the shoreline as he dared, conscious of the jagged rocks that could tear his boat to shreds.

''I have to put in to shore, but where? It's too far to go back. I'll have to wait it out. Lord, I need a harbor. A safe one to get out of this storm. Can You help me?''

Half an hour later Russ found the cove. Carefully edging

in, he barely missed gashing his hull on the jagged rocks hidden by white-capped waves. He jumped into the water, waded to shore and fastened the boat down by tying it to two huge trees. The rain poured over him in darkened sheets, drenching his body until he was completely chilled and worn out with the effort of fighting the storm.

Russ clambered back on board and stood on deck for a moment, watching as the storm raged full-strength. Then he hurried into the tiny cabin and shut the door. He found an old pair of shorts and a T-shirt and quickly changed clothes, shedding his sopping garments eagerly.

Wrapping himself in an old blanket he'd brought along for Drew, he snuggled into the small, narrow bunk. At least he was warm, and for the moment, safe.

Annie.

The reminder shocked him. She'd be worrying about him just as she'd always worried over Drew if he wasn't home on time. Russ reached for the radio.

"This is three-two-seven-nine-four. Come back." Over and over he relayed his call signals. "I'm safe. I am taking shelter in a cove. I repeat, I am safe. Anyone hearing this message please contact Charles Creasy of the Safe Harbor police. Over."

Though he said it repeatedly, no one answered when he released the button. There was only the crackle of static and the sound of thunder and lightning.

"Please, God, let Annie know. Don't let her worry."

He brought her small, smiling face into his mind, added the details he knew so well, the hands that had trusted him to hold them, the smile she'd lavished on him. Most of all, he remembered her eyes, soft, trusting, believing in him.

His grandfather's words echoed in his brain.

"You try to avoid responsibility by running away. But you can't run away from life. The only way to make it through is to take on whatever God gives you. Do it in His strength. All through our days God gives us gifts, special, beautiful gifts that we can either cherish and enjoy, or we can ignore, toss away. One day you're going to realize God has given you a gift like that. Then you'll have to decide what to do with it. Will you accept God's gift, or will you throw it away because you're afraid of what it might cost you?''

Gramps could have been speaking of Annie. Was she God's gift to him? Russ knew the answer. Allowing himself to truly love Annie could fulfill and sustain him. But it meant facing the tough times with her, sharing the good. It meant Russ had to be there, stand by her side, face up to it, even when it hurt.

Gramps's words from his last letter returned.

''It's not about pretending to be what someone else wants, Russ. It's about living up to your own standards, facing the fear and sometimes failing. It's about getting up and trying harder. It's about living.''

The truth cast the light of hope in his heart, and suddenly he understood what had taken so long to penetrate the fear, what she'd been trying to tell him. They could only make it through together. Without Annie, his life was rudderless. Giving back just a portion of the love she lavished on him made them both richer. She loved him. He knew that now as surely as the water fell in torrents outside.

And with equal certainty, Russ knew he loved her, loved Drew, with every atom of his being. He couldn't bear the thought that he might hurt them—worse, that he might miss out on the joy life with Annie would bring. But wouldn't running away hurt far more? Annie was part of himself. A future without Annie? Unthinkable. Drew needed a daddy. Even a messed-up one.

He caught the soft glow of his ring in the dimness of the one lamp he'd lit. He tugged it off, squinted to read the inscription once more, though he knew it by heart.

"For my inner harbor. Love always, A.M."

He slid the ring on, clenched his fist. An inner harbor, a place where storms were endured, where struggles produced strength, where bonds toughened, became resilient to the tossing of life. He wanted to be that for Annie, wanted her to feel as his grandmother had so many years ago, that he'd always be there for her, no matter what.

Doubts? He had thousands of them. But with God's help, he'd find enough love to surmount any doubts that could come up.

"Gramps," he whispered, remembering the old gent with a pang of joy. "You gave me the very best gift I could have had when you sent me to Annie. She's my safe harbor. I promise I'll treasure her always. In case I didn't tell you, thanks."

Russ stood, ready to meet the challenges God had sent him. He loved Annie and Drew, and he was not going to walk away without a fight. Not ever again. Pile the duties and responsibilities on him—he'd gladly shoulder them all for a chance to spend his life loving Annie, caring for his son.

He opened the door, peered outside, his heart sinking as he saw the fog swirling like a blanket, covering the water and land alike. He closed the door, sank down on his tiny bunk.

"Okay, Lord," he whispered. "I'm finally ready to take on the future You've given me. I'll do my best never to disappoint Annie again, but You know that cantata is tomorrow morning. I'm going to need a little help if You want me to be there."

"You have a knack for helping people face reality." Annie's long-ago words echoed in his mind.

Him? Russ chuckled. He'd faced reality, all right. And it wasn't very flattering to see the coward he'd become. But he'd gladly tell her all about it when he got back. And then they'd start over again.

If he could just get out of here.

Chapter Fifteen

Annie shushed the children for the tenth time, though if the truth were known, she really didn't care how much noise they made. She only wanted to go home and wait for Russ.

"He's fine, Annie. That part of the message was very clear. Then his radio gave out. We don't know exactly where he is." Charles Creasy had made a personal visit late last night to tell her the news, but until she saw Russ, until she held him in her arms and kissed him, she was clinging to hope. And with every moment that passed, it flickered a little more.

"Russ will be here, Annie. He will. I know it." Drew snuggled his head against her leg, his fingers threading through hers as she hugged him. "Russ loves us, Annie."

Did he? Or were they only a means to an end? Her heart ached at the thought, and she shoved it away. She'd told Russ she trusted him. All right. It was time for trust to begin working.

"I'm sorry, Annie. I know you wanted to wait for Russ,

but I think we have to get started.'' Justine rested a gentle hand on her shoulder, her eyes soft with commiseration.

Annie nodded. She had to do this. Now.

She shoved the worries away, drew in a deep breath and gave the signal for the choir to march toward the front and take their places. She waited until each child was in place, then turned toward the congregation. She would make no excuses, she decided. She would simply lead them, unaccompanied, as best she could.

''Ladies and gentlemen, our Easter cantata.''

She turned, faced the choir, waited for the clapping to die down as she straightened her papers.

Suddenly three loud chords rang through the sanctuary. Russ! Annie glanced at Drew, saw his wide grin of pure delight, his wink and the words he mouthed at her. *I told you he'd make it.*

She smiled, touched by his faith.

Russ was home.

Annie whispered a soft prayer of thanksgiving and gave the signal to begin. The notes swelled in rich, somber harmony as the children sang the beginning of the Easter story. Annie blocked out everything, allowed nothing to penetrate her consciousness but their dulcet, melodic voices raised in praise as the undertones of the old pipe organ egged them on to perfection.

The words of the age-old story came to life as one reader after another stood, recited the words in pure, clear tones. During each reading, Annie forced herself to remain still and silent, though her heart was singing full throttle. Then she rose and with the choir, worked through the next number. Drew's one solo line rang to the rafters with meaning, his voice doubly sweet for having been almost silenced.

Justine's soft, poignant homily offered each person something to rejoice over. The beauty and wonder of a gift so freely given seemed to touch the entire congregation. As one they recited the age-old greeting. *He is risen.*

Feeling as if only moments had passed since they'd begun the cantata and yet longing to see Russ, Annie held up her hand for the triumphant notes of their final song. The children's focus never wavered as they approached, then soared over the climactic ending of the "Hallelujah Chorus." And for a few moments, after the glorious notes had died away, there was utter silence in the small church.

Then, like a clap of thunder, the congregation rose and applauded their appreciation. The children bowed as she'd instructed, shiny faces beaming with delight at their performance. Annie stepped to the side as the children marched out, not daring to search the sanctuary for that beloved face.

"Annie, that was fantastic."

"You did a superb job, Annie."

"Best thing I've heard in years."

She thanked them all, but her heart hung, suspended, waiting for that one special voice.

"Annie."

She turned, gazed into his gleaming silver eyes and sighed.

"Russ," she whispered, noting his tattered T-shirt and baggy shorts. "Glad you could make it."

Russ stared at her a moment, then tilted his head back and burst into delighted laughter.

"You never say quite what I imagine," he told her, grinning with delight. "That's one thing I love about you." He wrapped his arms around her waist, tilted her head with one thumb and kissed her in a way that left Annie completely and utterly speechless.

"I couldn't stay away from you, my darling Annie," he whispered, staring into her eyes. "Not for long."

Annie stood, sheltered in his arms, and heard the wondrous words tumble from his lips.

"Not from you, and not from our son. I love you. I want to be married to you forever, Annie. I want to be the inner harbor you run to, the place you turn when life gets in the way. I want to show you how much I need you and Drew to be there for me, to keep me on the straight and narrow, to help me fix things when I mess up." He cupped her face between his hands, held her eyes with his.

"I want to really marry you, right here, in front of God and most of Safe Harbor. And I want everyone to witness my vows to you and to Drew. Is that a problem?"

She lifted her arms and surrounded his neck to draw his head close.

"Not to me, my darling," she told him, joy welling inside.

"Not to me, either." Drew grinned at them, then raced up to the nearest microphone. "Hey, you guys, come back here. Annie and Russ are getting married. Again!"

"I imagine you were up all night in the storm. You're sure you're not too tired to do this?" Annie frowned as she studied the lines framing her husband's beloved face.

"No." He reached out, caught her hand in his, brushed her knuckles with his lips. "I have to do this."

"I know." She scooted across the seat and laid her head on his shoulder. "So do I."

They sat in peaceful silence as the miles flew past. Then Russ navigated the streets of Green Bay until they found the site, the two spots they were looking for.

"Anne Marie Willoughby, Wharton Willoughby. At rest in the harbor." Annie brushed a tear away, smiled at Russ. "Do you think he knows about us?"

Russ wrapped one arm around her shoulders and drew her closer.

"He knows," he whispered. "Gramps was the smartest old coot I've ever known." He brushed his lips across her forehead. "He sent me to you, didn't he?"

"Yes, he did," she murmured. She lifted the huge sheaf of pure white lilies they'd cut from Annie's tiny flower garden and set them in front of the gray granite stone. "Thank you, Wharton," she said, brushing a kiss against her fingers then trailing them over the stone. She glanced at her beautiful wedding ring, diamonds flashing in the bright sun. "And thank you, Anne Marie. You've both given me the most wonderful gifts."

They stood together, thinking about the past. Then, with like minds, they turned and, hand in hand, walked back to Russ's truck.

Wrapped in the circle of Russ's arm, Annie stared at him, half bemused by the tender light glowing in those beautiful silver eyes.

"Where now?" she asked softly.

"Home. To Safe Harbor. With you."

* * * * *

*Will Gracie Adam find her heart's desire
and discern God's plan for her life?
Be sure to watch for her story,
HART'S HARBOR, coming next
month only to Love Inspired.*

*And now for a sneak preview,
please turn the page.*

Gracie Adam shifted, carefully adjusting her perch on a thick branch in a sturdy oak tree at the edge of the green, straining forward to get a better vantage point of what was going on at the bachelor auction.

Specifically, she wanted to see Kyle squirm on the bachelor's block.

She was late getting to the picnic, because she'd been helping out an indigent family on the dock who'd called her when they'd had a minor medical emergency. She couldn't—and wouldn't—turn this family down, but she hoped she had not missed the spectacle she was sure would occur when the good doctor made his debut.

She'd relied on an old childhood trick, one she had learned when she was six years old and which had stood her in good stead over the years—shimmying up a convenient tree to get a better lay of the land.

Her mother had called it tomboyish and unladylike. She'd always thought it rather practical, herself. And now was certainly no exception. She wasn't going to be able to get a glimpse of the gazebo any other way.

After nimbly shifting down to her stomach on the tree branch, her knees braced around the rough bark for security, she was finally able to get a good glimpse of Dr. Hart.

She had arrived just in the nick of time, as Kyle was already on the block.

And what she saw made her chuckle under her breath. Kyle's face was red, but he looked green in the gills. He looked like he'd swallowed a chicken. *Whole*.

Not that she could blame him. She'd kept an ear out for the bidding, and it was pretty outrageous, even for Safe Harbor. Some of those older gals were practically coughing up their pensions for a date with the handsome doctor, not that she could blame them.

And of course there was Chelsea Daniels. Princess extraordinaire. Miffed that she couldn't capture Kyle's attention the old-fashioned way, she was going to flat-out buy the man.

For a ridiculous amount of money.

Gracie watched Kyle shrug back into his jacket and attempt without success to retie his bow tie. She got the unspoken message, even if the other women cheering on the green didn't hear what he was silently trying to tell them with his actions.

He didn't want to be paraded around like a piece of meat. And though he was going along with it like the gentleman he was, it was killing him to do it. From the tortured look on his face, he'd like to be anywhere but here in Safe Harbor, and most especially not on the bachelor's block.

Suddenly, Gracie found herself experiencing feelings

she never thought to encounter when she climbed up this tree on the green.

She felt sorry for Dr. Hart.

She'd always been outrageously outgoing by nature, and she'd grown up in Safe Harbor, after all, with their strange traditions and irascible characters. It was all she'd ever known, and she was perfectly comfortable in this uncommon little part of the world. Up to and including taking her stand on the bachelorette block when it was her turn to do so, even flirting with the fellows to get a good price.

But Kyle was different. He came from another world entirely. He was educated, distinguished, refined. He wasn't some hick right off the farm who looked at the bachelor block as his opportunity to make his mark in the world.

Her heart swelled into her throat. She could almost physically *feel* Kyle cringe from where she crouched in the tree, as Chelsea made yet another bid. Gracie knew how much it cost Kyle not to jump right off that block and make a run for it.

The next moment, her decision was made, and her heart was firm.

She swung her leg around and shifted down, swinging herself so she was dangling on the branch from her arms, where everyone on the green could see her, if—when— they looked in her direction. There could be no mistaking what she was about to do.

"One thousand dollars," she said, her voice as crystal clear as her mind was made up, and as her heart was strong and true.

"The doctor has been sold. To me."

Dear Reader,

Hello again. I'm glad you joined me for *Inner Harbor*.
I hope you enjoyed Annie and Russ's struggle to know
God's plan in their lives. Aren't we humans funny? We
put such limits on ourselves, limits that God ignores.
But isn't that the way it should be? In Him, our options
are vast. He is always there, always listening, always
waiting for us to come back, snuggle into His lap and
listen. Then, when we know His way, we're ready, like
newborn lambs, to wobble onto our own feet and take
tiny steps toward the life He wants for us. As spring
brings rebirth, I wish for you new hopes and dreams,
fresh plans and the chance to plant much joy in this
world. And, of course, may God send you an abundance
of love.

Blessings,

Lois
Richer

HART'S HARBOR

BY

DEB KASTNER

Dr. Kyle Hart had come to Safe Harbor to find peace. But the town matchmakers had other plans for the dashing widower. So when Kyle and the spontaneous Gracie Adams masqueraded as an engaged couple to outwit the matchmakers at their own game, he found himself finding love and healing where he least expected it....

Don't miss

HART'S HARBOR

the third installment of

SAFE HARBOR

The town where everyone finds shelter from the storm!

On sale May 2003

Available at your favorite retail outlet.

A LOVE TO KEEP

BY
CYNTHIA RUTLEDGE

Lori Loveland didn't plan on risking her heart during her six-month stint as devoted nanny to Drew McCashlin's daughters. But once she let her guard down around the handsome single dad and his beloved girls, she found herself praying that six months could last a lifetime!

Don't miss
A LOVE TO KEEP
On sale May 2003
Available at your favorite retail outlet.